THE
MOTH
CAME
BACK

Native Prairie Mysteries
Book One

TARA RATZLAFF

**CAVEL
PRESS**

Kenmore, WA

CAMEL PRESS

A Camel Press book published by Epicenter Press

Epicenter Press
6524 NE 181st St.
Suite 2
Kenmore, WA 98028

For more information go to:
www.Camelpress.com
www.Coffeetownpress.com
www.Epicenterpress.com
www.tararatzlaff.com

This is a work of fiction. Names, characters, places, brands, media, and incidents are either the product of the author's imagination or are used fictitiously.

Permission given for cover photo image by Shooting Star Native Seeds.

Cover design by Scott Book
Design by Melissa Vail Coffman

The Moth Came Back

Library of Congress Control Number: 2022946244

ISBN: 978-1-684920-96-9 (Trade Paper)
ISBN: 978-1-684920-95-2 (eBook)

Printed in the United States of America

I would like to dedicate this book to my husband and daughter who put up with my absence while furiously writing and frequent zone-outs when plotting story lines.

ACKNOWLEDGMENTS

I'D LIKE TO ACKNOWLEDGE JENNIFER MCCORD, executive editor and associate publisher of Epicenter press for taking the chance on a first-time author. Thank you!

CHAPTER ONE

Pollinators and wildflowers have a symbiotic relationship;
where you have wildflowers, you will have butterflies.

THE MOTH WAS BACK. I'd spent Monday morning alternately sweeping for bugs with my net and crawling around on my hands and knees peering at the plant stalks and leaves. I'd lost this crop of prairie blazing star two years ago due to this moth and I'd learned my lesson. I had been faithful in checking every day for the last two weeks and unfortunately they were now here. The caterpillars that came from the eggs these moths would lay could destroy my entire crop in a matter of two days' time. I would have to be up early tomorrow morning spraying insecticide before the bees were active in order to reduce any chance of accidentally harming those valuable pollinators. It was a shame to have to spray out the other harmless bugs, but prairie blazing star was an excellent pollinator and if I could get the seed into the market, the benefits of it being planted all across the country by others would help offset any harm I did. The University was working on a more organic solution than insecticide for this particular moth, but so far they hadn't come up with anything.

I stood up, bones creaking and took a few minutes to appreciate the pale blue, pink and peach-colored sunrise along with the vibrant purple blooming expanse of the field I was in. In some ways it was a relief to have found the moth. I'd been concerned about it for so long and had even been having nightmares that I'd missed it and the next time I checked on the crop the seed heads were all missing. But I did wish it wasn't now. My plate was already full.

My name is Carmen Karlaff and my family and I have been farming native grass seed and wildflowers for thirty-five years. We were located about five miles from Arvilla, a small town in Northwest Minnesota, with a population of around 2500. Arvilla was approximately thirty miles east of the North Dakota border and twenty miles south of the Canadian border. Although I don't notice it, I've been told our close proximity to Canada gives our speech a Canadian accent. Our operation was more than a farm as not only did we grow and harvest the seed; but we also cleaned our own seed, marketed it, packaged it and shipped it all over the United States. We sold the majority of our seed to wholesale seed companies who would in turn combine the species we grew along with species from other growers into seed mixes that were used for projects such as prairie restorations, gravel pit reclamations and roadside plantings. But the primary use of our seed is government conservation programs such as the conservation reserve program and wetland restoration projects more commonly known as CRP and WRP respectively. We also at times buy in species we don't raise to make our own mixes and sell them direct to customers in northwest and north central Minnesota, and eastern North Dakota. A recent decision we had made was to branch out into tourism, making life even more complicated and busy. We hoped to eventually make tours of the farm available and were in the process of working on getting three small cabins built in one of our native prairies for birdwatchers and anyone else interested in observing native prairies and whatever wildlife that may decide to show itself. Just last night we had a picture of an elk on our game camera. It was exciting they were getting to be a more common sight for our part of Northwestern Minnesota. I was supposed to be meeting with the building contractors in a couple of hours to go over their quote for the final time. If the quote was good and I gave them my approval it sounded like they could start on the cabin foundations soon. My cell phone rang, disturbing my thoughts. I checked the caller id before answering, not wanting to take the time to deal with my younger brother Kirk if it was him. It was the number of the shared cell phone for the roguing crew. "What can I get you?" I answered, knowing that something was needed as the roguing crew rarely called unless they were out of something.

"Carmen you'd better get over here right now." Gary Pitterson, our longest employed regular roguer said. Every year we employed a group of four to six people to walk our fields all summer and remove weeds. I don't know what their technical title should be but our farm has always called them roguers, pronounced like row-ger.

"Is it that urgent?" knowing in my gut that by the tone of his voice any chance of making it home this morning to grab a snack was getting farther away. My stomach growled.

"We found a body in the big bluestem field." Gary told me, his voice sounding oddly devoid of emotion.

"A body as in a dead animal?" I asked knowing it was a pointless question as I wouldn't be getting this phone call if that was the case.

"No Carmen, it's a man. I don't know who it is, but to be honest I didn't take much time to look. I don't think I have ever seen him before," he said as his voice started to rise.

"Did you call the sheriff?" I asked, knowing for sure that any hope of going home to grab a snack was now gone.

"Yes, they are on their way. In fact I think I can hear the sirens."

"I'll be there in five minutes." I ran for my pickup, jumped in and raced down the gravel road. I rummaged through the junk on the passenger seat that always accumulated in a farmer's pickup, hoping for anything that might be food. Squished under an owner's manual for one of the combines was a granola bar. It had been there so long, and smashed under stuff, that it was more like granola than an actual bar, but hey, it was something. I poured it into my mouth like a baby bird being fed as I turned onto the main highway; well maybe it was more of a two wheeled cringe-inducing, tires-squealing turn.

Three miles later I turned off the highway onto the road leading to our seed cleaning plant and break room building behind which were our fields of big bluestem, auburn in color now as it was almost ready for harvest and purple prairie clover which had lost most of its purple bloom. Once I got past the seed cleaning plant I was met by the flashing lights of emergency vehicles. I pulled up behind the sheriff's vehicle, put the pickup in park and jumped out, looking for Sheriff Poole. This was difficult as Sheriff Poole was a short man, and big bluestem could grow up to eight feet tall. I noticed an area of the field that looked like it was moving and with no wind today I was pretty confident that was where everyone was. I started in to the field, trying to knock down as little as possible. As I got closer I could hear voices. I finally located Gary, the head of our roguing crew, the sheriff, our other two roguers, and a couple of EMT's standing around a form on the ground. My brother, Kirk, was another roguer and should have been there also. For a second my heart stopped as I thought he might be the body, but I realized Gary would have told me if that were the case.

Sheriff Poole turned around, "Hi Carmen, any idea who this is?"

As I stepped next to the body, I looked down. I had seen plenty of dead animals over the years, but the only dead humans I had been exposed to had been prepared with carefulness and respect by morticians. This body did not look as lovingly prepared. His knees were scrunched up to his chest with a look of panic on his face. He did look vaguely familiar, but I couldn't place why and I wasn't going to look any closer. I hesitated and finally said, "I don't think so. Do you know what happened to him? I suppose you'll have to wait for an autopsy."

"No, I don't think I will," Sheriff Poole responded.

I looked again, this time noticing the brown stain on the ground next to his arm and the bloody hole in his chest on the side that closest to the dirt.

"He was shot?" I asked dumbfounded, the granola bar crumbs starting to stir in my gut, and feeling very thankful I hadn't eaten any more than that.

"It appears that way," Sheriff Poole answered. "It could hardly be an accident either. There is no hunting season this time of year, and no close by neighbors that would be target shooting. I'm sorry to do this to you Carmen, I know how busy everyone is as harvest is mere days away, but I'm going to have to talk to every one of your employees. In addition I have to preserve this as a crime scene, which means you are going to lose around a half-acre of your crop."

"I understand. I don't like it, but I do understand," relieved that it wasn't one of the more valuable crops. I know worrying about the crop instead of the dead person didn't make me sound like a very good person. "I'll get everyone to gather at the break room by the seed cleaning plant and you can talk to them there."

"Thanks, it will be awhile yet, as I have to wait for a crime scene technician to get here first. I'll let you know when they get here. I'm sure it will be a couple of hours or so as the nearest town with a crime scene technician is Bemidji. In the meantime don't let anyone leave work. How many employees do you have anyway?"

"Right now our employees consist of four on the roguing crew, my dad and I, and our new foreman, Nick Banning, that we hired about a month ago. Nick isn't here today though. He headed over to Grand Forks, North Dakota this morning to pick up parts for a new combine header. He should be back late this afternoon."

"I only saw three roguers, who's the fourth and where is he?"

"My brother, Kirk, is missing. I don't know where he is, he was supposed to be at work today," I shrugged my shoulders.

"Get everyone you can in the break room please and try to encourage them not to talk to each other, I like to gauge people's reactions when I talk to them." Sheriff Poole said.

"I'm supposed to be meeting with some contractors in a couple of hours. Is that going to be a problem?" I asked him.

"Could you do it to tomorrow? The less people around that could muck up the crime scene the better."

"They aren't coming here. I'm meeting them at the site. It's about three miles away. Certainly that won't be a problem?"

"Alright Carmen," the sheriff said his voice getting testy.

I could tell the sheriff was getting frustrated but it wasn't my fault some idiot got himself killed on our property. It's pretty sparsely populated around here, and it wouldn't surprise me that someone took advantage of that for some sort of drug deal, or other criminal activity. US Highway 59, the main highway that runs north-south through the middle of our farm was a direct route to Canada with a lot of different traffic on it. If hadn't been for my obsession with checking the fields for Palmer Amaranth, which was the next super weed, the body wouldn't have even been found until harvest which was about two weeks away for this particular crop. I only decided yesterday that I was going to have our roguing crew walk all fields one last time looking for the chemical resistant weed.

The sheriff continued, "You can meet with them if you want, but if you aren't around when I need to take your statement, I'll be royally pissed."

"I'll be here in time." My cell phone pinged; I looked at the text and after reading it said to the sheriff, "The contractors are already on their way. I need to take off but I should be back long before your crime scene techs even arrive. You can question the roguing crew in the break room. I'm going to quick run and get some bakery rolls. I'll put them in the break room so they have something to munch on while they wait. Anybody in your department is welcome to help themselves."

"Thanks Carmen," The sheriff let me go, but I knew he wasn't happy about it.

As I walked back to my pickup I stopped and told the roguing crew to wait in the break room, and that the sheriff would want to talk to them at some point. I asked Gary where Kirk was.

"He called me early this morning and said he had something going on with his band today," Gary answered. "I told him it was alright as I knew it didn't need all of us to get through the big bluestem field."

I rolled my eyes, thinking it was a good thing Kirk didn't want any part of running this farm for as much time off as he took. I told them I would pay for their time if the sheriff's questioning took longer than their normal shift and that they should cooperate with the sheriff.

I drove to the local convenience store which stocked baked goods from my friend Edna who ran a bakery out of her home in Arvilla. I was relieved to find a couple dozen caramel rolls left. At first I thought it was amazing as they were the first items to disappear on any given day, but then I realized it was only 9:00 a.m. I'd been up since 5:00 a.m. and it felt like the day should have been almost over. I added them to our charge account and headed back to drop them off at the break room before meeting with the contractors.

When I got back to the break room I noticed the sheriff was on the phone, no doubt hoping to locate closer crime scene investigators. I figured I had plenty of time for my meeting with the contractors. I handed the rolls to the workers, realizing to late I should have saved one for myself as they swarmed the boxes, and I was on my way again.

CHAPTER TWO

Big bluestem was the dominant grass of the tallgrass prairie.

I SOMEHOW MANAGED TO BEAT THE CONTRACTORS to the site. I parked, and as I waited I looked around and realized to my surprise that I was feeling a little apprehensive about what we were about to do. The wildflowers were past their bloom and the indiangrass and big bluestem had turned a beautiful auburn color. Seeing the advanced stage these wildflowers were at disheartened me in regard to any chance of harvesting our still blooming field of prairie blazing star. Circumstances out of our control forced us to burn the field later than normal and the field had never caught up to the rest of our crops. I prayed there wouldn't be an early frost and that the crop would have time to turn its blooms into seed. As I continued to wait I looked around and saw a whitetail deer bounding through the grass heading for the trees. For years my family has enjoyed the privacy of this one-hundred acres of native prairie. It was surrounded by woods which helped keep it a place of solitude for us. We burned and harvested it every year, but that was the extent of anyone but our immediate family being in here. We've had a couple of requests over the years for people to hunt the prairie, but had always turned them down. Now we were venturing towards getting away from our strictly agricultural business and sticking our toes into tourism. We were going to build three cabins out here and run them as a type of bed and breakfast. Each cabin would be able to accommodate up to eight people and they'd be at least a quarter mile from each other for privacy. My best friend Jessica Golding ran the local restaurant, and between her and another good friend Edna Forting, the local baker, they figured they could provide breakfast and dinner. I made a mental note to make sure my advertising brochures and website explained that dinner for this part of the country was a noon meal so no one would be confused. I know other places called the noon meal lunch and the evening meal dinner, but for us the evening meal is called supper. With the interest in pollinators and bird watching increasing in popularity, our native prairie provided an ideal spot for people to observe the ecosystem of a prairie. And it wouldn't hurt our bank balance either.

Mitch and Mark pulled up behind me and as I walked over to shake hands with them, I could hear another vehicle coming. My dad's rattling two door pickup pulled up and parked behind mine.

"What are you doing here Dad?" I asked him as he walked up to us.

"I saw all the commotion at the break room and no one would give me any answers. They just told me to find you." He answered his eyes full of questions.

"We'll talk about it later." I could see the questions in Mark and Mitch's eyes too. I imagine they would have driven by everything on their way here also.

"Morning, Mitch, Morning Mark." Dad shook their hands.

"Hey Chet," they responded.

"Did you get a chance to look over the final plans? Did you find any problems?" I asked them both.

"Yes, they look pretty basic. The hardest part will be the septic and water." Mitch answered.

Mitch and Mark Carboot ran MM construction, a very reputable company and I was thankful they had been able to fit our project into their schedule. They were brothers, a couple years apart, very similar in build as both were husky, blond and around six feet tall. The similarities ended with their appearance, Mitch was the people person and I was pretty sure Mark did most of the physical work.

"I checked with rural water, and other than the expense of it, it won't be difficult to get it here. The septic system might be more difficult." Mitch said.

"I was hoping you guys would have some ideas on what to do about the septic system; any thoughts?" I asked them hoping they would come through for me.

"Well; we thought that the easiest option might be a large holding tank that you'll need to have someone pump on a regular basis. That way you wouldn't need any drain fields or additional permits." Mitch answered.

"That sounds like a practical solution. They wouldn't need to be pumped more than once a year. I sincerely doubt that anybody will be using the cabins for the five months of winter." I said with relief.

"What about snowmobilers?" Mitch asked.

"We considered that, but decided it would be too hard to keep them off our fields. If the snow cover wasn't adequate, they could cause quite a bit of damage to the plants. But we haven't entirely ruled it out yet. We decided to start first with the spring, summer and fall months. The access in winter months could be difficult also. I can't see Jessica or Edna getting out here in four-foot snow drifts with food."

"We'll be sure to build with plenty of insulation in case you decide later to open them for winter. We'll also make sure the tank is large enough to hold waste for eight months. Of course you'll have to heat them all winter so the water lines don't freeze. The propane fireplaces should be adequate to keep them warm."

Mitch said showing me just how much time he had put into the proposal.

"I get the feeling you guys want these open in the winter?" I asked smiling.

"We have some buddies who would love a place to stay for snowmobiling in the winter. You also might want to consider catering to people who snowshoe or cross-country ski." Mitch responded.

"That's a good idea, in fact I like that better than the noise of snowmobiles. Either one I will have to consider. Do you guys have any further questions for me? If you don't I should be getting back. Sheriff Poole is going to be looking for me and if I'm not back before he needs me I think he'll throw me in jail." I said only half joking.

"No that should do it. We'll get our final quote to you tomorrow, and if it's acceptable we should be able to start building next week. Any chance you are going to share what's going on at your seed facility?" Mitch asked.

"Sorry, the sheriff said I had to stay mum. Thanks for everything guys," I hollered as I walked back to my pickup.

"Wait up Carmen," Dad hollered. "I may as well ride back with you. If you are meeting Sheriff Poole there must be something going on I need to be aware of."

I stopped walking and turned around to say to him, "You'd be better off bringing your own vehicle. I have some other stuff to do and I won't be able to bring you back to your pickup later. I'm sorry but I can't say anything to you, the sheriff told me not to talk to anyone. He wants to tell people himself what is going on. He made that very clear to me."

I made it back to the break room, with Dad right behind me just as Sheriff Poole was getting out of his department-issued car.

Dad and I parked, got out and walked towards the break room door. Looking at the little building always gave me a sense of pride. We'd made the decision a little over three years ago to build the 18' x 18' building here at our seed cleaning facility to give our employees a place to take a break, eat their dinner, get out of the heat, and most important, a nice bathroom as the other one was located at our shop a couple miles away and it was a rustic bathroom, to put it nicely. The roguing crew had port-a-potties in the field, but they tended to avoid using them, preferring to wait and take advantage of nice indoor plumbing at break time and dinner. I can't say as I blamed them. The break room was also equipped with a table, chairs, microwave, pizza oven, and refrigerator.

"Glad to see you made it back in time. Have you talked to anyone yet?" Sheriff Poole asked as he caught up to us, looking straight at my dad.

"No, Carmen didn't tell me a thing, but I'm thinking it is about time someone did," Dad said as he looked around.

"Let's go in the break room as it looks like everyone is here with the exception of Nick and Kirk. Nick left at 5:00 a.m. this morning and Kirk has been gone all day with his band I believe. I doubt they need to be talked to." I said hoping it was true.

"Don't be so sure, I have no idea how long the body was laying there. I won't know until the medical examiner has a chance to look at the body," Sheriff Poole responded.

I hated to say it, but I heard myself saying, "As hot as it's been last night and today, the body didn't look like it had been there that long, a day, maybe two at the most."

The sheriff shot me a glance, as Dad exclaimed, "What body?"

"I've seen dead animals and they puff up fast in this kind of heat plus if the body had been there very long some animal would have found it, or at least there would have been more flies. I would guess sometime yesterday or last night." I defended myself, ignoring Dad.

"That would be one of the details we'd prefer you keep to yourself. Well let's get on with it shall we," Sheriff Poole said as he opened the door to the break room and motioned us through. Conversation halted as everyone looked up at us.

"Who was the body Carmen?" Gary asked.

"I'll let the sheriff tell you about it."

Sheriff Poole stepped forward and said, "The body that you guys found in the field I'm confident was murdered."

Dad exclaimed, "What?"

The sheriff glared at him and kept talking without addressing Dad's question, "I'd like everyone to take a piece of paper and write down what you've been doing for the last two days in regards to this farm, where you've been, who you were with, approximate times and especially make note of where and when you saw any strange vehicles."

There was a lot of grumbling. "Do it guys, the faster you get this done, the faster you get out of here." I told them.

There was silence as everyone started thinking and then some scribbling noises as they stated to write.

Sheriff Poole looked at me as I stood there.

"What?" I asked.

"You need to start writing too." He looked at Dad, "You too Chet."

"Oh," I said startled and kind of surprised. "We weren't even here."

"Again, we don't know when the body was put here," the sheriff replied frowning at me and pointing at the paper on the table.

Dad and I sat down and started to write.

CHAPTER THREE

*Little bluestem provides nutritious grazing and
can produce ¾ to 2 tons of forage per acre.*

IT HAD BEEN A BUSY COUPLE OF DAYS and it took a while to recall everything. The workers had been finishing one by one and handing the papers to the sheriff and as a final step either he or a deputy reviewed it with them.

I was the last one to hand mine in. Dad had already finished his, visited with the deputy, and had been gone for around thirty minutes. That was an added benefit of being retired; his list of activities wasn't very long. Sheriff Poole glanced over the paper I gave him and started with the questions. "You haven't ever seen the deceased before?"

"No," again for some reason I was hesitant to say that there was something familiar about him.

"You didn't see any strange vehicles around?" He continued with his questions.

"I can't say for sure. I don't know if you are aware but our farm is spread over several townships. The fields in those townships are all small acreages not always close to each other. Also a major highway runs through the middle of it all," I said as I pointed to the steady stream of traffic on the highway next to the seed facility. "I see strange cars all the time as it is a direct route to Canada. We do have some trail cameras around that I don't check very often. A couple of them are set up for security that I can check in the event I end up missing something or we think that something may have been stolen. I'd be happy to turn the SD card over to you. There is one located by the crossing off the highway in to this facility. Maybe you'll get lucky and identify a car coming in. To be honest there will be a lot of traffic on it as a gravel pit that we irrigate out of is at the end of this field road and is known to be stocked with Walleye. A lot of people come to fish and swim in the gravel pits."

"How many people know the camera is there?" He asked me.

"I'd say most of the locals do."

"Is there another way in?"

"Not really," I answered. "There used to be an old trail, but I think it is impassible now."

My heart dropped as the sheriff said, "My preliminary instinct is that it almost has to be one of your workers or a local. I can't imagine anyone else even knowing this field is here. From the highway, the bins, buildings, and break room hide the field. The ditch crossing into your facility and field road doesn't lend itself to looking like this was a place you could hide a body unless you knew the field was here. Let's go get the pictures from that camera right now and hope we get lucky."

My phone rang interrupting us. I looked at the caller id and saw it was our lawyer, Jacob Esling. I was thankful for the interruption as it stopped me before I got too angry at the sheriff for accusing my workers. "Hi Jacob, what's up?"

"You know how the gossip works in this town, what's going on out there? I heard that the sheriff and some emergency vehicles are on the scene?"

"I'm not at liberty to say."

"Sheriff Poole is nearby I take it?"

"That would be correct."

"Okay, I'll leave it alone, but the real reason I called is to let you know I got all the easements drawn up and signed from the adjacent landowners for travel across their property to get to the cabins."

"That's great, were there any problems?" I asked hoping the answer would be no.

"There were a few special conditions for two of the landowners, but nothing that was out of the ordinary. When they heard that you weren't allowing anyone to physically be on their property, that guests staying in the cabins would be just passing through, and that you would maintain the trail, they were more than happy to be accommodating. Of course it helped that both landowners own businesses in town that will benefit from any extra tourism no matter how small."

This was true, while I loved our small town, with a population of 2500 it could use all the business it could get. We weren't known for our beautiful scenery, as the topography in our part of the world was flat with broad expanses of farmland broken up by wooded farmsteads. The primary draw for any tourism was a state park with a small man-made lake seven miles away. My hope was that we would help bring a little more tourism to the area by providing the opportunity to view wildlife and the beauty of native prairies. I didn't think there was anything better than watching a deer and her fawns frolicking in a prairie of golden-brown native grasses and purple, yellow, blue, and white blooming wildflowers, but I may be biased.

"I better let you get back to Sheriff Poole. Give me a call later and let me know when you can stop by to sign the easements." Jacob said curiousness evident in his voice.

"I will, hopefully I won't be needing any other legal work from you," I said with a sideways look at the sheriff. "Thanks Jacob for all the work." I said as I hung up.

Sheriff Poole standing next to me hadn't moved, but he was now looking irate at being interrupted, "I hate to be a bother, after all a mere dead body isn't that high of a priority," he said voice dripping in sarcasm, when I looked back at him after hanging up.

"Right this way. I need to get the computer out of my pickup." I walked over to the pickup, retrieved my computer case and walked over to the camera with Sheriff Poole close on my heels. The camera wasn't hid on purpose, but unless you knew it was there you wouldn't notice. It was on the same pole as a rain gauge and it looked like it was part of that setup.

"Let me do that Carmen, I've got enough game cameras, I know how it works and I don't want to take any chance of someone claiming the evidence wasn't handled properly."

He took the SD card out of the camera, stuck it into my computer and let the pictures download. The sun was too bright to see the computer screen so we walked back to the break room, went in and sat down at a table and started paging through the pictures. It didn't take much time. To my surprise, aside from the usual farm pickups, there was only one vehicle that I couldn't identify. However it was going at such a fast rate that it wasn't more than a red blur.

"I guess this isn't going to help too much. On a positive note I can't believe there was just one vehicle that was unrecognizable. Typically this field road is like a freeway with people going in and out to fish."

"At least the presence of one unknown vehicle gives you a slim chance that none of your employees is involved." Sheriff Poole said.

"I am positive that none of my employees had anything to do with this," I said trying to make my voice sound forceful.

"I hope you are right Carmen, but it's my job to check everyone out. I'm going to find out what I can about this red vehicle. Maybe someone can do something with this picture to make it clearer."

"I hope so as knowing that it is a red vehicle isn't going to help too much," I said. "Our new foreman Nick has a red pickup and my brother Kirk also drives a red piece of crap beat-up Ford Taurus. And when I think about it, two days ago I was in town picking up some parts and I noticed that over half the pickups at the café were red. I happened to notice because four were parked right next to each other and then I started looking."

The sheriff ignored me and said, "It's good that everything has a time stamp so we will start by trying to rule out your regular workers. I assume it is normal for them to work in groups so everyone should have someone to alibi them, and we'll go from there. Anybody with a red vehicle better have a good alibi for the time this one goes by. I believe you mentioned your foreman is a new employee. How much do you know about him?"

"Enough to know he wouldn't kill anyone." I answered hoping this was true.

"I'll need to talk to him when he gets back and I will be bothering your crew again. I'll need to verify their statements with the time and date stamps to make sure everyone is accounted for."

"I understand. The roguing crew is about done for the season, maybe a couple of days left. Is there any chance you can interview them on their own time instead of mine?" I asked knowing that question was futile.

The sheriff grunted, because really what kind of answer could there be to that. He pocketed the SD card, walked out of the break room and got into his patrol car; I presumed to wait for the coroner and crime scene investigators.

CHAPTER FOUR

Butterfly milkweed was thought to have been boiled and eaten as greens and the roots possibly used as a medicine by the Indians.

I SAT IN THE BREAK ROOM ENJOYING the silence for an all too brief moment when the door banged open and in walked my brother Kirk. He got all the height in the family, standing at six feet two inches with curly black hair and if the comments on the band's Facebook site could be believed was widely regarded to be very handsome. In addition he was a genuine nice guy, although most days he annoyed me so much I had a tough time remembering that.

"Did you know they found a body?" he asked me.

That's my brother, king of the obvious. "No I've just been sitting here wondering why the sheriff was here," I retorted.

"No need to get sarcastic," he stated.

"Yeah, well I'm a little frazzled. I have enough on my plate without dealing with this too. By the way, where have you been all day? You were supposed to be helping the roguing crew today."

Kirk got a funny look on his face.

"Where were you?" I repeated.

"I heard that a new bar is opening in Parkville. They are looking for bands to book for Saturday nights. They're going to pay unlike where we are playing this Saturday night, so I took the day off and drove over to get our band first on their list."

My brother and his buddies from high school had an undying desire to make it in the music world. And while I admired their tenacity, I was a little short on admiring their musicality. They specialize in extreme hard rock. I don't know that they are necessarily that bad, but I can't make heads or tails of any of their lyrics and after ten minutes of trying I have a throbbing headache.

"You know you are supposed to check with me or Dad if you aren't going to be around." I stated.

"I know. I did let Gary know, but I figured I would zip over there and be back before you or Dad knew I was gone. But my car got a flat tire and Wizard got out of the car while I was trying to change the tire. I then had to spend a half hour trying to catch him and coax him back into the car. To top it off, all I had was one of those stupid small single-use spare tires and could only drive about twenty miles per hour."

Wizard was my brother's Weiner dog. For some reason Kirk insisted on taking Wizard with him everywhere he went and Wizard made a habit of escaping every chance he got. He is deceptively fast in spite of his short legs and fat belly, and to everyone's surprise, hard to catch.

"So did you know who it was?" he asked.

"No, I didn't. You'll have to take a look and see if it's anyone you recognize. Sheriff Poole is going to want to talk to you too."

"I already talked to him. He caught me as I was driving in. He showed me a picture; it wasn't anyone I recognized." Kirk paused, then said, "What are you thinking?"

"There was something about him that was familiar, but I'm sure I had never seen him before," I said, disappointed that Kirk hadn't recognized the body either.

"You know, now that you mention it, I had the same reaction.

Do you think we knew him a long time ago, or maybe he has a relative in the area?" Kirk asked. "Anyway it's weird, I imagine it will turn out to be some stranger that was trespassing and had a heart attack or something."

I guess the sheriff hadn't shared many details with him. "No, he'd been shot," I told Kirk. "He'll probably think you killed the guy since you were missing." I sighed.

I looked out the window bemoaning the fact that this had happened on our property in silence. Kirk had sat down and now repeated, "He was shot?"

"Yes, that's why Sheriff Poole is interviewing everyone. He also took the SD card from the camera."

"Will that do any good? If the body has been there awhile the camera has a limit on how many pictures it holds," Kirk stated.

"The sheriff thinks it was pretty recent, but I suppose the autopsy will say for sure. I don't think whoever put it there thought it would be found for a while. If it was a local they'd know that we don't harvest the big bluestem for a few more weeks and with any luck some wolves or coyotes would have gotten rid of the body. They wouldn't have known that we were making one last pass for Palmer Amaranth. Best circumstance it was a stranger who didn't know that the grass was an actual crop; if that had been the case the body would never have been found."

"Either way it's a little insane," Kirk said shaking his head.

"I guess we'll have to wait and see what the sheriff comes up with. I know it sounds unfeeling of me but I just want this over. I have enough to do." I heard another vehicle drive in, and when I didn't hear any car doors open or shut, I got up to look. A couple guys in uniforms were talking and gesturing in their vehicle. They got out of the vehicle and walked over to the sheriff's patrol car. "It looks like the crime scene investigators are here." I said as I walked back to the table and sat down by Kirk.

My comment about being busy must have reminded Kirk of the

cabins as he asked, "What's going on with the cabins? I know your meeting was today with the contractors."

"If their quote is good they'll be starting next week. Back to you though, I really do need you to be with the roguing crew tomorrow. Harvest is coming fast and the fields have to be gone through one more time."

"I will, I will. What are you going to be doing?"

"First, I need to be up and spraying the prairie blazing star by 5:00 a.m. The moth is back and it has to be sprayed early in the morning before the bees get active. I need to check in with Nick to see if he needs help getting the new header parts installed on the combine. I also need to get together with Jacob to get the final easements for the cabin project and get the building permit filled out, although with any luck I can catch him in his office yet today."

"Is there anything else?" he asked. Proving once again how annoying he could be.

Dad walked back in the break room. I resembled Dad the most, both of us about five feet seven inches tall, and blonde. Dad and I were sturdily built while Kirk inherited the slenderness of our mom. Curly hair was the only physical trait we had in common with Kirk.

"Did you hear what happened?" he asked Kirk.

"Yeah, the sheriff just got done talking to me." Kirk answered.

"It's too bad, everyone is shook up and I know we don't need any hassles before harvest." Dad said looking at me.

"I know, Dad." Apparently lots of people were intent on telling me things I already knew today. "Did the sheriff or a deputy talk to you after you got your paper filled out?"

"The sheriff did. I told him the truth that I hadn't been over this way for three days and that I didn't have anything more to offer and then I waited in my pickup until you were done," Dad said as he sat down next to me.

"Did he accept that?" I asked.

"Well he didn't appear particularly happy, but I can't help with what I don't know. Is Nick back yet?" he asked.

"I haven't seen him yet. I'm pretty sure it'll be late tonight. Why don't you go home and relax. You've been up most of the day." Dad had suffered a heart attack last year. In my mind Dad had always been so indestructible that it was a real shock for me to see him in a hospital bed. It took me eight months, but in the end I convinced him it was time to retire, which is why we hired Nick. Dad now did take more time off than before, but at times he seemed to be fighting it a little. He had reduced his hours, thanks in part to wanting to spend time with his new girlfriend Karla Harmen, but couldn't help himself from trying to be involved in decisions I made. I was doing my best not to take it personal; after all, Dad had been in charge of this farm for many years. I knew it was tough for him to let go and I did welcome his opinion. It hadn't involved any serious conflict yet, as we had been in agreement on most things so far, but I was dreading the day we weren't. Karla was also doing her best to help him slow down, but she wasn't much of an example. She hadn't slowed down and was continuing gung-ho with the cattle farm she ran with her son James, who was one of my closest friends. We'd been neighbors our entire lives. Within the last couple of months Dad and Karla had become a little more than neighbors. While I approved of it—after all, Mom had been gone for six years—it felt strange to me that after living a half mile away from each other for forty-plus years with no real contact they discovered a connection now. In fact at one point some twenty years ago or so, they had quite a feud going. Some of her cows got out and trampled down our blue grama field. I don't think I'd ever seen my dad so mad. At times it amazed me to see them together now.

"That sounds like a good idea. Karla and I are heading out for supper tonight in Parkville. It wouldn't hurt to get a little nap in before we leave."

"That sounds fun." It was kind of sad that my sixty-three year old dad had a more active social life than myself. "What time is it anyway?" I asked as I looked at my phone. "It's only 3:00 p.m." I groaned, "It feels like this day is lasting forever."

"Well you've had a long day," Dad said. "Are you going to check in with Jacob yet today?"

"Yes, that's where I'm heading now."

"Okay. Don't wait up for me tonight," Dad grinned at me as I walked out of the break room.

I climbed into my pickup, sat for a few minutes and let the air conditioning cool off the interior. My water jug was on the floor of the passenger side. It was almost too much effort to reach down and over to get it. I fumbled around with one hand and grabbed it, grunting with the effort. It was deliciously cold. I took a long, long drink, put it down and started to put the pickup in drive, when the phone rang. It was Nick.

"Hey Carmen, I'm going to be later than I planned, the trailer I was using for the combine header parts got a flat tire. It took me a while to track down a spare and get it changed. I wanted to let you know I won't be back until late."

Apparently flat tires were the normal for the day. I didn't want to get into everything over the phone so I settled for saying, "some strange things have happened today, how about when you get back you stop by the house and I'll let you know what's been going on, unless you have other plans for the evening?"

"No, that'll be fine. I should be there around 7:00 p.m."

Nick Banning was our new foreman. It was a trial period for all of us. With Dad wanting and needing to slow down and Kirk not wanting, nor able to be anything other than an occasional hired man, we needed a mechanic who could also help manage the farm. I couldn't handle everything when agronomy was my strong suit and not anything mechanical. I had originally wanted nothing to do with farming; even though I'd enjoyed being associated with the uniqueness of our farm. As a teenager the years of walking fields as a roguer had left me with little appetite for wanting to farm as a vocation. After high school I started out as a business major at the University of North Dakota in Grand Forks which was about an hour southwest of here but it never felt like I was a good match for being in dress clothes all day in a business setting. I stuck it out for a semester and then transferred to the Crookston campus of the University of Minnesota to pursue an agronomy major with a minor in business; thinking I would pursue a job working for a chemical/fertilizer company. Everything changed my last year of college when my mom died unexpectedly from cancer. Dad needed help on the farm and Kirk had already made music his passion so I moved home after graduation and threw myself into helping to run things. Mom had been the musical one in the family. She encouraged Kirk and it felt like a betrayal to Mom to push him into farming, not to mention, due to his disinterest, his help would have been negligible. It was mind-boggling but the four years away had helped me appreciate our farm and its challenges and I had moved from reluctance to enthusiasm in no time at all. Although my agronomy and business degrees, plus my prior experience made me more than competent with most things running this farm threw at me, stereotypical as it may sound, I was no good with anything mechanical. I could operate equipment and I knew when something wasn't running right, but I was of no use when it came to fixing or repairing. So far Nick was working out well; he was knowledgeable and dependable and had proven his worth many times over the last couple of months. He was a difficult man to read though; I didn't have a good grasp if he was enjoying being here as much as we were glad he was here. We didn't know much about him personally other than that he was from a small town in Oregon by the Willamette Valley and his references checked out. He had a diesel mechanic degree and the references from the two previous farms he worked for had nothing but good to say about him. It was also a positive that both farms were turf grass farms with irrigation systems similar to ours. I was praying he wasn't somehow tied up in this murder—harvest would never happen if that was the case—was my selfish thought. As I was about to put the pickup in drive I thought I may as well get something accomplished today, so I stopped again and called Jacob before driving in to town to make sure he was in and if it would be convenient to stop by to sign the easements. He said it was. I finally put the pickup in drive and drove to Jacob's office in Arvilla which was five minutes from most of the farm acreage. My stomach growled reminding me that I had missed dinner, but this late in the day it would have to wait now until I was home for supper.

I walked into his office and was surprised to find the front reception desk empty. I say surprised because Jacob, while I liked him, was a very stuffy guy. Not having Gwen, his receptionist, sitting at the front desk during business hours wasn't normal, but maybe she was in his office helping him with something. Jacob was a handsome man, about ten years older than I was. He was a little taller than my five feet seven inches and kept himself in tip-top shape. Most unnatural for our rural small town, he was rarely seen in anything other than a suit and tie and his impeccable black Cadillac Escalade. The one saving grace that kept him from completing the stereotype of a stodgy lawyer was his designer sunglasses and his pride and joy, a yellow Corvette Stingray. People in this part of the country would never spend seven hundred dollars on a pair of sunglasses or own a vehicle that couldn't be driven on a gravel road. He had announced a couple of weeks ago that he was going to run for State Representative and while I felt he had the qualifications to do the job, I wasn't sure he'd be able to connect with voters on the campaign trail. That may be ignorance on my part as my outfit of choice was jeans and a t-shirt with my hair in a pony tail; and the people I associated with were the same. But, I don't tend to get out much beyond my immediate community, and the district he would be representing covered a good chunk of northern Minnesota. I am sure there are plenty of suits and tie people that would find my jeans and t-shirt apparel inappropriate. However my main concern was that I got my property easement paperwork finished before he got too busy on the campaign trail. I knew my chances of getting a hold of him for any help once the campaigning started would be nonexistent.

I walked around the front desk calling his name. As I got closer to his office I could hear voices. As I went to knock on the door, it opened before my hand could connect with it and a girl I recognized as Gwen, his secretary, came out crying. She brushed past me and rushed down the hall.

Jacob saw me standing there.

"I can come back another time." I said.

"No, no that's alright. I had to let her go. I feel bad, but between a few serious mistakes that have happened and her inexperience it was time to find someone else. It is essential that I get someone competent in here to can handle things when I'll be gone so much the next six months. But you're not here to hear about my problems. Have a seat and I'll find your paperwork in this pile somewhere." He proceeded to shuffle through his stack, finding the right file on the very bottom.

"Okay, here it is, you need to sign on the last two pages. All the easements are in order. The Olson's requested that there was a litter condition put in your easement across their property. They were pretty serious about it, so you better make sure you have someone checking it out to make sure any guests aren't chucking stuff out their windows as they drive through."

"I don't think that will be a problem. The type of clientele that we will be attracting shouldn't be litterers," I said to him with a smile.

"I didn't think so, that's why I went ahead with the condition instead of contacting you over it."

"Thanks, anything else?" I asked.

"The Limbroghs asked that the Juneberry trees on their property have some sort of signage to keep the berries from getting picked."

"That should be fine. We have a lot on our own property if someone feels the need to pick berries." I said thankful for such minor concerns.

"They know that, but are concerned that since they are right next to the road it might be too much temptation. Again, I didn't think you'd have a problem with it, so I went ahead with the paperwork. Otherwise all other parcels are fine with a road going through them as long as you were picking up the liability insurance."

"Yep, it's already in place. I talked to my insurance company last week."

"Sign in these two spots and you are good to go," Jacob said as he handed me the paperwork.

I reached down to sign the papers, stopped and asked, "Do you know where I get a building permit?"

"The courthouse processes them, but I should have an extra form here." He turned around to his filing cabinet, opened a drawer, found the form, and handed it to me. "It'll have to be mailed or delivered to the courthouse though. I don't have anything to do with processing them."

"Thanks Jacob, I should have taken care of this a few weeks ago, but better late than never."

"It won't be a problem, I've never heard of them not approving a building permit. More building means more tax base for the county." He smiled at me as I handed him the signed easements back. "I'll get you a copy of the easements in the mail tomorrow after they've been recorded. It's been a pleasure and I wish you the best with your venture."

"Thanks again Jacob. Good luck to you with your secretary search and your run for office."

"It should be an interesting adventure. I'll walk you out. It's time to lock up and head out anyway," he said as he stopped and looked around his office.

"Is something wrong?" I asked him.

"No, just my usual search for sunglasses and keys, I keep telling myself to put them in the same place every day, but it never happens. To my continual frustration I'm organized with every other aspect of my life except those two items which are somehow always misplaced," he said with a shrug.

I smiled, "That's why the rest of us leave our vehicles unlocked with the keys in them and buy ten dollar pairs of sunglasses."

"Everyone else doesn't look cool either." He said with a laugh.

As I left Jacob's office the enormity of my undertaking hit me. There was no backing out now. I had just enough time to head over to the courthouse before it closed and submit the building permit. After filling it out with the help of the county administrator and paying the application fee, I turned it in. He didn't think there would be a problem but they would let me know in a day or two. I walked out of the courthouse, looked at my phone and decided it was time to head home for supper.

CHAPTER FIVE

*Early pioneers used prairie cordgrass to thatch their roofs
and to cover their haystacks and corncribs.*

NICK WAS STANDING BY HIS PICKUP, busy scratching the ears
of Tabitha, a small female calico that was the only privi-
leged one of our three farm cats that got to come in the house,
when I drove into the yard of the two-story old farm house
where I lived with Dad and Kirk. Yes, I know; twenty-eighty-
years-old and living at home with daddy sounds very sad. But
honest it was necessary. Existing places to live were few and far
between, unless you had the money to build, which I did not, but
also Dad genuinely wanted us here. Losing Mom had been hard
on him and the last thing he wanted was to be rambling around
a big house all alone.

I parked, got out of my pickup and walked over to Nick. As
I did I couldn't help but notice again that Nick was a handsome
man, at least I thought he was. He was about five feet ten inches tall
with dark brown hair and a lean muscular build. "It sounded like
there was some excitement around here this morning." He said as
I walked up to him.

"How did you hear about it?" I asked.

"I ran into Gary when I dropped the combine header parts off at the shop. He was cleaning up the van and filling it with gas. I happened to be there at the same time. What a weird thing to have happened. Gary said no one knew who it was. Have you heard anything else from the sheriff?"

"No, but I wouldn't be the first person they tell, seeing as for lack of anyone better, myself and most of the workers are the prime suspects." I answered him.

"He thinks that?" Nick asked in amazement, looking like he wanted to sit down.

"I don't really think so, but I guess he has to start somewhere. You do need to get a hold of him as he wants to talk to you too."

"I'll give him a call as soon as I leave here," Nick said.

"I wish I could figure out why the guy looked so familiar," I said bugged by the faint feeling that I should have known who the body was.

"An old worker perhaps," Nick suggested.

"No. I don't think so, anyway," I shook my head. "How was your day?"

"Okay, but long. I debated about the wisdom of going myself, as we could have hired a shipping company, but I'm glad I went. They had the parts for the wrong header sitting out. If I hadn't gone, harvest would have been delayed or we would have had to use one of the other combines for the prairie blazing star, yet it was a long slow, boring drive when you can't drive over thirty miles per hour."

"You're welcome to come in for a glass of lemonade or an iced tea." I offered.

"I'll pass on those, thanks, but a glass of ice water sounds good. It's been a hot one today even though I spent most of the day in an air-conditioned pickup cab."

We walked into the house where the blasting of the central air felt glorious. It wasn't normal to be this hot in Minnesota in

September, but every once in a while we'd get a couple days of high ninety degree temperatures. For us cold weather climate people it was just about unbearable.

I grabbed two bottles of water and a couple glasses that I added ice to, handed Nick one, grabbed the other for myself and we both sat down at the kitchen table. Our kitchen was no doubt outdated with white linoleum, dark brown cabinets and butcher block countertops, but it was comfortable and where we spent most of our time. One day I would have to make the time to sand the top of our kitchen table and refinish it, as it still bore the marks where Kirk and I in our younger years had carved lines into the top to make sure we didn't encroach into each other's space.

"That hits the spot," Nick said sighing and setting down his now-empty glass. "Did you get a chance to scout for the moth?"

"Yes, and it is here. I'll have to get up early tomorrow and spray."

"I can do it for you." Nick offered, helpful as always.

"I know you would, but your pesticide application license hasn't been processed. I'll take care of the spraying, but thanks for your offer."

"Did you meet with the contractors?"

"I did. They think they can start next week." I answered him grinning.

"You sound excited. It has the potential to add a lot of work to your plate."

"I know, but I am thrilled. As more people are getting into this type of farming, the prices are going down for our crops, so I think this will be a good way to bring in some extra cash, plus it'll be good for the local businesses. It is always nice to bring some more people in to the area to spend some money, and it won't be that much extra work once the cabins are finished. Jessica and Edna will handle the food. I haven't figured out who is going to clean the cabins but I'm certain I can find some teenagers to do it. But yes, it will be a bother while everything is getting built. Mark and Mitch are the best contractors around. I know I'm paying a little more for them, but it will be worth it as they are honest and competent and will handle most problems that come up during construction without bothering me much. They've done quite a bit of construction for us and we've never had a problem." What I didn't need complicating things was a dead body, but I didn't say that out loud.

"On an unrelated note, have you noticed Gary has been absent quite a bit lately?" Nick asked.

"No, Kirk hasn't said anything."

"He hasn't been here much to even notice. I don't mean to step on toes but Kirk hasn't been very reliable either."

"I know, undependable is Kirk's trademark unless its music related. I've been planning on talking to him."

"You don't need to talk to him; after all you hired me to be the foreman here, but being new and him being your brother . . ." Nick's voice trailed off.

"You treat him like any other employee. Chew him out. Fire him if you have to. I love my brother, but sometimes I think it would be good for him to have the safety net of this farm gone. He'd either have to get serious about his music or actually find a career. But what is going on with Gary?" I asked.

"I'm not sure, all I know is in the last two weeks he's gone from being a reliable employee to a pretty hit and miss one. His personality has changed also, almost like he's resentful of having to work here."

"That's odd. He's always indicated that he's happy to work here. We also gave everyone a raise when they started walking fields four months ago. I make a point of ensuring we are paying a top wage for this area. Weeding fields isn't fun work and I want to make sure the pay reflects that." I said, puzzled by Gary's behavior.

"Well if you don't know of any personal reasons I'll have to talk to him tomorrow. I thought I'd check in case he'd mentioned something to you. I didn't want to come down too hard on him if he was going through something terrible in his personal life." Nick put his

glass of water down on the table and said, "I guess I'll head out and
I better get a hold of the sheriff yet tonight."

"Thanks Nick, and thanks for stopping by and catching me up
on things."

"I'll see you in the morning," he said as he walked out the door.

I watched as Nick walked out to his pickup and drove away. Dad
and I had gone round and round about hiring a foreman. I hadn't
wanted to and wasn't sure we could afford it, but our accountant
had taken one look at me after last year's harvest, ran some numbers, and told us we could swing it. It took a few months to find
Nick. We were surprised when we had quite a few applicants, but
in retrospect we shouldn't have been, as good paying jobs weren't
that prevalent in our area, but most of the applicants were familiar with traditional crops like wheat, corn and soybeans and didn't
have a clue about what our farm entailed. They tended to look at us
with a puzzled expression when we started talking about big bluestem, indiangrass, sideoats grama, blue grama, purple prairie clover, wild bergamot, white prairie clover, leadplant, prairie blazing
star, prairie cordgrass, and little bluestem; all crops we raise. Nick,
however, at least came from a background of turf grass farming
and while it wasn't the same as what we did, he at least didn't have
the conventional farming ideas ingratiated into his thinking, plus
he'd had experience with irrigation. So far I was counting my bless-
ings. He'd been a wonderful asset and taken a lot off of my plate. My
musings were interrupted by a face in the window. Tabitha liked to
sit on the grill and look in the window when she wanted inside for
some attention. I opened the door and she blasted in. I filled her
food dish that we kept in the kitchen special for her. I poked my
head in the fridge while Tabitha inhaled her food. It sounded like
she was enjoying her food while I wasn't having much luck finding
something to eat. It was a good thing I loved eggs, as it looked like
that was my only choice.

I fried two eggs, made some toast and treated myself to both
butter and peanut butter on it. This was my favorite meal, breakfast,

dinner and supper. I was putting my dishes in the dishwasher when I heard a knock on the door. Tabitha looked at me, and just like she knew her chance of getting any cuddles on the couch was over, she headed up the stairs to her favorite place to nap, on top of my bed. The knocking intensified.

"Hurry up and open this door, I know you're home!" shouted a voice I knew well.

CHAPTER SIX

*Purple prairie clover varies in height from one to two feet
and has a purple cone-type seed head.*

M Y BEST FRIEND JESSICA GOLDING was standing at the door. She was five feet two inches tall, petite, dark short hair, pretty much the exact opposite of me in appearance but her best feature was that she was the happiest person I had ever met. More to the point, life had dealt her so many knocks it was even more impressive that she always maintained such an optimistic attitude. Her older brother had run away about twenty years ago after a nasty drunk driving accident, when he ran into a girl on a bike, leaving her paralyzed from the waist down. Her father passed away a few weeks after his disappearance. The doctors said it was an undiagnosed heart defect, but Jessica had once told me she thought the stress and shame he felt over his son leaving broke his heart. I'm sure Jessica's father's fatal heart attack explains why I was so petrified when Dad had his and pushed him to consider retirement. If the loss of her brother and father wasn't enough, her mother struggled with depression, mourned for years, and passed away about three years ago. Yet somehow Jessica remained the most cheerful person I know.

"Why didn't you call me? I can't believe I heard something like this through the grapevine," she said in indignation.

"I assume word of the body that was found in our field has spread?" I asked her knowing full well that was what she was talking about.

"It is true. I was really hoping it wasn't. Did you know who it was?"

"No, but he did look kind of familiar." I said again wondering why that was.

"Was it creepy or gross?" she whispered as if whispering made it less creepy. "I heard he was shot." She paused and spit out, "I guess I'm trying to ask if you are okay?"

"As well as I can be, but I'd rather not talk about it anymore. It's the sheriff's problem now and I have enough of my own," I said trying to sound firm.

"I'm not sure I believe you. After all the mysteries you've read you can't tell me you aren't a little intrigued by this," Jessica said knowing me like a best friend does.

"I have to admit to a little bit of interest," I finally said.

She looked at me, laughed and said, "You don't lie very well."

I smiled, "Ok, I'm very interested, but between harvest and the cabin construction I don't need another distraction."

"I can help with one of your distractions. Edna and I have come up with some ideas for menus for your cabins, things that will be easy to transport and able to be heated up in microwaves if necessary, or if preferable, ready-made stuff that can be left in freezers that they can pop in the oven. We thought when they make their reservations you could give them a choice between having their freezer stocked or food brought in once each day. You are planning on supplying breakfast and dinner each day, but not supper, correct?"

"Yes, I want the town to benefit from this also and if we supply all their food they'll have no reason to go to town."

"That's what we thought. We were thinking baskets with scones and muffins, fresh fruit and homemade jams for those who don't want to mess with cooking, and some breakfast quiches for those who like a warm breakfast. The dinners would consist of dishes that could be frozen if needed to be, things like lasagnas, potpies or even meatloafs," She stopped, took a breath and looked at me her eyes twinkling.

"I can tell you are excited Jessica; so am I, and I am so grateful for all the work you and Edna have done, but please take a breath and relax. It's been a long day and I have to get up at the crack of dawn tomorrow and spray. So what I would like right now is to sit on the couch and relax. Most of all I'd like it if my best friend would sit down with me and talk about something fun, like how the fund raising is going for the pool repairs or the latest gossip from town."

"I'm sorry to tell you this Carmen, but your murder is pretty much the gossip," Jessica said as she watched me clean my dishes.

"There is nothing to be sorry about; I guess it was stupid of me to think it would be anything else. You are being an outstanding friend helping out with these cabins. I'm just beat." I said rubbing my eyes.

We plopped down on the couch with big sighs, looked at each other and burst into laughter, "You'd think we were eighty years old. In all seriousness, are you making any headway with the fundraising?"

Our town pool was special to us. Not many towns our size had pools and it was a big draw from neighboring communities in the summer for swimming lessons, activity for kids, and cooling off for everyone. But the pool had cracked over the summer and expensive repairs were needed. Nobody wanted their taxes raised for a pool project so we were hoping to raise the funds.

"We are about $50,000.00 from our goal, the fundraising along with the grant from the state means we've raised the majority of the funds. We were kind of stalled on anything else as we've had bingos, raffles, bake sales, and community suppers and frankly the committee was getting tired out. But Jacob offered to pay for a Hawaiian vacation for 4 along with plane tickets for a final raffle. We are going to charge $50.00 per raffle ticket so I'm hoping that will do it," Jessica answered excited by the prospect of being done.

"Wow that's amazing. He may be kind of stuffy but he sure is willing to help out. I know lawyers make a lot of money, but he does donate a huge amount back to the community," I said amazed.

"Well he doesn't have any family, so in a way the community is all he has," Jessica answered.

"That's both sad and incredibly generous."

"Well if you want to be a little more cynical, he is also running for public office," Jessica said laughing.

"That is true," I agreed. "But I do believe Jacob likes to help the community."

"I'm sure he does. Speaking of nice guys, have you seen much of James lately?"

James Harmen, Karla's son, was considered by most people in town to be my boyfriend. The truth is neither one of us was interested in each other that way, but it was nice to have a plus one to attend events with. It also eliminated the need for everyone to be trying to hook us up with other people if they thought we were a couple. Jessica of course knew this, but being a romantic at heart she sometimes acted like she was waiting for that to change . . .

"No, it's been hectic getting ready for harvest and working on getting the cabins going," I said "James hasn't had much time either. He and Karla have been doing a lot of fencing. That storm a couple of weeks ago caused a lot of trees to fall down on their fences. So instead of repairing just the downed fence areas they decided it was time to take on a complete overhauling of all their fence lines."

"How are you going to ever develop any sparks if you don't ever see each other?" she asked with a weird look on her face.

"I think you know you can give up on that," I said with a smile.

"What about Nick? Is there anything possible on that front?" she asked.

"Well, I can't deny he is handsome, but I don't know much about his personal life."

"It sounds like you have considered it though," she said again with the weird look on her face.

"It would also be pretty uncomfortable as he's our employee and I work with him almost every day."

"That's true, but he's nice to look at." She looked at me questioningly.

"Why don't you go for it?" I asked her wondering what she was up to.

"No, he's not my type," she answered blushing.

"Well, who is? I've never heard you get excited about anyone since Sawyer Periman." Sawyer had been her high school boy-friend. They had dated for a few years and had tried hard to make it work after graduation. They split up when Sawyer left for a job in Minneapolis and Jessica had no desire to live anywhere but here. She wasn't interested in any higher education but had always wanted to cook, so she bought the restaurant she had waitressed in all during high school shortly after graduation when the previous owners had retired. She loved feeding people and took pleasure in the fact that her restaurant was known for old-fashioned home cooking like meatloaf and meatball dinners, homemade soups, and chicken dinners all at reasonable prices. Her breakfasts were my favorite, especially her omelets. You never left hungry from her restaurant. The lone drawback was that she was only open for breakfast and dinner.

"Carmen," she paused, "Are you sure there is nothing between you and James?"

"James?" I said surprised, why hadn't I ever put that together before? "Absolutely not, you know that. Are you interested in James?"

"I've always liked him, but it has always been the two of you. I could never quite believe that it was platonic?" she asked blushing at my scrutiny.

"Trust me. Nothing would make me happier than if my two favorite people got together. Not to mention it would never work for James and me to get together." She looked at me puzzled, "Carmen Harmen," I said with a frown shaking my head.

Jessica looked at me strangely at first. When she figured out I was putting James' last name with my first name she burst into laughter.

I laughed with her and once we stopped I said, "What can I do to help make it happen between the two of you?"

"Leave it alone, please Carmen," Jessica said blushing even redder. "He's been coming in for dinner almost every day at the restaurant. I think he might be interested. But I wanted to talk to you first."

"Consider yourself free to pursue with my blessing. I think you two would be great together. But, I do have to kick you out. It's 10:00 p.m. and I have to be spraying by 5:00 a.m."

"Oops, I didn't realize it was so late. I better get going too." She stood up to leave and said, "Thanks for being so cool about James."

"There is nothing to be cool about; James is a friend, a super-close friend, but only a friend. In all sincerity I hope it works out for you two. You can always invite him to Parkville on Saturday. Kirk's band will be playing."

"I want to date him not kill him," Jessica said laughing as she walked out the door. "I'll have to think about it."

Life is funny I reflected, wondering why I had never thought of James and Jessica together before. They would be perfect for each other. The day ended up not being so bad after all.

CHAPTER SEVEN

Leadplant is a palatable range plant and its decrease is an important indicator of overgrazing.

THE ALARM JERKED ME OUT OF A SOUND SLUMBER way too soon Tuesday morning. Tabitha jumped off while I struggled to get out of bed, but found myself ensnarled in my sheets. It had been way too short of a night and I had vague memories of dreaming about running away from a giant gun on wheels. It was clear that yesterday's events were weighing on my mind. I kicked my legs out of the sheets, forced myself upright and stumbled to the bathroom. I deliberately took a cold shower to help me wake up. I was running late so I skipped breakfast, but I couldn't resist coffee; although a more accurate statement would be that I needed coffee even more than I needed food to survive the day. I was pouring it into my thermos when my cell phone rang.

"Good morning Nick, what are you doing up so early?" I answered after looking at caller ID.

"I couldn't sleep. I talked to the sheriff last night and it sure felt like he was doing his best to find a reason for the new guy in the community to be responsible for the dead body," he said sounding discouraged.

"Oh, no, I got the feeling yesterday that he was determined to make sure one of my employees was responsible. Are you okay?"

"I'm fine. It didn't sink in at the time, but it must have bugged me a little as I woke up thinking about it and I couldn't get back to sleep. Maybe you'll have to use some of your mystery book experience to figure this out for the sheriff," Nick said, knowing about my love for mysteries as we had once discussed our respective reading preferences while waiting to load seed for a customer one day. He preferred science fiction, which besides being my employee, was another reason why I shouldn't be romantically involved with him.

"Somehow I don't think the sheriff would appreciate my help." I said laughing.

"That is true," Nick said. "Anyway, I wanted to let you know that I've got the Spra-Coupe all ready for you. I wasn't sure which insecticide you were planning to use, but the Coupe is out in the field waiting for you. You just have to swing by the shop and pick up whichever one you need."

"That wasn't necessary, but is much appreciated. How did you get back to the shop?"

"Your dad was up tinkering this morning. He said he couldn't sleep either, so I had him give me a ride."

"Awesome, I am running late, so this will get me back on schedule. Thanks again Nick."

I drove out to the field, drinking in the quiet of the early morning. The sun was barely starting to rise. I would be finished long before the bees got going. It was a small field, just five acres and the actual spraying would only take thirty minutes. Moving the equipment took most of the time, but Dad and Nick had helped with that. Though by the time I finished spraying, got the sprayer cleaned and rinsed, I was getting hungry.

I called Nick, "Are you around to give me a ride back to my

pickup if I drive the Spra-Coupe back to the shop or are you in the middle of something?"

"It's not a problem to pick you up, but the sheriff is here and wants to talk to you. You can bring your pickup and when you are finished talking to him I can take you back out to get the coupe."

"That will work. Do you have any idea what he wants?" I asked feeling a little nervous.

"He hasn't said, but he looks kind of upset."

"I'm beginning to think that's his normal countenance," I said with a laugh. "Let him know I'll be there in ten minutes."

I jumped in my pickup and drove as fast as I could back to the shop, after all if the sheriff was there I could hardly get a ticket. Sheriff Poole was waiting for me by Nick's pickup when I drove in. I was pretty sure he frowned, as he would have seen me speeding on the highway before I slowed to turn.

"Did you put any more thought into who you thought the dead man was?" he asked me with a funny look as I walked up to him.

"No I told you yesterday I didn't know who it was."

"Well his name was Matthew Golding." He said watching me close.

"That's the same name as Jessica's missing brother," I paused. "Is it really him?"

"I find it difficult to believe you had no idea who it was yesterday," he said ignoring my question. "After all Jessica is your best friend. How could you not know what her brother looked like?"

"Jessica's brother," I repeated as I was stunned for few minutes. I shook my head to clear it as the sheriff was waiting for a response. "To answer your question he was a lot older than us. He disappeared when he was like seventeen or eighteen years old. I think he was a senior or maybe a junior in high school. Jessica and I were seven years old. I rarely ever saw him. Why would I remember what he looked like? Have you told Jessica yet?"

"That is why I'm here. She isn't home. Do you have any idea where she'd be?"

"She was at my place last night but she left around 10:00 p.m. She didn't say anything about going anywhere. You checked the restaurant?" I asked him.

"They haven't seen her either, and we didn't see her car anywhere. The coroner confirmed that Matthew was killed sometime Sunday night; he doesn't have an exact window of time yet. Do you have any idea where Jessica might have been Sunday night?"

I ignored his question but I was starting to get a little apprehensive about why he couldn't find her. After all, her brother had been murdered. Maybe something happened to her too.

"I was wondering if you could call her?" the sheriff asked, "I don't have her cell phone number and I didn't want to start a pile of rumors by asking other people for it. They might start wondering why the sheriff was asking for her phone number."

"Hang on." I grabbed my phone and dialed Jessica's number.

She answered on the fourth ring. "What's up Carmen? I'm on my way to the restaurant right now, running late and I can't talk."

"Will the restaurant function without you a little longer? I need you to swing by our shop first?" I told her.

"I'm sure my staff can handle it. What's wrong?"

"I don't want to get into it but the sheriff wants to talk to you and I think it would be better if he talked to you here."

"Now you have me worried. I'm about four miles away. I'll be there shortly." She hung up.

I turned to the sheriff, "She will be here soon. Do you mind if I listen in? I know it's been over twenty years, but I'm sure it's going to be a shock and I'd like to be here for her."

"That's up to her," the sheriff answered. "She may not want you to hear this."

That was a strange answer, plus the sheriff was looking awkward.

Jessica's car pulled up to where we were standing. "What's up sheriff?" Jessica asked as she got out of her car.

"I wanted you to know that we identified the body that was found in Carmen's field."

"Okay," she said as she looked at me questioningly.

I shrugged my shoulders.

"The body has been identified as your brother, Matthew."

"My brother," Jessica took a step back and put her hand over her mouth.

"Your parents left you a rather sizeable estate when they passed away, didn't they?" Sheriff Poole asked her.

"What?" she asked confused.

"I understand you are quite a wealthy young lady?" He continued.

"I don't understand what any of that has to do with this. You've just told me my brother is dead and now you're questioning me about my money?" Jessica asked bewildered.

"When we were at your house this morning looking for you, I noticed an old red pickup parked alongside your garage."

"It was Matthew's pride and joy; we could never understand why he left without it. It's there because no one had the heart to get rid of it."

"Does it still run?" Sheriff Poole asked her.

"I have no idea, I have never moved it."

"There was blood in the box in back. We're testing it right now. I'm wondering if your wayward brother showed up after all these years and was expecting some of your inheritance and you killed him so you wouldn't have to share it and then you transported the body to Carmen's field."

Jessica gasped, "You have got to be crazy. I would never kill my brother, and I have never touched that money. My restaurant does fine, and I left all that money in the bank on purpose, planning to share it with Matthew someday. I always hoped that he would come back. Are you sure it is him?"

"No question," the sheriff answered stoically.

"And you think I killed him", Jessica's voice was starting to rise.

"I think you are a good suspect." The sheriff stared at her.

"I understand he was shot." Jessica said after failing to stare the sheriff down.

"Yes, that is true," he answered clearly wondering why that mattered.

"That by itself should prove it wasn't me. I know nothing about guns. I don't even know how to load one, much less shoot one."

"That doesn't matter," the sheriff said. "My guess is he brought it with him to force you to turn over some money. After all, he's been on his own all these years. He's probably been bumming around working odd jobs and got sick of having nothing. Somehow you got the gun away from him and shot him."

"You are crazy!" Jessica was now yelling trying to make the sheriff see sense. "First of all I would never shoot my brother and second even if he did come here and ask me for money I would give it to him."

"We'll find the gun sooner or later." He said.

"I hope you do, as my fingerprints won't be on it." Jessica's voice was now back to normal.

"Nevertheless, until we get the results from the blood I expect you to stick around," he stated, his voice devoid of any emotion.

"Where would I go? This is my home," Jessica replied sounding exasperated.

"Where were you on Sunday evening?" he asked ignoring her question.

"I was doing inventory at the restaurant and noticed my shipment of beef hadn't made it on Saturday like it usually does. I was able to track down that it been delivered to a restaurant in Parkville. I knew the owner and they agreed to meet me there so I could get it. I didn't get home until 1:00 a.m."

The sheriff grunted, said he'd be checking on her alibi, reiterated for her not to go anywhere, and turned around and walked back to his squad car.

"Carmen what the heck is going on?" Jessica asked as she turned to me.

"I have no idea. Where were you by the way?" I blurted out.

"What, you too?" She looked at me in exasperation.

"Good heavens, no. I know you couldn't do this. I'm assuming since you have the same clothes on as you had on at my house last night, you were gone last night. Someone could have planted the blood." I stopped, "but that doesn't make any sense. He died Sunday night; wouldn't you have noticed the blood yourself?"

"I never look at that pickup. The closest I get to it is when I mow and trim around it, and last night I was with James." She said with no hesitation, not hiding anything.

"Wow. That was fast. You didn't even leave my place until 10:00 p.m." I smiled to let her know I was kidding.

"It's not what you think. After our conversation last night I decided I wanted to talk to James as soon as possible," she smiled, looked down at the ground and continued. "When I left your place I saw that the lights were on at his house. I decided what the heck, and I turned into his driveway." She looked up and said, "I'm so glad I did; it turns out he feels the same way as I do and we spent the whole night talking. He was taking care of a calf that had been abandoned by its mother and we spent the night in the barn talking until we fell asleep. You caught me as I was heading home to change clothes."

"I'm so happy for you both," I said as I hugged her and removed a piece of straw from her hair.

"I can't believe this is happening though. Matthew is dead. I can't wrap my mind around it. Where has he been and what he has been doing all this time?" She paused and said, her voice shaking, "I can't believe that he was finally home and someone killed him before I even got to see him. Do you suppose someone followed him here?"

"I sure hope so, otherwise it's possible one of our neighbors or friends did this. Not to mention if we don't figure out another suspect, the sheriff is going to blame you."

"This is so unbelievable; to think we were just joking about you investigating. I do need to get to the restaurant though," Jessica said her shoulders drooping.

"Are you sure you can work?" I asked her.

"I'll be fine, I don't think the reality of this has hit me yet, it's going to be tough to wrap my mind around it all. Matthew has been gone for over twenty years, what made him come home now? I think staying home instead of going to work would be worse. I'll have to process this later. Right now I want the busyness of work so I don't have to think."

"I'll come over tonight. What about James, should I let him know?" I asked her.

She considered for a few seconds, "No, not yet."

"You shouldn't wait. The grapevine moves fast in this town and I think he'd be hurt to hear about Matthew from someone else," I said disagreeing with her.

"I know, but I don't want to talk to anyone or even think about this right now. Maybe you should let him know." She decided sounding drained.

"I'll do that and we'll both come over tonight." I said as I hugged her.

"That sounds good." Jessica smiled a tremulous smile, turned and left.

I hoped the sheriff found a different focus than Jessica, as there was no possible way she would kill anyone, especially not her brother. I turned to look at Nick. He was waiting in front of the shop and, in his usual style to never be idle, was busy repairing some ends on the extension cords for the bin fans, using the tailgate of his pickup as a bench. He looked up at the sound of Jessica's car leaving and caught me watching him.

"Are you ready to go?" he asked.

"Yeah," I walked over and got into his pickup while he moved what he was working on and closed the tailgate.

As we backed out he looked at me. "You are starting to look a little frazzled."

"Thanks a lot," I muttered.

He immediately apologized.

"I know you didn't mean it that way. It is all so surreal, Jessica's long-lost brother is dead and the sheriff thinks she did it."

"I know. I couldn't help but overhear. Has Poole been a sheriff long here? If he has been, he should know Jessica isn't that type of person."

"He's been the sheriff for about two years now. He grew up here but left for a job in Minneapolis. I heard he was a patrol officer there and when he retired he moved back home. When the previous sheriff died of pancreatic cancer, Poole was the best qualified person to run for office. The other deputies weren't interested, and he won by a landslide. I don't think he compre-hended that it wasn't necessarily an endorsement of him, but that the other candidate was the seventy-eight year old town drunk who has run in every sheriff's election for the last twenty years with a campaign promise of – no more drunken disturbing the peace arrests will be enforced if he is elected. I haven't heard any-thing negative about his job performance, other than some have said he's not the most congenial person. I don't imagine he's up to solving a murder though. I think Jessica is an easy solution and someone is trying hard to make it easy for him to pursue her as the primary suspect."

"What possible reason would the sheriff think Jessica had for killing her long lost brother?" Nick asked. Obviously he hadn't been able to hear everything.

"According to the sheriff, Jessica's parents were rather wealthy and he thinks she killed him to prevent having to share the inheri-tance. But she told him she hasn't touched any of the money, she was hoping Matthew would come home someday. She is telling the truth, never once in all the time I have known her has she ever acted like she had any extra money."

"That's not that great of a reason, he must have some other evi-dence that points to her?" Nick asked.

"He also found some blood in the back of Matthew's old pickup that has been sitting in their yard forever. I don't even know what made him think of searching the pickup in the first place other than he was looking for a red vehicle," I mused. "Someone must have told him about Matthew's old pickup and the inheritance. I wonder if he had a search warrant, maybe it doesn't matter when it was outside? Anyway he believes she shot him when Matthew showed up unexpected and asked for his share of the inheritance and even more crazy the stupid sheriff thinks she transported Matthew's body to our field. That by itself should exonerate her, she knows we harvest that field, plus she's not big enough or strong enough to move Matthew's body. Stupid sheriff," I finished talking, fuming by the time I was done.

"True. Why did her brother leave anyway?" Nick asked trying to calm me down.

"My dad said that Matthew was a good kid, but he ran with a, I wouldn't say a bad group, just adventurous. After all, Jacob was in the bunch and look at what an upstanding citizen he turned into. The story I always heard was that one night they were out at a party drinking and it got out of hand. People figured Matthew must have been upset for some reason as he didn't normally drink that much and was always responsible about not driving when he had been. Anyway, he told people he had to leave as he had to be to work at the lumber yard the next morning. Jacob said he tried to give Matthew a ride, but Matthew insisted he could drive. Unfortunately he ran into a girl that was biking home."

"Did you know the girl?" Nick wondered.

"No. I think she was about four years older than Jessica and I. When you are seven you don't pay that much attention to anyone other than yourself, your family and your friends."

"What was she doing by herself out that late?" Nick asked puzzled.

"I guess she was at a slumber party, got homesick and didn't want to wake up the host parents for a ride."

"Did she die?" Nick asked.

"No, but she was paralyzed from the waist down. The girl was wearing dark clothes and biking on the wrong side of the road, so there was some sympathy for Matthew. It was said that they could see by the skid marks that Matthew had tried to swerve as he did end up in the ditch, unconscious, and wrapped around a tree. His blood alcohol was quite a bit above the legal limit. He was seventeen, so technically a minor but he was old enough that he could have been tried as an adult which would have meant serious jail time. He took off instead of going through the trial. Jessica's parents lost their bail money. Worst of all her dad; a very strict, moral person, who was so ashamed that Matthew took off rather than facing the consequences, suffered a fatal heart attack a few weeks after the accident. Her mom never was the same again. She grieved until she died about three years ago."

"How do you know so much of this if you were only seven at the time?" Nick asked.

"Jessica spent a lot of time at our house. Her mom tried, but she couldn't find any effective treatments to lift herself out of depression. I remember my folks talking about this among themselves when they thought I wasn't listening. They also used it as a cautionary tale when I was getting my driver's license to be responsible and how quick stupid actions and choices could change the course of your life."

"Wow," Nick shook his head. "She's had a tough life. How does she stay so upbeat?"

"I don't have any idea, but that is Jessica. She's always been that way, but this might be the actual needle that breaks the camel's back. I can't imagine being a person of interest in your own brother's murder. I mean, I admit that I've had thoughts of throttling Kirk, but I could never actually do it." I said trying to introduce some levity into the conversation.

Nick responded with, "Some days I might help you."

I laughed.

Nick let me off at the Spra-Coupe. Before getting in it I stood in the field next to it and dialed James' number. While it rang I took a few seconds to appreciate the sweet aroma of the blooming field and was thankful to see a few bees already active. It looked like I had sprayed early enough.

"Good morning Carmen, what can I help you with?" he asked when he answered on the fifth ring.

"Morning to you too; congratulations on the good news about you and Jessica getting together," I said to him before getting into the bad news.

"You must have talked to Jessica already this morning. I knew she wouldn't be able to keep it from you for too long but I didn't think it would be quite this fast," James said with a chortle.

"Well, yes, but that's not exactly what caused us to visit this morning," I told him hesitating on how to break the news.

"What do you mean?" James asked his voice now serious as he picked up on the tone of my voice.

"You heard about the body that was found in our big bluestem field I assume?" I paused.

"Yes, Jessica told me about it last night," James said.

"It turns out it was Jessica's brother Matthew," and I proceeded to tell him about the sheriff believing Jessica killed her own brother and why.

"Is she okay?" James asked.

"She is putting on a good act, but she is pretty shook up. It's a lot to process. Of course she left for the restaurant but it might be a good idea if you checked in on her after a while."

"The veterinarian will be here soon. I've got a sick cow, but I'll drive to town right after he leaves. Thanks for letting me know Carmen; I'll call her right now and let her know I'll come as soon as I can."

"Thanks James, I know she'll be glad to hear from you." I hung up and got in the Spra-Coupe.

I drove it back to the shop trying to think how I could help Jessica. I knew she couldn't have done this. What was even more concerning, I was starting to realize that it couldn't be a stranger, only a local would know about the pickup in Jessica's yard. Maybe Matthew had tried to come home first and the killer followed him there. Jessica lived a couple miles out of town, I wondered if there were any security cameras on any of the stores that would show Matthew in the vicinity. Another thought came to my mind; how did he get to town? I can't imagine he walked, so he must have had a vehicle somewhere unless the killer brought him. That should be some evidence for Jessica's innocence. It wouldn't make sense for her to go get her brother, bring him home and then kill him. I sure hope the pickup in her yard doesn't run. If it doesn't, someone else with a red vehicle must be the killer. If real life was anything like the mysteries I read Sheriff Poole wasn't going to take my thoughts and ideas well. It didn't matter, I was going to talk to him but first I needed to get through the rest of this day.

CHAPTER EIGHT

Switchgrass provides excellent nesting and cover
for quail, pheasants and rabbits.

I MET BACK UP WITH NICK AT THE SHOP after I had spent the rest of the morning scouting the fields for any more potential weed problems. I was thankful all the crops looked good. We discussed how much longer the roguing crew would be needed. It was a seasonal job and over the years the people on the crew varied from students home from college for the summer to retirees. The primary requirement was that they had to be eighteen or older. Dave, Gary, and Kirk were the only consistent workers from year to year. Depending on our crop acreage our crew varied from four to six people. It wasn't a fun job walking the fields and removing weeds either using herbicides or with a shovel depending on the type of crop. I had first-hand experience as I had started walking fields when I was thirteen. We didn't let minors work with herbicides but family members were exempt. The actual physical contact with the herbicide was virtually non-existent as we carried wicks that contained the herbicide in the handle. The herbicide would flow through the handle and saturate a cloth strip at the bottom. Once the cloth was wet we walked through the fields touching the weed with the wick. We used the wicks for the first three or four weeks of the growing season, after that the crops would be too tall and the weeds couldn't be touched without harming the crop. For the remainder of the season weeds were either dug out or their seed heads chopped off. Depending on the type of weed it may have to be carried out of the field also. The schedule helped to make up for the hard work as they started at daybreak to get most of the work done before the heat of the afternoon leaving summer afternoons open and we didn't require them to work weekends. Between the pay and the hours, we didn't have too much difficulty finding workers.

Nick and I decided to have them walk through the purple prairie clover one last time. Nightshade, a nasty weed, had a habit of hiding until right before harvest. It should take about two days and they'd be done for the year.

"Were you happy with their work this summer?" I asked Nick.

Typically we give the crew a bonus at the end of the season as a thank you for their hard work and as an incentive to come back the following summer. If we found good people we wanted them back if they were willing.

"I've only been here a couple months," he reminded me, "but I'd take your brother off the bonus list."

I laughed, "He hasn't gotten a bonus in years. What about Gary?"

"I don't know yet, I'm planning on talking to him today. I need to find out the reason for his uncharacteristic behavior. If it's a good personal reason, I'm willing to cut him some slack. You said he's been a good employee for many years and he has been for most of this one."

"Thanks. I appreciate you talking to him, let me know how it goes as payroll is next week."

"I will."

"Are the combines ready?" We had numerous combines as so many of the crops could ripen at the same time depending on the weather. It was helpful to have a different combine for each species to save time. Cleaning a combine to prevent contamination between fields could take a half day or more. We had about fourteen combines, some were for parts, and they were all over thirty years old. We can't justify spending hundreds of thousands of dollars on a new combine for a mere six-acre field, so instead we ran a fleet of very old combines that we modified to suit our crops. It was a definite improvement to our equipment budget, but keeping that many aged combines running or even being able to locate parts was a full-time job. Nick was an answer to prayer as so far nothing had fazed him and he had been able to find or manufacture parts and fix everything we had given him. He had also taken the time to get an inventory of common parts for our ancient combines on hand for harvest.

"They are ready with the exception of one, and I'm just waiting for a part. We are in good shape for harvest I believe," Nick said, confident as usual.

"How about the bins and fans, have you had time to check them out? I was supposed to help you with them and I never did," I asked apologetically. Obviously I'd been a little preoccupied as this was the first time I had even thought about that part of the harvest since we talked about it two weeks ago.

"All taken care of," Nick responded with a smile, knowing I had forgotten. "One fan does make me a little nervous. It runs, but it sounds a little off. I've gone through it, but I can't find anything wrong so I'm hoping it'll make the harvest. If not, we do have a backup since you won't be harvesting the prairie where the cabins are being built. We can count on that as a spare bin and fan if needed."

See what I mean about Nick being capable.

"Thanks again Nick, we sure appreciate all you do around here. You've been a lifesaver. The biggest stamp of approval is that Dad trusts you, which is obvious, as he is starting to spend less and less time here. You being here is a big part of why he is starting to enjoy his somewhat forced retirement."

Nick blushed, I had noticed before that he didn't accept compliments very well.

He finally said, "If that's all, I'll head back to the last combine. UPS might have delivered the part by now."

"That sounds good. I'd better check what the contractors are up to." As Nick walked back to the shop I pulled my cellphone out of my pocket and called Mitch. "Hi Mitch," I said when he picked up.

"Hi Carmen, what can I do for you?" He answered genial as always.

"Do you guys have the final quote ready?" I asked him.

"I emailed it to you twenty minutes ago," Mitch answered.

"That's great. I'll take a look and get back to you as soon as I can." I hung up; excited, yet also scared. Everything came down to this quote. I decided to drive back home so I could look at it in the comfort of my office and print it out instead of peering at it on my phone. I was really hoping the quote would match our budget. I didn't know where any more money was going to come from if I needed it. I also realized it was almost dinner time and with any luck Dad would be home and have something cooked.

I drove in the yard and was glad to see Karla's pickup parked in front of our tiny one-stall garage. That was a good sign there would be food. Dad wouldn't have her over at this time of day if he wasn't going to feed her. Sure enough when I walked in the kitchen I could smell potatoes frying and Dad's famous chili.

"Hi guys, it smells delicious in here," I said as I stood in the doorway.

"Hello Carmen," they both said as they looked up from the kitchen table. "Go ahead and help yourself to some food."

Dad and Karla were very similar in height and appearance. Their now-grayed hair and tanned skin testified to years of outdoor work. Karla was two years younger, a lot more slender than Dad and very fit. Life on a cattle farm clearly agreed with her.

"Thanks, I will. I didn't even realize how hungry I was until I walked in and smelled everything."

"Did you get the prairie blazing star sprayed?" Dad asked.

"Yes, I was finishing when the sheriff arrived at the shop and Nick had to call me to come back as the sheriff wanted to talk to me."

"What did he want?" Dad asked.

"He knew who the body was," I replied

"Was it anybody we knew?" Karla questioned.

"It was Matthew Golding," I said, waiting for a reaction.

"Isn't that Jessica's brother that disappeared?" Karla asked scrunching up her face trying to remember why the name was familiar.

"Yes and even more shocking, the sheriff thinks Jessica killed him." They both stopped eating and stared at me.

"Now where in the world would he get a crazy idea like that?" Dad asked.

I explained how the sheriff had me call Jessica to come to the shop as he couldn't find her. I didn't mention that she'd been with James. I thought Jessica and James deserved to let Karla know on their own. I also told them about his believing he thought Jessica had killed her brother so she wouldn't have to share her inheritance.

"That is just too stupid for words," Karla said becoming agitated. She surprised me by saying, "I suppose she was in the barn with James when the sheriff was trying to find her." She stopped and looked at me.

"It's okay. I think that the two of them are great together, but how did you know?" I asked knowing James has his own little house near Karla's and that they had been in the barn on the other side of his house.

Karla looked relieved and said, "I got up in the middle of the night and saw lights on by the garage. When I started to walk out to check I saw Jessica's car." She stopped and said, "For many years I hoped you and James would get together, but you have always acted more like brother and sister and Jessica is a wonderful girl."

"She is, and James and I are good friends, but that is all," I emphasized. "Honest, I am thrilled for them. Anyway the sheriff is pretty set on her as the main suspect. Do you think it would do any good if I checked to see if there are security cameras on any of the businesses along the route from town to Jessica's house? Maybe it will show a red vehicle and who was driving it."

"What does a red vehicle have to do with it?" Dad asked.

I explained about the camera at the seed plant showing a red vehicle and how Matthew's old red pickup that had been left in Jessica's yard had blood in it. "That is another reason the sheriff thinks Jessica did it. Although for all he knows the blood could have come from a mouse that a cat killed," I said disgusted.

"It sounds like you are getting pretty involved," Dad said with a questioning voice.

"How can I not? I know Jessica isn't a killer."

"We'll check for cameras, Carmen. We were planning on going for a drive this afternoon anyway. But are you positive you don't want to ask the sheriff to do it?" Karla asked.

"I'm not sure the sheriff will listen to me, but maybe if we find some cameras he can at least be convinced to look at them."

"We'll look around and stop in a few businesses and ask," Dad said.

"Thanks guys. That will free up my afternoon to look over the quote for the cabins. Mitch said he emailed it to me. I hope it is under budget so we can move ahead on this project. As soon as I finish eating I'm going to look at it; on second thought I can't wait. I'm going to take a bowl of chili and some potatoes and eat in my office."

"We will get going right after we clean up the kitchen. Let me know how much the quote is," Dad said as I walked out of the kitchen carrying my food to the tiny office that was a converted porch after we eliminated a third doorway on the house.

"I will. Good luck with the security camera search. I sure hope you find some." Shutting the door to my office so I could better concentrate I turned on my computer, opened the email, found the quote and hit print.

Taking the paper off the printer I flipped first to the very last page. I couldn't help but let out a whoop of glee, as the estimate was four thousand dollars under budget. I knew I couldn't avoid the tedious work of reviewing each and every line item to make sure nothing was missing. But first I opened the office door and hollered to Dad that the quote was under budget.

"That's great news Carmen. I'll talk to you some more when we get home," Dad yelled back.

Looking for a reason to postpone the tedious line-item review and feeling guilty for being excited about something when Jessica was going through such a horrible time I decided to call Nick.

"Hi Nick. Did the combine part get delivered?" I asked when he answered the phone.

"Not yet but sometimes UPS delivers later in the day. Did you need help with something?" he asked.

"No. The estimate for the cabins came in under my budget. I was excited and I guess I wanted to share it with someone. Of course I have to review it one line item at a time, but at first glance it looks promising," I answered wondering why my excitement had turned to hesitation.

Nick must have picked up on the change in the tone of my voice as he said, "That's good isn't it? You don't sound that excited. Are you having second thoughts?"

"Absolutely not, I mean I'm a little apprehensive about the extra work and the expense of building the cabins but I'm looking forward to it also. I've even been able to utilize my business minor with this venture."

"I would have thought you use that every day as this farm is also a business; you do handle all your sales, shipping, receivables and payables plus payroll," Nick said wondering what I meant.

"Yes, but these cabins are my own. The farm, and the operation of it, were all implemented by Dad and I just took over. I'm excited, but I feel bad to be excited when my best friend found out her brother has been murdered and that she is the main suspect."

"I can understand that," Nick said, "but from the little I know of Jessica she would be the first person cheering you on."

I considered that for a moment and said, "True. How did you get so wise?"

"Many years at the school of hard knocks," he answered sounding resigned.

"Thanks for talking to me Nick. I'd better get back to reviewing the estimate," I said not feeling that as an employer I could reasonably follow up on his statement. I hung up thinking about what I knew about Nick. From his employment application I knew he was thirty-two, was a certified diesel mechanic and his previous employers had nothing but good to say about him. I recalled that there had been a gap from when he graduated high school until he stared his mechanical training at age twenty-five. Dad and I had argued about asking him about it. I had wanted to question him, but Dad had felt that whatever youthful indiscretions he may have been up to was his private business as long as he passed a background check, which he did. Still, my insatiable curiosity wondered at times what he had done for seven years. Based on his answer I was pretty sure he'd had a tough life before getting back on track. I sighed and put all thoughts of Nick aside, it was time to concentrate on the estimate.

Two hours later with the makings of a headache I came to the conclusion that to the best of my ability everything in the quote looked in order.

I picked up the phone and called Mitch, "Everything looks wonderful," I said when he picked up the phone. "I'm signing the quote right now. Do you want me to fax or email a signed copy back to you?"

"Emailing would work best. And Carmen, if it is alright with you can we start tomorrow? We finished up our current job earlier than I thought we would."

"That should be fine, wonderful actually. I stopped by and signed the easements yesterday with Jacob so everything is a go. I do need to check on my building permit. They said there wouldn't be a problem, but I better check. If you don't hear otherwise, go ahead and start tomorrow."

"Great, we will be there unless you let me know different."

I hung up the phone and dashed out to the kitchen to share my good news, forgetting that Dad and Karla were already gone. Kirk walked in, with his wiener dog, Wizard, trailing behind him. Wizard rushed past Kirk and headed for his water bowl muddy footprints trailing behind, which was amazing as it hadn't rained for a long time. Leave it to Wizard to find mud during a drought.

"Apparently you had Wizard in the field with you," I said pointing at the tracks.

"Yes I did. He has fun and he relieved the monotony of the job. I hate picking the nightshade weed. It is too much bending and I especially hate having to carry it out of the field." He quit grumbling and noticed my expression. "What's with you? I'll clean up Wizard's tracks."

"The cabin construction starts tomorrow," I answered, back to being excited and almost wanting to jump up and down.

"That's neat sis, I know you've been excited about this. Do you suppose you'll want to hire my band to play for the occupants around the camp fires in the evenings?"

"If we want the venture to be a failure from the get-go and all the wildlife to flee the vicinity to protect their ears that would be a good idea."

My phone rang interrupting our usual banter. I looked at my caller ID, it was James, "what's up?" I asked.

"Could you come to Jessica's restaurant, she's not doing very well and I can't convince her to leave and go home."

"I'll be right there."

"What's wrong now?" Kirk asked when I hung up.

"The body that was found in our field was Jessica's long-lost brother, Matthew."

"That's insane," was Kirk's stunned response.

"I know, and even more insane, Jessica is the sheriff's prime suspect." Even Wizard stopped drinking and stared with water running out of his mouth. "That was James; I need to get to Jessica's restaurant. She needs some help." I grabbed my keys and headed for the door, stopped, turned around and reminded Kirk, "please don't forget to clean up Wizard's tracks," and I left.

CHAPTER NINE

Switchgrass can produce moderate to high biomass quantities lending itself for use in bioenergy production.

I WALKED INTO JESSICA'S RESTAURANT expecting some sort of chaos but at least on the surface everything was running as normal. The Formica topped tables were full, several people were sitting at the counter by the pastry shelves and coffee makers and I could see orders being placed on the high counter at the opening to the kitchen. I noticed James peeking out of the swinging kitchen door. He saw me and motioned for me to come into the kitchen. I forced myself to calmly walk through the tables of patrons, smiling at everyone I knew. When I entered the kitchen Jessica was sitting in the corner on top of a large box of take-out containers. It looked like she might have to order some new ones as these were looking a little crushed. She wasn't weeping but you could see the evidence that she had been. She looked up at me with a dazed look while her kitchen staff bustled efficiently around her like the well-trained staff they were.

"Hi Carmen, what are you doing here?" Jessica asked and looked down again before I could even reply.

"James asked me to stop by. He thinks you should maybe go home, but you don't want to?" I answered her.

She looked up at me again, "It is too busy to leave."

"Jessica; look around, your staff is more than capable. I don't think you're helping too much right now anyway." James had moved over to stand beside her.

She gulped and took a shaky breath, "I know but I didn't want to go home to an empty house."

"I told you I would come over," James said putting his arm around her.

"I know, but you are supposed to be leaving for the cattle sale in South Dakota in a few hours. You've been talking about that bull you plan on buying for weeks. You are not missing that."

"You are more important than a bull," he said sounding insistent.

"That may be", she looked up adoringly at him, "but you are not missing it".

I could tell by the eye rolls of the staff that were bustling around that this argument had been going on for awhile. I decided to put an end to it.

"James you go to the sale and Jessica I already told you I would spend the night at your place," I reminded her.

"I know Carmen, but that is tonight, I don't want to be by myself right now either," she said apologetically.

"That isn't a problem. I can come over now. Let me help you. Jessica we're going to your house right now. We'll swing by my place first and I'll grab some clothes," I said as I reached out my hand to her.

"Thank you Carmen. I'm sorry to be such a bother," she said as she grabbed at my hand and started to get up.

"You are never a bother. Now go get your stuff. You can ride with me. I assume you are parked somewhere where your car can be left overnight."

"Yes, it's fine where it's at. It's right behind the restaurant."

"Let's get going," I said pulling her along.

"I need to talk to my staff first." She was starting to drag her feet.

"Nope, we are going right now. Again, if you haven't noticed, your staff," I pointed as her main waitress Phyllis hustled by carrying a plate full of meatballs, potatoes and gravy, and George, who helped anywhere needed was busy cooking, "has been performing perfect without you, let's go. You have trained them well."

She finally lost the dazed look and noticed her kitchen was humming along as normal.

"You're right," she laughed. "Let me get my purse."

Jessica was quiet on the ride out to our farmstead until we turned off the main highway and she said, "I was fine until the coroner called and asked me what I wanted to do with Matthew's body. I didn't think the sheriff would release the body so soon," she said, her voice trembling a little.

"I told them I'd get back to them. I was so glad James showed up and called the funeral home for me and got it arranged for them to pick up Matthew from the coroners."

She subsided into quiet again for a couple seconds, and then she continued. "A few minutes later the funeral home called me and asked when I wanted to meet to discuss funeral arrangements. I lost it at that point. I think up to that moment it was all so surreal, and then it sank in that Matthew wasn't ever coming home." She started crying softly.

"We'll figure it out tonight and I'll go with you to the funeral home tomorrow."

"Oh thanks Carmen. I know James wants to help and it's sweet of him but our relationship is so new. I know this sounds strange but I don't want the darkness of this to ruin everything."

"It won't. James has been our friend for many years. He is a first-class guy. I understand, but make sure you don't cut him out of this, that would hurt him a lot."

"I don't think I could even if I tried," she said with a smile. "He really is wonderful."

We pulled up in front of my house, "wait here, I'll run in and grab a bag of clothes."

I jumped out of the pickup and raced into the house. Dad and Karla weren't back yet. I hoped that meant they were having some luck with the security cameras. Kirk and Wizard were gone also, no doubt practicing with the band. He had cleaned up after Wizard, and even more amazing, must have taken the time to mop the entire kitchen floor as it was sparkling. I packed a quick overnight bag and left a note on the table for Dad. I peeked out the window. Jessica hadn't moved. She was sitting in the pickup staring straight ahead. I decided I had time to call Nick.

"Hi Nick, is there anything urgent going on that I need to be aware of?" I asked when he picked up.

"No. Nothing that can't wait. Why, what's up?"

It struck me how immensely reassuring his voice was, he always personified control even on the bad days when every piece of equipment around him was breaking down. I explained to him what was going on and that I wouldn't be around until tomorrow afternoon.

"Not a problem. The part I was waiting for came and I got it put in the combine. We are good to go whenever Mother Nature decides that the crops are ready."

"Thanks a lot Nick." I belatedly remembered the construction, and I slapped my head, "I forgot that I have to meet with the cabin contractor tomorrow too, but if you need anything you can call me at least."

"I'm sure there won't be any problems. Take care and tell Jessica I'm sorry."

"I will and thanks Nick." As I hung up I realized I hadn't yet called to check on the building permit. I peeked again at Jessica. She was in the same position staring off into space, so I called the courthouse. I got through right away, and they were able to answer that yes, it had been approved.

I hung up and walked out to the pickup where Jessica was now looking at her hands folded in her lap instead of staring out the window. We drove in silence to her place. I think Jessica was just starting to doze off when we pulled into her driveway.

She came to with a start, looked up at the two-story house so similar to ours, except hers was painted brown while our house had white steel siding and we didn't have a basement, and said, "I don't even have a suit to bury Matthew in. In fact, he's been gone so long I don't even know if he was a suit kind of guy. I'm realizing I don't know anything about him."

"We'll check with Sheriff Poole—maybe they know by now where he's been all this time and you can find out something from people that knew him from wherever that was."

"That's a good idea."

"Why don't you go in and I'll call the sheriff right now." She got out of the pickup and walked towards her front door, her entire body projecting misery.

I dialed the sheriff's number knowing full well he probably wouldn't tell me anything even if he did know something.

The dispatcher answered. "Is Sheriff Poole in?" I asked.

"Not right now, can I take a message?"

"Yes please, this is Carmen Karlaff. Could you have him call me when he gets back in?"

"I'll give him the message, but it may be tomorrow before he gets back to you. He had to drive over to Parkville."

"Ok, make sure he gets the message please."

"I will," she said and took my phone number.

"Thank you." I hung up wondering if the sheriff was on the hunt for information on Matthew or if it was something unrelated. Guess I would have to wait until tomorrow. I was sure hoping to have some information for Jessica tonight though. Maybe we could figure out who some of his friends from high school had been. They would be about ten years older and more than likely unfamiliar to us unless they hadn't moved away. If some of them were living around here we could talk to them and at least get a feel for who Matthew was back in high school. After all he was seventeen or eighteen when he left. That might help give Jessica some sort of ideas on what type of funeral he would want—at least it would be a start and something to keep her distracted with tonight.

I got out of the pickup, grabbed my bag from behind the seat and headed towards the house. Opening the front door, I was happy to see that Jessica had changed into some comfortable clothes and was helping herself to some cookies. "What did the sheriff say?"

"He wasn't in the office. I left a message for him to call back but the dispatcher said it would be tomorrow. I thought maybe we could do some investigating ourselves. Do you know if you have any yearbooks of Matthew's?"

"What do you want those for?" she asked puzzled.

"Maybe we can figure out who his friends were and see if any of them live here in the area. I know he was good friends with Jacob, but if we can find more classmates we can talk to them to find out what they remember about him. My hope is that it will help you get started with some funeral planning while we wait for the sheriff to give us any information on the missing pieces of his life since he's been gone." I didn't mention my belief that I doubted he was going to share anything with us.

"It sounds like a good place to start. I'm sure we still have them. Mom and Dad always sponsored an advertisement in the school yearbooks for their business so I'm pretty sure we got a free one every year. They should be in Dad's old office."

We walked down the hallway to her dad's office. While Jessica had updated most of the house the office looked much the same as I remembered it looking when I used to spend nights here as a kid; dark paneling, with bookshelves along two of the four walls and a massive oak desk. Jessica had moved over to the bookshelves. "Well maybe we didn't get a free one every year, or at least they didn't save them if we did. There isn't a single one anywhere. I have mine in my old bedroom, but they won't help. There was too many years age difference between us."

Jessica had moved into her parents more spacious bedroom on the main floor after her mother died. She'd completely redecorated it to make it hers. She also had admitted that sleeping by herself upstairs in her old bedroom where she couldn't hear anything had been too creepy, so even though she hadn't wanted to, it made sense to move into her parent's bedroom.

"Well maybe they put the yearbooks in Matthew's old bedroom."

"He doesn't have a room anymore. Dad was upset when he ran off before the court case and he turned his bedroom into a game room."

"That's how you got that cool room. I was always jealous of that room when we were kids." I said blabbing, trying to hide my shock.

"It is a neat room, but it almost broke Mom's heart when Dad wanted to throw everything away. Mom managed to sneak some of his boxes in the basement. Let's go look through them."

We went further down the hallway to the end where the door to the basement was.

"This could be nasty, I never did like going down to the basement and after Mom died I moved all hers and Dad's bedroom stuff down there. Other than changing the furnace filter I don't come down here anymore," Jessica said.

She turned on the lights and we walked down the steps. She hadn't been exaggerating, dust and the general feel of neglect pervaded every step.

"How can you, a confirmed neat freak, deal with this lurking under you?" I jokingly asked her.

She laughed, "As long as a door can be closed, I'm okay with not knowing the condition of what's behind it. I think Matthew's stuff is over in the corner tucked way back in the shadows. Mom didn't want Dad to find the boxes."

We moved some old lamps, a nightstand and an old typewriter.

"Here they are." She stood looking at them for a moment, her eyes filling with tears.

"Why don't you go upstairs and I'll look through the boxes. If I find anything I'll bring it upstairs to you," I suggested.

"No, I want to be here, I need to look at this stuff anyway. It's time to deal with it."

She grabbed the first box and opened it. It was full of trophies, most of them from his years in little league and in later years baseball along with some wrestling trophies.

She smiled as she held up one for the high school science fair. "I remember this one, athletics came easy for Matthew so the sport trophies were normal for him, but he was so proud of winning something for academics." She pushed that box aside. The next box was full of clothes, and right on top was a stained sweatshirt. "Oh my, what did Mom save this for?" Jessica said as she recoiled from the box.

"Why, what is it?" I asked her.

"It's the sweatshirt he was wearing the night of the accident. It has his blood stains on it." She dropped it on the floor.

"Yuck. What an odd thing to save," I said wrinkling my face.

"I think maybe Mom was saving it for the court case. She never could believe Matthew was responsible for the accident and I'm guessing she hoped it would be needed if there would have been a trial or investigation. She didn't want to believe her son could have been part of something so horrific. She also wondered why so much blood, when all he had was a small cut on his forehead. Dad would get so mad at her. I remember him telling her that she should wake up; it was obvious Matthew was responsible, otherwise why did he run off?" She folded it up and put it back with the other clothes and quietly said, "At least Mom tried to defend Matthew, Dad just condemned him."

I looked at her, not knowing what to say. She rarely mentioned the devastation the accident had caused her family. I swallowed and said, "You know if we don't find the yearbooks, or you want to quit, I'm sure the library will have them also. I can go look myself."

"No, let's keep on, there are three boxes left and anyway it's better to keep busy," she said continuing to move boxes.

We pulled out the three remaining boxes. Two of them were more standard teenage room stuff, posters, trinkets, alarm clock, school tablets, and some models. The third box was where we finally found what we were looking for. Better yet, besides the two yearbooks, the box also held Polaroid pictures.

"Let's take this box upstairs and go through it."

"Okay, but first help me move these other boxes. I know I need to throw them, but I feel like I should look through them more thoroughly one last time. Let's put them over by those boxes of canning jars. I keep meaning to get rid of them too. Maybe if the stack of boxes is bigger I'll do something with them as I will be able to see them from the top of the stairs."

We moved the boxes we weren't interested in and carried the box of pictures and yearbooks upstairs. As we reached the top of the stairs my phone rang. Jessica grabbed the box out of my hands so I could answer the phone. Glancing at caller ID, I saw that it was the sheriff. I mouthed his name to Jessica as I answered.

CHAPTER TEN

Indiangrass was a major component of the tallgrass prairies of the central and eastern United States.

"HELLO SHERIFF POOLE," I said as I greeted him.
"I heard you called." He didn't sound pleased.

"Yes, we were hoping that you had found something out about where Matthew has been all these years."

"Not surprising, we haven't found out anything yet. We sent his fingerprints in, but unless he's committed another crime it's unlikely that will give us anything. I believe with his fingerprints being in the system from the accident he wouldn't have worked at any place that would require fingerprints. That gives him another good reason to have been fed up with his life and have come back to get some of his inheritance from his sister. We are putting out some press releases hoping someone out there will recognize him, but if he came from far away the likelihood of any of those press releases reaching someone who knows him would be pretty scarce. I'd like to know how he got to town although I believe Jessica would know. He must have had some help to have survived all these years and I'm sure she is the person who did."

"Sheriff, if you don't know better than to suggest that, you are going to waste taxpayer dollars on the direction you are taking this investigation. Jessica did not have anything to do with this. Thanks for calling back," I said as I angrily hung up the phone.

"No good news?" Jessica asked.

"No, and he can't get past you being the primary suspect, so we need to come up with some other ideas to get him looking in another direction. The one positive is that he did share the little information of what he had done so far. Let's get this box on the kitchen table and start making some lists."

I handed Jessica the yearbooks and put all the pictures in a pile. "You look through the yearbooks and flag anyone that wrote something in there that indicated they may have been a friend and mark any pictures of him with someone. Do you have any sticky notes around?"

"Yes, there should be some in the drawer by the refrigerator." She pointed at the drawer.

I found the sticky notes, handed them to her to use on the yearbooks and I started leafing through the pictures. "I'll put the pictures in two piles, one pile of pictures showing Matthew with people I don't know, and one pile of anyone I might recognize. If I don't recognize them, I doubt they live in the immediate area. I'll also put aside any pictures with family. We know they aren't responsible."

It didn't take very long, as there were only about one hundred and fifty pictures. I finished before Jessica. I looked over at her. She was methodically going through the yearbooks page by page. I waited in silence until she was done. She finished, closed the last book, and looked up.

"I marked all the pages Matthew was on. It looks like he had a lot of teammates as he was on the football, wrestling, and baseball teams. But John Harling, Gary Pitterson, Jacob Esling, and Mitch Carboot are pictured with him the most. I know Jacob is the lawyer here in town and that Gary is one of your roguers, but

I'm not sure I recognize the rest. How about you, what did you find?" she asked me.

"Mitch is my contractor, but I don't know a John Harling. I found Mitch and Jacob in these pictures, I bet Gary is in them too, I thought a guy looked familiar but I couldn't place him." I handed her the stack of pictures of people with Matthew. 'Do you recognize any of these people?"

Jessica flipped through the pictures and pointed, "These two look like the John Harling pictured in the yearbook. A couple of these I recognize from the yearbook as teammates but none of the names were of people that stayed around here that I know of. The girl in this picture is Maggie Onster. She's the town librarian now."

"Did she and Matthew date?" I questioned her.

"Not that I know of, but I wouldn't have. I was too young."

"Well the good news is that three people who at least appeared to be good friends with Matthew are local. I can ask Mitch some questions tomorrow afternoon. I'm supposed to meet with him anyway. Do we have time to catch Maggie in the morning before the appointment with the funeral home?"

"Yes, the library opens at nine in the morning and my appointment isn't until ten."

"Maybe we can catch Jacob too. I'll also make sure to grab Gary and talk to him before their shift is over tomorrow afternoon."

"So we have a plan, but what are we going to ask them?" she wondered.

"Our first objective is to help you plan the funeral so I think general questions about what he was like, and what he liked to do. Maybe we should ask if anyone wants to talk at the funeral. That might be kind of awkward though as it was a long time ago. We also need some clues as to what he's been doing. Let's ask them if he talked about what he'd like to do for a living, or where he talked about living someday or maybe even if he ever talked about wanting to see any certain places. Most important, we need to ask if they've ever heard from Matthew in the last twenty years."

"The more I listen to us, this sounds hopeless. Do you remember anything about classmates you haven't seen in twenty years? Not to mention if Matthew was keeping in touch with anyone around here he would have heard about Dad, and then Mom. I can't believe if he knew about them passing away that he wouldn't have at least reached out to me," Jessica said, her shoulders and expression drooping again.

"I know, but right now you are the only suspect the sheriff is even willing to look at and we have to find out something that will make him focus his attentions elsewhere. You know we are missing the prime suspects. What about the girl he hit with the car, or even her family? Maybe he contacted them out of guilt to apologize and they decided to get revenge. It shouldn't be hard to find out their names. Are you sure you don't remember them?"

"No, I was so young. Of course I remember Mom and Dad talking about it, but after Dad died, Mom never talked about the accident again," Jessica answered.

"Weren't you curious about it as you grew up?" I asked her.

"No, I just wanted to forget." She shrugged her shoulders.

"I understand. It will be a good excuse to talk to Maggie at the library. I'm sure they have old newspapers on file and we can look up the accident. At least we have a plan of sorts," I said closing up the yearbooks and putting them and the pictures back in the box.

We spent the rest of the evening talking about the funeral. I think we both came to the conclusion that there wasn't much point in trying to get anyone else involved in the funeral by asking them to speak. Jessica was the last remaining family member left. Of course my family would come and Jessica's friends, but I couldn't see too many other people coming. Jessica agreed so after going back and forth between a full-blown funeral or a family service she decided a simple family service would be best. She would bring some family pictures to put up on a board to look at when people walked in. She grabbed their family photo albums and we spent some time picking them out. She decided to have the service at 7:00 p.m. on Friday night so no meal would have to be served. We would ask Edna to supply some doughnuts and cookies from her bakery. Jessica would bring juice and coffee from her restaurant. By the end of the night we felt we had everything taken care of. Jessica decided to have Matthew cremated so she wouldn't have to make a decision about burial plots or clothing. He would join her mother and father on the mantle. She figured after some time had passed she'd decide on a burial plot for all three of them, but she wasn't ready to deal with that yet. We headed to bed. I don't know about Jessica but I felt better knowing we had a plan of action for the next day.

CHAPTER ELEVEN

Prescribed burns are essential to control weeds and increase plant viability in native prairie habitats.

I WOKE UP WEDNESDAY MORNING a little disorientated by the amount of light streaming in the windows. It took a few minutes to remember where I was. I could hear noise coming from downstairs; Jessica must be up already. I checked the time; it was 6:45 a.m. I grabbed my overnight bag and headed to the bathroom. Twenty minutes later I was downstairs where Jessica had some pancakes and scrambled eggs ready.

"How are you doing?" I asked as I studied her face.

"Ok I think. I already checked in with the restaurant, things are going fine. It sounds like it is busier than normal."

"Curiosity seekers I would bet, I'm sure the rumor mill has been running rampant."

"Hopefully they'll tip my staff well anyway."

"What time does the library open again?" I asked feeling stupid for not remembering." My memory was not always the best.

"It's open at 9:00 a.m.," Jessica answered with a smile knowing how bad my memory could be concerning anything not farm-related.

"Good, let's check with Jacob first, I know he's in by 8:00 a.m. every morning."

"He could be gone. He's been doing a lot of campaigning lately," Jessica reminded me.

"I have his cellphone number, I'll text him," I said as I scrolled through my contact list.

Jessica started cleaning up the kitchen while I sent a text to Jacob. He answered immediately.

"Jacob has an appointment at 9:00 a.m., but he's there already and willing to visit with us if we get there right away."

"Give me five minutes and I'll be ready to go." She finished putting the last dishes in the dishwasher while I put everything away in the refrigerator.

As I washed down the countertop I said, "After our visit with Jacob I'll take you back to the restaurant so you can get your own car. When we are done with Maggie and the funeral home I'll need to leave right away to meet with Mitch and Mark. They are starting construction on the cabins today."

Jessica grabbed her purse and keys, while I grabbed my bag. She locked the door and we walked to my pickup. While the outside temperature was in the mid eighty's, the sticky humidity was gone and there was a crisp feel to the air. As we drove to town I noticed the trees were starting to turn yellow and gold. Fall and harvest were on their way. Seven minutes later we pulled up in front of Jacob's office that although painted in a tasteful taupe and black color scheme you could tell it had once been a nail salon. The second story of the building now converted to apartments had "Cathy's Cuticles" in faint pink showing through the taupe paint.

Jacob hadn't hired a new receptionist yet, but he heard us come in and hollered for us to come back to his office. He stood up as we walked in, "So sorry to hear about Matthew, Jessica."

"That is why we are here. I don't know if you are aware, but right now Jessica is the primary suspect and we're trying to find a new direction for the sheriff to look," I said as we sat down.

"How can I help?" he asked as he sat down.

"We were hoping you could remember anything about Matthew that might give us an idea of where he may have been all these years. We thought if we could find out where he's been living there might be somebody there that could tell us what was going on in his life. Maybe somebody followed him here and killed him for a reason that has nothing to do with Jessica. Do you remember if he ever talked about any place he wanted to live or visit when you knew him in high school?" I asked.

"Oh man!" Jacob exclaimed with a big sigh. "I haven't thought about those days for a long time. Matthew and I were inseparable back then. I'm not sure we talked much about the future. We were more concerned with hunting, wondering what girl did or didn't like us and sports." He leaned back and held his hands over his head. "Let me think, Matthew did talk about Colorado, but I think that was mainly because he wanted to try fly-fishing and he'd seen a fly-fishing program on TV one night that was about Colorado. Other than that, I just don't recall anything else. Like I said, at that point in our lives we weren't thinking too hard about the future. I certainly never dreamed I'd become a lawyer. Matthew was so talented in anything he tried. It would have been fun to see what he would have become." His face grew pensive.

"What happened that night?" Jessica asked him. "I was so young and Mom and Dad didn't talk about it much in front of me."

"I've thought about that night many times. I should have tried harder to keep him from driving." He looked down at his hands on his desk. "We went to a party that night at Gary's house. Gary's parents were gone for the weekend. We didn't drink as a norm or go to many parties, but Gary was a friend and he was kind of an outcast at school so he begged us to come, knowing more kids would come if we came." He reddened, "that sounded egotistical didn't it? But we were popular, Matthew more than me. He was so genuine and a friend to everyone. Anyway, we were both competitive, some drinking games started and Matthew and I dove in.

I stopped almost immediately because I had to drive home and knew my mom would be waiting up for me but Matthew kept playing and losing. Then Matthew said he had to leave as he had to work the next morning. Gary and I tried to stop him from driving. I even followed him out of the house and tried to take his keys but he wouldn't let me. He left and I went back in for about another hour, but I thought I'd better check to make sure Matthew wasn't in a ditch somewhere, so I got my coat, said goodbye to a few people and left. I was the first one to find the accident. Matthew was unconscious and the girl was lying in the middle of the road. I called 911 and that's about it." He looked up, clearly uncomfortable with the story even after all this time.

He continued talking, "After the accident, I saw Matthew one more time when he was in the hospital, and the next thing I knew he was gone. I still can't believe he ran. I think that's one of the reasons I became a lawyer. I wanted to help people in those types of situations to not have the devastation that happened to your family. Yes, he did something wrong, but he could have served his time and was young enough to have had a life left when he got out." His voice trailed off.

"So you haven't heard from him ever in all these years?" I asked knowing he would have said so if he had.

"No, I wish he would have called. I always hoped he would show up some day." He swallowed, and said, "I guess he did try to come back home, too bad we may never know why. He never got in touch with you either Jessica?"

"No, never," she answered sadly.

I could see that they both were getting maudlin. I stood up, "thank you for your time Jacob. We'll let you get back to work."

"Sorry I wasn't more help." He stood up and escorted us out. "If I think of anything else I'll give you a call."

"By the way, have you had any luck finding a receptionist?" I asked looking around at the pile of files that was starting to stack up.

He shrugged, "I haven't had much time to look. To be honest I'm not looking forward to the search, competent employees are hard to find. It can't be helped though; Gwen was incompetent, unreliable and needed to be fired. Her computer skills weren't very good and she rarely made it to work on time. It sure was bad timing as it would be nice to have someone here when I'm going to be gone so much."

"You mean with your election?" Jessica asked.

Jacob nodded.

"I hope you find someone and good luck with your campaign," Jessica said. He nodded at us and went back in to his office.

We had talked to Jacob longer than I expected and it would be quicker to walk to the library than to try and find a parking spot there. "Let's walk over to the library and when we are done we can come back to my pickup and I'll take you to your car at the restaurant," I said to Jessica as we stood on the sidewalk contemplating what Jacob had told us. It was a beautiful day, with a light breeze and sunny skies. The library was two blocks away and with any luck the walk would help get rid of the sad expression in Jessica's eyes. "Do you know Maggie very well?" I asked Jessica.

"Not on a personal level. She comes to my book club, but she tends to keep to herself. She's an excellent librarian though. She's very good at recommending books and I know the high school kids are thrilled with the help she has given them on their research projects. Funny after all these years of visiting the library she's never mentioned that she knew Matthew."

"There is quite an age difference between you and Matthew. She probably didn't realize you were his sister. If she thought about it at all she may have assumed you were just a relative," I said.

"That's true. She has always been very nice to me. I don't think she's married, but again we've never talked about anything personal."

We stopped in front of the library, "Are you ready?" I asked as we both stared at the brick one story building.

"Yes, let's get this over with." She straightened her back.

As we walked in there were several people milling around the front desk. "Which one is Maggie?" I asked. It was obvious Jessica was the more voracious reader in our friendship, seeing as I didn't even know who the librarian was, but my schedule didn't lend itself to reading very often. I loved to read, but didn't have much time and when I did have time, I chose to read my favorite genre which was mysteries. I had an extensive list of favorite authors and tended to order the books I wanted rather than take the time to drive to the library. I almost always had five or six books on hand stacked on my nightstand.

"She's the tall brunette standing by the telephone," Jessica said nodding her head to point in the right direction.

We walked up to the front desk, and waited. When it was our turn, we stepped up to the desk and Jessica asked, "Maggie could we talk to you in private please?"

She looked at us funny, and said, "Sure. We can use my office." She gestured for us to follow her.

We went down a long hallway to an office located at the far end in a corner. She sat down behind a large glass desk and we sat down at the chairs in front of it. Her office was sparsely decorated with one token landscape artwork on the wall and nothing personal visible.

"What can I help you with ladies? Is there an issue you have a complaint about?" She asked us as she folded her hands together on top of her desk.

"No, nothing like that," I started to say, but Jessica interrupted me.

"I believe you knew my brother, Matthew Golding, in high school?"

Maggie looked puzzled at first, and then her face cleared. "You're Matthew's sister? Why did I never connect that in all these years? Yes, I knew Matthew. He was one of my best friends. I heard he was found dead a couple days ago, I was hoping it wasn't true."

"I'm sorry but it's true. You can understand that it's brought up a lot of memories for me, and with the difference in mine and Matthew's ages, I'm trying to get a picture of who he was at that age. We looked through some pictures and it appeared that Matthew and you were acquainted. I was hoping you could tell me more about him. I was so much younger than him; I didn't get to know him very well."

"Matthew was a great guy. I was devastated when he left."

"Were you dating?"

"No, but we were good friends. My home life was pretty bad, my mom was an alcoholic, and my dad showed up just long enough to take any money she did manage to earn. Matthew was always willing to listen, provide a shoulder to cry on and even feed me a meal once in a while. You know I never could figure out what happened that night. Matthew never drank."

"Were you at the party?" I asked her.

"No, I avoided all alcohol. I wanted nothing to do with it after experiencing what it did to my home life. I would have bet my life that Matthew felt the same way. I tried to visit him when he was in the hospital. I wanted to ask him what happened but your dad wouldn't let me see him. I think he thought I was part of the party that night."

"Have you heard from him at all over the years?" Jessica asked her leaning towards the desk.

"Not in a long time," she answered surprising us.

"Does that mean that you did hear from him?" I asked shocked.

"He'd been gone for about a month when I got a postcard. All it said was that he was sorry and that he wanted me to stay strong and wrote that my family life didn't define who I was. He also encouraged me to pursue my dream of college. I cherished that postcard. Matthew gave me the courage to leave for college. It wasn't easy but I did it. I think part of the reason I moved back here was that I always hoped Matthew would come back."

"Did you keep that postcard?" I asked her.

"I'm pretty sure I have it somewhere. I know I would never have thrown it, but finding it might be impossible." She shrugged her shoulders.

"Do you remember anything about it?" Jessica asked starting to get excited.

"If memory serves me correctly, I think it was from North Dakota, but I don't remember any more than that."

Jessica and I looked at each other. I could tell we both were thinking we hadn't learned much.

"Thanks for your time Maggie," Jessica said as we started to get up.

"Did I help at all?" she asked us.

"I honestly don't know. But we'll let the sheriff know that at some point he was in North Dakota," I told her.

"Why is the sheriff involved?" she asked.

"Matthew was murdered and the sheriff suspects Jessica. We were hoping something from his high school years or even better from wherever he's been these past years would give the sheriff a different direction to look." I answered her.

"Do you need me to find the post card?" she asked.

"No. Since it was so soon after he left I doubt it was sent it from anyplace he settled in or he wouldn't have risked sending it. We'll let the sheriff know about it. If he wants to see the postcard he can talk to you. Can you tell us anything else about Matthew, who his friends were, and if any of them live around here?"

"I know he hung out with Mitch quite a bit, and he went hunting with Gary a lot. Other than hunting they didn't do much else together."

"What about Jacob?" I asked thinking it was strange that she left him out.

"I know that everyone considered them best friends but I'm not so sure it wasn't only on Matthew's side," Maggie said with a frown on her face.

"What do you mean?" I asked as both Maggie and I sat down again.

"Jacob was always trying to one up Matthew, at least that's how it appeared to me," she said after pausing trying to find the right words.

"How so?" I asked.

"I don't know how to explain it, but Matthew had this magnetism about him and to me it felt like Jacob didn't think he was Matthew's equal, like Jacob felt he was in Matthew's shadow but wanted to get out of it." She paused searching for words. "For instance if Matthew was telling a humorous story about something he and Jacob had done together, Jacob couldn't ever let Matthew tell the story, he would try to interject, but the story would drag on and then Matthew would take over the telling and get everyone laughing again. I got the impression that Jacob didn't really like Matthew—he just liked being in his circle and at the same time he resented Matthew's easy comradeship with others. It's how I saw things anyway." She shrugged her shoulders.

Jessica and I looked at each other. "Well that's interesting, but you have to understand that's not the impression we've gotten from others."

"I know, but you have to remember I wasn't around them together that much, I could have been wrong."

"It at least gives us a few things to think about. Thanks so much for taking the time to talk to us." We walked out of the library and stood on the top step outside the doors.

"What did you think of that?" I asked Jessica.

"I'm not sure. I've always thought Jacob and Matthew were good friends."

"I've done quite a bit of business with Jacob over the years, and not that the topic came up often, but when it did he always indicated the same," I said puzzled.

"Maybe she was jealous of Jacob and wanted to be the one spending time with Matthew," Jessica said.

"Could be, but don't forget we haven't talked to Gary or Mitch yet. Maybe they'll give us more insight. But right now we'd better go

back to get your car and both of us drive over to the funeral home."
As we walked down the library steps I could hear our names being
called. "Oh no." I nudged Jessica, "don't look now but I think we are
going to be accosted by crazy Melanie."

Jessica nudged me back, "that isn't nice. She just has a different
way of looking at things." Sometimes Jessica is too nice for her own
good.

Melanie was a short, petite, eclectically dressed woman around
forty years of age. She had been a fixture around town as long as I
could remember. She was always wearing brightly-colored, flow-
ered tunics that rarely matched whatever bright colored pants she
was wearing. She ran a meditation studio, but I always wondered
how she could make a living with the limited population in this
rural area.

"Jessica, Carmen, I'm so glad I caught you," Melanie puffed as
she ran up to us.

"What's up Melanie?" I asked.

"I understand you are building some cabins for bird watchers
and Jessica is supplying the food."

"Yes, along with Edna," Jessica answered her.

"I was wondering who you were going to get to provide the
meditation sessions?" she asked.

"I hadn't planned on any meditation sessions," I answered her
with an incredulous look at Jessica.

"Oh no, you simply must have some. How can you expect
return visitors if you haven't dealt with the unrest of their psyches?
Meditation is the path through which they will be able to truly
enjoy what nature has to offer. I can come right out to the cabins
and put on sessions at daybreak before my studio opens here in
town."

"I don't think that's necessary," I said trying with no success to
cut her off.

"It is so necessary, of course some people can't be helped, they
have such black auras," she said as she looked down the street.

I tried to see if there was anyone in particular she was looking at, but didn't see anyone. Melanie finally drew a breath, and I jumped in. "How about we do it this way, why don't you give me some pamphlets, brochures or business cards and I'll put them in the cabins. That way they can contact you direct if they are interested."

"That sounds wonderful Carmen," Melanie said as she hugged me.

"We do have to get going," I said as I extracted myself from her embrace. Jessica and I took off as fast as we could.

We could hear Melanie calling after us, "Thank you!"

CHAPTER TWELVE

Blue grama is the state grass of Colorado and New Mexico.

THE VISIT TO THE FUNERAL HOME hadn't been as distressing as I'd expected. Jessica picked out an urn, settled on Friday evening for a small service like we had discussed, and worked out the various other details for the small service. We finished in about forty-five minutes. The last thing Jessica had left to complete was to write up an obituary. "Are you going to be okay?" I asked her.

"Yeah, it'll be busy today and that will help."

"I'll give you a call later after I talk to Mitch and Gary."

"Okay, thanks again Carmen. I sure appreciate all your support," Jessica said as she hugged me.

"That's what friends are for." I smiled at her and drove away.

If I hurried I could get back home for dinner and find out if Dad and Karla had any success with locating security cameras. I would still have plenty of time to get to the meeting with Mitch and Mark. With any luck, Dad would even have some food made. I made a mental note that I needed to find time to make Dad a meal for a change before I got busy with harvest. I arrived home and was pleased to see Dad's pickup there. Upon entering the kitchen the smell of Swiss steak and baked potatoes wafted over me.

"Is there enough for me?" I asked eagerly wondering if my tongue was hanging out.

"There's plenty, help yourself," Dad said looking up from his plate and motioning towards the stove where the food sat.

"Isn't Karla here?" I asked looking around.

"No, James was having some problems at the sale and she had to go home to get some paperwork wired."

"Did you guys have any luck finding security cameras?" I asked as I grabbed myself a plate and filled it with food.

"We stopped at every business along the route from town to Jessica's house. There were some cameras but they all basically pointed at their front doors, which I guess is to be expected. The body shop on the corner may have something, but it was closed today. It's a long shot but we noticed they have a lot across the street from their shop that they store vehicles in. We could see two cameras and one of them pointed across the street towards that lot, so depending on how low the camera is pointing it may show some street traffic. Karla can't make it, but I'm planning on stopping by there tomorrow. How is Jessica doing?"

"Better, I think. We did get the funeral planned; she's going to have a short service on Friday evening. We talked to a couple of Matthews friends this morning, Jacob and Maggie the librarian. Did you know Mitch and Gary were buddies of his, also?"

"I guess I'd forgotten about Mitch, but I knew Gary was. He had just started working for us. I remember he took it pretty hard when Matthew disappeared."

"I'm planning on talking to them this afternoon."

"About what?" Dad asked.

"I want to ask them some questions about what they remember about Matthew from high school. I also want to find out if they have any idea where Matthew went when he left and if they'd ever heard from him over the past twenty years."

"What do you hope to gain from this?"

"I guess I'm hoping to stumble across another suspect for the sheriff besides Jessica."

"Shouldn't the sheriff be doing that, after all it is his job. I know you want to help Jessica, but it's not like she's been arrested. She's a person of interest, which for all you know he may have many. Are you sure you aren't nosing around because you are intrigued by the thought of an actual real-life mystery?" Dad asked me as he leaned back in his chair and studied me.

I considered his words and said, "If I'm honest, you are right that I'm a little fascinated with an actual murder, which does make me sick to my stomach," I paused, "but I do believe my primary motivation is to help Jessica. You weren't there and you didn't hear how the sheriff talked to her. He truly believes she killed Matthew and if the blood he found in the pickup in her yard matches Matthew's I know he'll arrest her. He also released Matthew's body, which I can't imagine he would have done if he had any doubt in his mind that Jessica killed him. Trust me, he isn't looking for any other suspects. Jessica doesn't deserve that so if my asking some questions can send the sheriff in a new direction I'm going to do it."

"Okay," Dad said and went on to caution me by saying, "If it is something to do with where he's been living all this time it's going to be difficult to figure out."

"While I'd love to think that someone from Matthew's new life followed him here and killed him, I doubt it."

"Doubts about it being somebody from out of town, or doubts about the sheriff finding a person from out of town?"

"Both; the sheriff isn't even looking. I don't believe someone from out of town would follow Matthew all the way back here just to kill him, and why would Matthew be heading back here if he thought he was in danger. After being gone this long, he wouldn't bring that back to his family. I think he came home for some reason, and someone wasn't happy about him showing up. I'm questioning his old friends because I think someone from here killed him and why would they do that unless something happened from when he used to live here?" I said not knowing if I was articulating myself very well.

"Or he was keeping in touch with someone here and he was coming to talk to them. For all we know about the last few years of his life he could have been coming here once a week, doing something stupid like dealing drugs and it finally caught up to him," Dad said.

"Do you believe that?" I asked Dad as I finished up with my dinner.

"Not really—other than that accident, Matthew was a great kid. I can't see his personality changing that much."

"I do think it is something to do with that accident. Do you know what happened to the family of the girl that was hurt? Jessica couldn't remember their name."

"They moved away right after the accident. They got the little girl into a rehab place in Colorado and they moved out there with her."

"Do you remember the last name?"

"Not offhand, but there was enough news coverage about it, I'm sure you can find out. I doubt it was a big enough story that any major newspapers picked it up to be on-line, but the library should have old local newspapers on file."

"We were going to look into it when we were at the library this morning, but we didn't have enough time after we talked to the librarian, Maggie. I'll check into it tonight. Right now I've got to go meet with Mitch and Mark."

"They're starting on the cabins today?"

"Yep, I'm looking forward to it, not the actual building process, but I'm excited about the new venture."

"As I've said before, I'm not so sure you need more work," Dad said, sounding worried.

"To be honest, Nick has been such a lifesaver that I don't think there will be a problem. It won't be that much extra time for me as he's taken up so many of my farm duties."

"Yes, he's seems to be a great addition."

"What do you mean by seems to be? Are you having any problems that I'm not aware of?"

"No, at times I wonder if he's too good to be true."

"I think you may be having a tough time accepting your retirement and acknowledging that you can be replaced," I laughed at Dad.

He stuck out his tongue at me. "I do wish he'd open up more about himself with us. He's so reserved and almost too helpful. Makes me wonder what he's hiding."

"I brought all this up before we hired him and you said everyone deserves a second chance, remember?" I reminded Dad.

"I do," Dad admitted.

"He's been awesome so you leave him alone. But speaking of work, what's my baby brother been up to?"

Dad started laughing, "Next time you see your brother be sure to ask him about Wizard's latest adventure."

"What happened now?"

"Just ask him about it, Wizard got the best of him as usual."

"Okay, I will, but right now I have to get going," I said putting my dishes in the dishwasher.

As I drove out to the cabin site I thought about what Dad had said. Was there something off about Nick? No, I didn't believe it. He's been nothing but hardworking in his time with us. I pulled into the prairie where Mitch and Mark had their crew hard at work. They already had the topsoil stripped off and were starting to haul in the gravel for the foundation under the concrete of the future cabins. I had to admit it was hard to see the prairie disturbed, but they were doing a good job keeping their work area contained to the immediate space around each cabin. I got out of the pickup and walked over to Mitch and Mark who were busy looking at the blueprints.

"You guys don't mess around. Is everything going well?" I asked when I caught up with them.

"Hey Carmen, good to see you, we do have a couple questions on the blueprints here."

"Not problems already?"

"Not really, we were looking at the rooflines on the cabins and thought that with a little additional expense we could put some small five foot extending concrete slabs on the front of the cabins and extend the roof lines to give you small porches."

"What does little expense mean?" I asked knowing I didn't have a lot of extra in the budget.

"That's what you caught us trying to scratch out. It looks like about six hundred dollars for each cabin. It wouldn't be much extra, just adding a little more gravel and concrete and extending the roof lines a little longer. It wouldn't be a tall porch, but it would give some cover for a couple of rocking chairs."

"That is doable. It would also make the cabins look quite a bit more attractive. But realistically speaking, with mosquitoes you'd have to be quite a die hard to want to sit outside, at least in the evenings, but let's go ahead. In the dry years when the mosquitoes are tolerable they'd work well."

"We'll go ahead with them and start stripping off a little more sod and black dirt and get some more gravel hauled in."

"Do you have anything else? You asked me to stop by; I was worried there was a serious problem."

"We like the people who hire us to stop in and check to make sure everything looks good fairly regular. We'll be pouring the concrete tomorrow and once that's poured there's no turning back."

"I'll walk around a little bit and make sure the cabins are located where I envisioned them," I said as I started walking away.

"Why don't you take a couple of flags and mark which way you want the front of the cabins to face," Mitch called after me.

"No problem." I went back and grabbed the flags from him and headed for the sites. I didn't want the cabins to look directly at each other. However, knowing that the back of the cabins would be kind of unattractive with the propane tanks being located behind them, I set the flags so that the cabins were kitty corner from each other. You could see the front of each of the cabins from the side of the others. You'd have to turn your head to look. I finished up and headed back to Mitch and Mark.

"Hey Mitch, do you have a couple minutes to talk about a personal matter?"

"Uh, sure I guess." He looked at me questioningly. "Is something the matter?"

"No. I'm sure you heard about the body that was found in our field?" I asked him.

"Yes, I heard they identified the body, but we haven't been in to the restaurant recently to hear the latest gossip."

"It was Matthew Golding," I said watching his face.

"Are you serious?" he asked looking shocked. "What the heck, why was he back here, how did he die?"

"We don't know why he was back, but someone shot him and the sheriff appears convinced Jessica did it," I said answering his questions.

"You've got to be kidding. She wouldn't hurt a fly. I haven't had that much contact with the sheriff, but I didn't think he was stupid."

"He's been questioning her and at least as far as I can tell he's not trying too hard to look elsewhere. That is why I wanted to talk to you. I'm trying to figure out what kind of a person Matthew was. I was so young when he left I don't remember anything about him and we saw in some pictures that it looked like you were one of his friends."

"Boy that was a long time ago." He leaned against his pickup and took his cap off. "Yeah, Matthew was a good guy. We had a lot of fun together, especially in football."

"Who were some of the other people you ran around with in high school?" I asked when he quit talking.

"Well, Jacob of course, Gary sometimes. We did some stuff with our class as a group but most of the time it was Jacob, Matthew and

I. Although come to think of it Gary may have spent more time with Matthew than the rest of us. They hunted a lot on weekends and during the season breaks between sports. Jacob and I hunted too, but not to the extent Gary and Matthew did. You know when people talk about good times in high school it is because they partied, but it wasn't that way with us. We had fun hunting, playing pickup games of basketball, and simply hanging out. I never understood what happened the night of the accident. Matthew didn't drink. I saw him with one that night, but I assumed he was only holding it and he wasn't drunk. He must have swerved for a deer or something."

"Yet according to Jessica, his blood alcohol level was way over the limit."

"It still doesn't make much sense," he said shaking his head.

"Jacob told us they were playing a drinking game."

"Not that I saw, but I could have missed it. Everyone was spread out on every floor of the house," Mitch said. "I guess it was true that he was drunk if his blood was tested at the hospital. It was the common repeated story when people talked about the accident, but I didn't want to believe it. I know Matthew's head took quite a crack. He told me he couldn't remember what happened that night when I stopped to see him in the hospital. He was distraught over the accident. I never did understand what made him run."

"I imagine knowing you were going to be spending a good chunk of your youth in prison would be a good reason."

"I know that, but Matthew wasn't the type to not take responsibility. We had fun, and sometimes that fun would involve some not-so-nice tricks on our classmates, most of the time at Jacob's instigation. Matthew was always the one tempering us to make sure no one would be humiliated, and if something did get out of hand and someone else was going to be blamed he always stepped up and admitted it. That drove Jacob crazy. One day when we were about twelve we were playing basketball in the playground of the park. We'd pulled the picnic table over to the basket and were trying to dunk from the top of the table. We accidently smashed the back-board. We all ran away and no one knew who had done it, so they were going to ban kids from playing in the park unless there was an adult present. Matthew felt bad so he confessed. We all had to cough up our allowances, and clean the park for that whole sum-mer to pay for it. Jacob was so mad." Mitch laughed.

"Do you have any idea of where he might have been all these years? Did he talk about going anywhere after graduation?"

"Not that I can think of. At that age who thinks about the future? All I know is that he loved fishing. I'm sure wherever he's been there was a place to fish nearby."

"I'm not sure that helps much."

"I agree, but maybe I'll think of something else later. I'll let you know."

"Oh yeah, what about your classmate Maggie Onster? Do you remember her being around you guys very often?" I asked, men-tally slapping myself as I just about forgot to ask Mitch about her.

"I kind of forgot about her. She and Matthew used to spend some time together I think, maybe Jacob sometimes, but never with the rest of us."

"Did she and Matthew date?"

"I don't think so. Matthew never said anything but I vaguely remember him getting a little tired of her at times, but he was too nice to ever say anything to her. Isn't she the librarian in town? You could talk to her." Mitch stated.

"Jessica and I did. She claims that Jacob was jealous of Matthew and that maybe they weren't the best of friends like everyone thought. Did you ever notice that?" I asked him, watch-ing his face.

"Not that I recall. I never had any impression that they were anything but close. Most of the guys in our class got along well together," he said looking over at the construction going on with-out him.

"Thanks Mitch. I'll let you get back to work now."

"Not a problem, after all you are paying me," he said with a smile.

I started to walk away and Mitch called after me, "is Jessica having a funeral?"

"Yes. She's having a small service on Friday evening at 7:00 p.m. at the funeral home."

"Thanks I'll be there."

"That is very nice of you Mitch, Jessica will appreciate it."

I finished walking to my pickup thinking that I wasn't sure I was getting anywhere. All anybody could say was how wonderful Matthew was, which didn't surprise me—after all Jessica was too, and I've been her best friend for years. It was 2:00 p.m. The roguing crew would be done at three, I could catch Gary then. In the meantime I headed towards the shop to see if Nick needed help with anything.

CHAPTER THIRTEEN

Wild bergamot is considered a medicinal plant
by many Native Americans.

NICK'S PICKUP WAS PARKED NEXT TO THE SHOP when I drove up but I didn't see any sign of him outside. I parked next to his pickup and walked into the shop. I could hear a lot of pounding coming from the back. I walked towards the noise and found Nick working on one of the combines. He hadn't heard me come in. I stopped for a second and admired the view. His shirt was stretched tight across his back, emphasizing his muscles. Plus, it was nice to see someone else besides me working on a combine. I cleared my throat. Nick jerked and cracked his head on the combine step.

"I'm sorry, did I startle you?" I laughed.

"What do you think?" Nick said rubbing his head, but smiling.

"It was just so nice to see somebody else working on a combine, and even better someone who actually knows what they are doing," I said smiling.

"Now that you're here, you can get over here and help. Maybe you'll learn something."

"I'll try. What do you need help with?"

"I need to get this bearing off, and I can't quite reach both sides. Could you crawl under there and hold the other end with the wrench."

"Not a problem," I said crawling under the combine. "Why are you doing this anyway, I thought you said all the combines were ready to go?"

"They are. I was finished but when I looked at the maintenance records from last fall I saw that I had to grease this one as it had been missed. I think I know why now; it doesn't want to come off."

I crawled under the combine with the wrench. "Did you ever get a chance to talk to Gary about what's been bothering him?" I asked him.

"Yeah, I did, he wasn't very forthcoming. Just apologized for being late to work and said it wouldn't happen again. I thought maybe he had some medical issues or something. I even floated it out there to see if he'd bite on it as an excuse, but no go. I decided to let it go for now. Tomorrow is their last day of work. No sense in firing him, but we may have to next year if nothing changes."

"I'll be talking to him later about Matthew. Maybe he'll be more open with me." I was pleased that Nick was talking about next year. He must be happy working here.

The bearing came off as we were talking and Nick grabbed it before it fell.

"Thanks for helping. It's about time you got some grease on you," he said to me.

"Ha-ha. I know I haven't been around too much. Thanks for keeping everything going."

"You have a lot on your plate. How is your investigation going?"

"What do you mean, investigation?"

"Everyone knows you are trying to help Jessica. I can see why. I haven't lived here very long and even I know it is absurd that the sheriff thinks Jessica killed her own brother."

"As much as I hate to say it, in his defense I'm not coming up with any other suspects either. Everyone loved Matthew."

"Maybe the girl he ran into or someone from her family would bear a grudge."

"Yes, I'm working on that angle. But they don't live here anymore and so far I haven't been able to track them down. Until Jessica and I find them, my only other lead is talking to Gary since he was a friend of Matthew's also. Has my bonehead brother been around?"

Nick grinned. "Yeah, he was here for the morning shift but had to suddenly leave at noon."

"Why what happened?"

"I think I'll let him tell you that." He said his grin even bigger.

"Can I guess it has something to do with Wizard?" I asked confident it was a good deduction.

"That would be a good guess," he said chuckling.

I heard noise out front. "It sounds like the roguing crew is here. I'd better catch Gary before he leaves."

I ran out front, and hollered at Gary, catching him as he was getting into his car. He stood up not looking too pleased to see me. I ran up to him.

"Hi Carmen, Nick already talked to me. I'll get my act together. I was late a couple of times; gee you guys could chill a little."

His tone took me aback. Gary had always been a pretty good-natured guy.

"I also wanted to talk to you about something else. I'm sure you've heard by now that the body you guys found was identified as Matthew Golding."

"Yeah, I'd heard. I should have recognized him, but I didn't look that close."

"Did you also know that the sheriff suspects Jessica of killing him?"

"What", he snorted, "that's ridiculous."

"I know, but that's why I wanted to talk to you. As I understand it, you were good friends with him back in high school. I was hoping you could tell me something about him."

Gary leaned back on his car, folded his arms, stared towards the bronzed, brown-colored field of maturing indiangrass behind the shop and finally said, "That was a long time ago."

"I know, but I'm hoping something from those years you spent time together could give us some clue as to where he's been all this time."

"What do you mean?"

"Jessica and I already spoke to Jacob and Mitch. It sounded like you guys all spent a lot of time together, but Mitch thought you spent the most time with him outside of school hours."

"Yeah we did. Matthew was a great guy. We had a lot of fun, hunting mostly."

"Did he ever talk about what he wanted to do or maybe where he wanted to live?"

"Nah, we didn't talk about that kind of stuff. We were busy enjoying life and being young."

"Do you know what happened the night of the party and the accident?"

"Sure. Matthew drove drunk and hit that girl, end of story," Gary answered getting impatient with me.

"Everyone we've talked to says that it wasn't normal for Matthew to drink like that. Do you have any idea what might have set him off?"

"I've wondered that myself. Jacob was bugging him that night, but that was nothing unusual."

"I thought they were good friends?"

"They were, but at times I thought that Jacob was jealous of him. Everyone liked Matthew, and sometimes I think that bugged Jacob, at least I thought so. When something good would happen to Matthew, Jacob would start to act stupid and try to get Matthew to do things he wouldn't normally do that would make him look stupid."

That fit with what Maggie had said. "Would peer pressure from Jacob have made Matthew drink too much?"

"No, I don't think so. Matthew was used to Jacob acting like that."

"Anything else you noticed that night?"

"No. My girlfriend at the time and I were fighting that night. My attention was focused on that. Plus, the party was getting a little out of hand and I was getting worried about how much trouble I was going to be in for hosting a party. The last time I saw Matthew he was with Jacob talking to a group of other kids."

"Were they playing a drinking game?"

"Not that I noticed, but like I said I wasn't paying that close of attention. I'm amazed I can recall as much as I did, but with everything that happened, that night is pretty well etched in my memory," he answered.

"Have you ever heard from him over the years?"

"Nah, he disappeared after that accident and that was it." He looked down at the ground.

When he wouldn't meet my eyes, it made me think he was being less than truthful. "Come on Gary if you know something, please tell me. Anything could help Jessica."

"What did Jacob have to say when you talked to him?" he asked me.

That was an odd question. "About the same as you, Matthew was a good guy, but no idea where he went."

"Yeah, well he wouldn't have known."

"Does that you mean you do? Come on Gary, what do you know?"

He sighed, "Alright, Matthew contacted me about a month ago. He was all excited because he had some new information about the accident. I didn't make much sense of what he was talking about. To be honest I was so stunned to hear from him that I couldn't process what he was saying. He said he was coming this way soon and asked if I could put him up. I told him it was a bad time for me."

"Why didn't he ask Jessica?"

"I asked him the same thing, but he said he had some stuff to work out and he didn't want to involve Jessica yet in case it didn't work out."

"What did he have to work out?"

"I don't know. He didn't say."

"How was he getting here?" I asked thinking this story was sounding very strange.

"He said he had bus tickets and that someone was picking him up in Parkville."

"Did he say who it was?" I asked thinking whoever it was could have been the killer.

"No. I wish now I would have asked him," Gary said his eyes showing sadness.

"I do have to tell the sheriff about this," I told him.

"I kind of figured you would," he said and looked down at his feet.

"You knew the body was Matthew didn't you? Why didn't you tell the sheriff any of this?"

"No, I didn't know. Not for sure anyway, but I did suspect it might be. I thought he looked familiar but I didn't want to get involved. I've got some of my own problems going on, and I thought that if I told the sheriff I knew Matthew was coming to town I would have been the prime suspect."

"What's going on Gary? You've always been a stand-up guy and employee. Now you are moody, showing up late to work and now withholding information from the sheriff."

"Ah, what the heck, I might as well tell you. Cynthia relapsed a month ago, that's why I couldn't let Matthew stay with me. She moved out two weeks ago taking most of our savings with her. I don't even know for sure where she went."

"I'm so sorry Gary." Cynthia was his wife, she'd been sober for about ten years. "I wish you would have told us."

"What could you have done?" he questioned looking at me directly.

"You could have taken some time off of work," I said recognizing that he was correct. Other than offer sympathy there wasn't much I could do.

"That's the last thing I wanted. I need to get out of the house. I know I should have talked to the sheriff, but it was one more thing I didn't want to deal with. I do wish I would have paid more attention to Matthew though. It almost sounded like he thought he wasn't responsible for the accident."

"Why would he have thought that?" I wondered out loud.

"I have no idea. But he was coming home for some reason. I'll run in to town and talk to the sheriff as soon as I can, okay. Maybe it will help Jessica and get the sheriff looking elsewhere."

"Thanks Gary, I won't tell the sheriff anything you said until you've had a chance to talk to him yourself; and please, if there is any way we can help you out right now, don't hesitate to ask."

"Thanks Carmen, I do appreciate it", he paused, his eyes avoiding mine, and said, "If you are serious about wanting to help there is one thing: our roguing work is going to be done soon—Is there any chance you need some help with harvest? I hate the thought of sitting around my empty house all day."

"I'll talk to Nick. I'm sure we can find something. I'll get back to you."

"Thanks Carmen." He got into his car and left. I hoped he was heading to the sheriff's office.

As Gary left, my brother drove up, all the windows open in his car. I waved him over. "What's this I hear about you leaving work before your shift was done?"

"Oh crud, nothing stays a secret around here does it?" Kirk answered looking at the ground.

"What happened?" I asked bracing myself for a good story.

"My buddies decided to save some money and rented the equipment to pump their septic tank themselves. Unfortunately they didn't have a very long hose, and even worse they didn't tell me they had done it. I stopped by there this morning before work to drop off an amp that they needed to fix. When I opened the car door, Wizard darted out. I didn't even know he'd snuck in the car, but I still didn't think anything of it. He took off like he always does. When I went to leave, I whistled, Wiz came running and we left."

"Didn't you notice the smell?" I asked as I burst out laughing.

"No, I was running late and was now going to be even later since I had to swing by home to drop off Wizard. My air conditioning doesn't work so I had the window open and my radio cranked; I wasn't paying attention. I got home, stuck Wizard in my bedroom and took off. When I got to work I checked my cell phone before getting in the van and saw that Dad had called, and you can imagine why. He could smell something when he walked in the house after his morning walk and tracked it to my room. I had to go back home and spend two hours cleaning my bedroom and airing out the house. I got back here in time to catch the guys before they went back out in the field after their morning break."

"How is Wizard smelling now?"

"He's fine, but my bedroom isn't so great. It's a good thing I have a gig tonight."

"I hope you left all the windows in the house open and the door to your bedroom shut."

"Don't worry, yes, I did."

"Is that dog really worth all he puts you through?"

"You know I love him."

"I know, and every day he shows you how much he loves you," I said laughing.

CHAPTER FOURTEEN

Prairie blazing star has bright purple flowers,
can grow up to five feet tall, and is an excellent pollinator.

I GOT HOME THAT NIGHT AROUND 7:00 P.M. I had swung by the construction site again on my way home and was happy to see that the foundations for the cabins were all formed, with the gravel for the sub grade hauled in and leveled off. Mitch told me that they'd be pouring the cement tomorrow. I told him again how thrilled I was at the pace they were moving, and as usual he didn't take praise very well. He tried to tell me that the weather was responsible for their speed. They were rushing to get as much done as possible due to a chance of rain the day after tomorrow. As dry as we were, I couldn't even bring myself to hope it wouldn't. At this point I'd happily accept rain slowing down the construction and harvest.

I walked into the kitchen and found Dad sitting at the table snacking on some peanuts, with Wizard on the floor by Dad's feet begging. Despite Kirk's efforts there was a definite odor emanating from him.

"Shouldn't he be getting punished?" I asked.

"He can't help it if his owner is an idiot," Dad responded.

I smiled, "True, have you eaten anything other than the peanuts?"

"Not yet."

"Good, it's my turn to cook for you for a change. I think I'll thaw some ground beef and grill us some hamburgers."

"That sounds terrific, anything I can do to help?" Dad asked.

"Sit there and relax. You've been doing all the cooking lately. We'll have some simple lettuce salads to go along with the burgers." I grabbed the ground beef and put it in the microwave to thaw.

"How is Jessica doing?" Dad asked.

"She was doing as well as could be expected when I left her late this morning. I'm planning on calling her after supper," I said as I started chopping up some tomatoes and cucumbers for the salad.

"So how did your questioning of Mitch and Gary go this after-noon?" he asked, watching me as I chopped.

"Mitch didn't have anything to add, other than the same old thing that no one could believe Matthew was drunk."

"It seems like you keep circling back to that accident. Do you truly believe the accident has something to do with his murder?" Dad asked frowning.

"I think that the accident has something to do with why he came back for sure. Gary told me that Matthew had called him and told him he was coming back and wanted to stay with him. Gary was under the impression that Matthew didn't think he hit that girl and he was coming back to talk to someone."

"Why wouldn't he have stayed with Jessica?"

"That's what makes me think his death has something to do with what happened the night of that party. Gary said he didn't want to stay with Jessica as he didn't want her involved or get her hopes up if he was wrong about his part in the accident."

"How about you, did you find out anything about the security camera yet?" I asked Dad.

"No, the owner of the body shop is on a cruise. Just our luck it is the first vacation he and his wife have taken in ten years. Good for them, but bad timing for us. I tried to talk Sheriff Poole into getting a warrant to access it, but as you already know he's sold on Jessica being the guilty party, so no help there." Dad paused, and after few seconds of silence said, "You know there were a lot of people who thought something was fishy about that accident."

"What do you mean?"

"They never found any paint that matched that girl's bike on Matthew's car, and some of the skid marks looked like there might have been another car involved."

"Jessica never said anything about that."

"I doubt she knew. I was good friends with Sheriff Poole's predecessor. He and his wife, and your mom and I would play cards together once a week. The information wasn't known by the public. But when Matthew took off it put an end to any speculation that he wasn't responsible. It didn't help that he was drunk as well; the blood tests don't lie."

"From what everyone says about Matthew's character, I'm starting to think something happened at that party that made him behave in a way that wasn't normal for him."

"It will be tough, if not impossible, to find out what that might be. It was a long time ago," Dad said, looking thoughtful.

"I know. But based on what Gary said, I think Matthew had come to doubt his guilt too and was coming back here for a reason." The ground beef had thawed and I had formed it into patties while we talked. They were ready, so I picked them up and went out to the grill. As I stepped out the door I heard the phone ring. Dad answered the phone as the door shut behind me. Tabitha showed up looking for some attention while I put the burgers on the grill. I set a timer, knelt down, pet her and walked back in the house with Tabitha following me. Dad was hanging up the phone.

"Jessica is coming over. She says she has some news."

"Did you invite her for supper? There is plenty."

"Yes, I did and she said she had some cheesecake she'd bring over."

"Great, she makes the best cheesecake." I got out the dishes and set the table for the three of us. I cut up some romaine lettuce, added the tomatoes and cucumbers I had cut up and put it in a big bowl. I also set some pickles, buns, and the salad dressings on the table. Dad mixed up some lemonade. Wizard pranced around waiting for anything edible to hit the floor. Tabitha sat by her dish looking at him with disdain. A cat would never deign to beg with so little decorum.

I had just brought the burgers in the kitchen when Jessica burst through the door. She stopped, sniffed and said, "It smells a little . . ." she paused.

I broke in, "poopy?"

"Exactly." She looked puzzled. "Are you having trouble with your septic system?"

"No, you can blame it on Wizard." I explained what had happened.

She laughed, "That sounds like something that would happen to Kirk and Wizard."

Not able to wait any longer, I said, "So what is the news that brings you over here?"

"I had the most amazing phone conversation a few minutes ago."

"Phone conversation with whom?" I asked, thankful to whoever it was because they succeeded in bringing some joy back to Jessica's spirit.

"Pamela Wicks, the girl that was on the bike," she furthered explained when she saw our blank looks.

"She called you?"

"Yes. She said Matthew had tracked her down about three months ago. He was asking what she remembered about that night."

"Why didn't she let the police know he contacted her?"

"She didn't think it was really him at first. She thought it was a sick crank call and hung up on him. He called back the next day, and again the next day, until he was able to convince her. He told her that he'd been seeing a therapist, trying to get his memory back about that night and he wanted to know if she had any memories. He couldn't be clear about the details, but he was pretty sure he had a repressed memory of another car that was following him. He was sure that he hit the tree when he swerved to avoid her. He thought the other vehicle may have hit her instead of him. She told him that he needed to turn himself in. He said he was planning to. He said that he missed his family, but also that he was becoming more and more convinced he wasn't responsible for the accident. He asked her to see his therapist."

"Did she do it?"

"She told him she didn't need to. She was almost positive there were two cars, but by the time she was alert enough in the hospital to tell anyone, Matthew was already gone and she assumed he was guilty, like everyone else. He told her he was coming back to talk to someone that had also been at the party and that he'd turn himself in once he knew the true story. She was expecting to hear something from him and finally tracked me down on the internet. Matthew never left her a contact number. When he did call her it must have been on burner phones because the numbers were never the same. When she did try to call one of numbers that was on her caller ID, it wouldn't work. She was shocked to hear what had happened." Jessica started to cry and said, "Do you realize all this time Matthew was gone for no reason?" She sat down with a thump.

"Someone else caused that accident," I said, the hamburgers in my hand forgotten.

Dad said what we were all thinking, "Someone in this town is a murderer."

CHAPTER FIFTEEN

*Some prairie plants can put down twenty-five foot deep roots,
each year some roots die, making great quantities of
organic matter, creating rich and fertile soil.*

W E SAT DOWN TO EAT IN stunned silence. The burgers had
somehow stayed warm, but I couldn't begin to say what
they tasted like as we all ate on auto pilot.

I chewed for a few minutes and said, "Matthew's death must be
tied to that accident. It was a senior class party and we have four
suspects that live locally. We found that out when we went through
the year books, Mitch, Maggie, Jacob, and Gary. John Harling was
another good friend but I don't know who that is so I'm assuming
he doesn't live around here."

"The Harling family moved away about fifteen years ago," Dad
said recognizing the name.

"It could have been somebody else, somebody that followed
him here. Maybe they found out that Matthew was coming here to
ask questions and they thought it would be a good time to kill him
as it would be blamed on a local," Jessica said.

"I don't see that being plausible," I disagreed. "First, if Matthew was in that kind of trouble he would never have brought it back here to his family. Second, I'm sure Matthew wouldn't have been going by his real name, so who would have known to try and frame you, Jessica. Third, it just makes sense that it was something to do with that accident, at least to me. I talked to Gary today and what he had to say verifies Pamela's story that Matthew was coming back to town."

"What did Gary say?" Jessica asked.

I then told her that Gary had said Matthew had contacted him too about coming back.

"It's hard to believe someone we in all likelihood know is a murderer," Dad said when I finished talking.

"Look, I don't want to think it is one of them either, but come on, this is a small community, and I doubt a stranger could be in town long enough to kill someone and no one even know that they were here."

"Matthew made it back without anyone knowing," Dad pointed out.

That set me back, "True. We appear to be going in circles and making no headway."

"Not necessarily, you can pass all this information on to the sheriff and he can track down everyone in that class and find out where everyone was that week."

"I think we all know the sheriff isn't going to do that," I said.

"I'm not sure that's fair," Dad said. "If Gary and Pamela both talk to him he can't continue to be that close minded. At least pass on the information to him and in the mean time you can discretely check out the other four."

" Three, Maggie said she wasn't at the party," Jessica interrupted.

"Why are you assuming it was one of them? Have you thought about it being someone that wasn't at the party?" Dad asked. "Anyone who lived here could have been out on the road that night."

"But who would Matthew be coming back to talk to. He had to have remembered something from the party that made him want to question someone. If he knew who was in the other vehicle he would have named them, or gotten a hold of the sheriff himself."

"But we talked to everyone. They all had the same story; something happened to upset Matthew, he drank too much and left the party on his own," I said. "The only differences in the stories we were told relate to how much alcohol people thought he drank and that not everyone believed Jacob and Matthew were best friends, all pretty minor stuff."

"We'll need to talk to everyone again. Somebody must have lied to us," Jessica stated, her voice hard with indignation.

"When is Pamela going to let the sheriff know about this?" Dad asked.

"She said she was going to call and talk to him tomorrow," Jessica answered.

"Between her and Gary, that should get some of the pressure off you as a suspect. You certainly weren't old enough to be involved with an accident twenty years ago," Dad said.

"Let's hope. Sheriff Poole is pretty determined to pin it on me." She yawned and said, "Thanks' for the supper. I'd better get home, I haven't been pulling my weight at the restaurant these last couple days and I want to get a good night sleep tonight."

"Are you going to be okay by yourself tonight?" I asked.

"Yes, I think so. Pamela's phone call was such a load lifter; not only does she have an alternate motive to present to the sheriff, but just knowing that Matthew wasn't responsible for that accident is a mental weight lifted from my mind that I don't think I even realized I was carrying. I wish Mom and Dad were alive. Although maybe it is for the best, it would have been horrible for them to have to go through the loss of Matthew twice. I know it happened a long time ago but it's always in the back of your mind. If he hadn't run away, things could have been so different."

I nodded in agreement, "I hate to ask as I know the funeral service is on Friday night, but do you think you will be okay with going to see Kirk's band play on Saturday?"

"Yes, I think it will be good to get away and there is no doubt Kirk's band is loud enough that I won't have to hear myself think." She smiled and said, "James is planning on coming, too. We'll figure out a time and transportation later. I need to get going." She left with more spring in her step than I'd seen in a few days. It was good to see.

"What do you think of all this?" Dad asked after Jessica had left.

"I'm not quite as optimistic as Jessica that this completely clears Matthew of his believed part in the accident, but I do believe someone from that night killed him. I am going to talk to everyone again."

"Are you sure you should be involving yourself in this anymore? One of these people could be a murderer. That person may have killed Matthew so that whatever happened that night would never come to light."

I stopped for a second, "I know it sounds stupid, but I never thought of it like that. I was mad the sheriff was trying to blame Jessica and wasn't thinking about the danger."

"Why don't you wait and see what the sheriff does with this new information and then you can decide how far you should pursue this, but leave it alone for now, okay?"

"You may be right. I'll leave it alone for a day and give the sheriff a chance. I have enough to do tomorrow anyway. It's been three days since I sprayed the prairie blazing star and I need to check to make sure I got the moth taken care of. The blue grama should be checked also; if ready we could start combining sooner than expected. I am so thankful Nick got all the equipment ready."

"I know I sometimes have my reservations about him, for whatever reason, but I'm glad he's been such a help to you," Dad said.

"He has been awesome. Some days I'm not sure I'm even needed anymore," I said with a laugh.

"Maybe you want to ask him to go with you guys Saturday night. He hasn't had much of an opportunity to meet people around here yet."

"Good idea, I'll call him when I'm done with the dishes."

"I can do them," Dad offered.

"No you can't, you've been doing too much of the cooking and cleaning around here. It's way past time to take my turn."

"Well if I'm not needed around here, I'll see if Karla wants me," he said with a wink.

"Have fun."

He stopped and asked, "You don't think your mom would be bothered by my dating?"

"Absolutely not. Mom would be glad you are happy. I think it's great too. It did surprise me though, to be honest. James and I have always been good friends, but I never had the impression you and Mom got along with Karla too well."

"No reason why you would have. Karla worked very hard to keep that ranch going on her own. After all, her husband died when James was around ten. She didn't have much time to join in with any community activities. She and your mom didn't have anything in common. I wouldn't say we disliked Karla; we just never got to know her."

"Well I'm glad for both of you," I said finishing putting the dishes in the dishwasher and washing the table and counters.

"I know Karla asked you earlier, but are you sure you are okay that Jessica and James are dating? Not that I'm unhappy for them but like everyone else I assumed you and James would get together at some point."

"No, there was never a spark. He's like a brother, perhaps a better one than I have," I said with a laugh. "I can't believe I didn't realize that he and Jessica would make such a good couple after all the years we spent hanging around together."

"Just don't stay so busy with the farm that you forget to have a life," Dad cautioned.

"Relax Dad. I'm doing exactly what I want to do with my life. I am only twenty-eight. I'm not over the hill yet."

He laughed.

"Go see Karla and get out of my hair."

"I will. What are you going to do with a night to yourself?"

"Since it is already nine o'clock it isn't going to be much of a night but first I'm going to call Nick about Saturday night, and then I'm going to relax and read a book."

"Have a good night," he said as he walked out of the kitchen to call Karla in privacy I assumed.

A couple of minutes later I heard the front door shut and his pickup leave. I finished sweeping the floor that looked like it had been neglected for weeks rather than a day, made sure the grill was turned off, looked around for my phone, and found it lying underneath Wizard. I figured I could let him out to do his business while I called Nick. Tabitha must have changed her mind about being inside as she followed Wizard out. She'd be more amenable to being inside once winter showed up. I stepped out on the porch and dialed Nick's number while Wizard ran around the yard sniffing to make sure nothing new had invaded his territory, and Tabitha slunk off towards the tree row to hunt.

"What's up Carmen?" he answered.

"Jessica, James and I are heading to Parkville on Saturday night to see Kirk's band play. I was wondering if you'd like to join us? They start playing around eight."

There was a slight pause and Nick said, "I'd like to get out for an evening, but is it safe to listen to his band? I kind of like my hearing."

"That's why we don't stay long." I laughed and said, "We show some support, eat some greasy fried food, and leave after a few songs. That way the integrity of our ears can be maintained."

"That's sounds wise. Sure, I'll go with, it'll be good to see some of the night life that is offered around here."

"I hope you won't be judging the community too harshly after your exposure to this particular form of entertainment. We do have a lot of other better-quality options."

Nick laughed, "I'll keep that in mind. See you tomorrow at work."

I hung up the phone surprising myself by how much I was looking forward to Nick coming with us. I'd better be careful. I didn't want anything to screw up our working relationship. I whistled to Wizard and we went back inside. I put Wizard back in Kirk's room as I didn't want to have to share the couch with his aroma. I made sure he had some water in his dish and then I walked upstairs to grab my book. Coming back downstairs, I curled up on the couch and started to read. I made it about twenty pages before I started to nod off. I gave up and went to bed.

CHAPTER SIXTEEN

Wild bergamot can be used to treat colds
and is often made into a tea.

Thursday morning dawned to a beautiful fall day. The week had been going by fast with a lot packed in, it was hard to believe it was only Monday, 3 days ago, that Matthews body had been found. I was putting some scrambled eggs on my plate when Kirk came shuffling out of his bedroom with Wizard trailing behind him.

"Aren't you going to be late for work?" I asked him as he was wearing a bathrobe and obviously wasn't dressed for work.

"No, the band and I have been practicing every afternoon and evening after work. I asked Gary for the day off so we could practice all day today too."

"Why so much practicing?" I asked knowing the guys were faithful to their practice sessions but never quite to this extreme.

"There is a chance a record producer from Minneapolis might be at the show on Saturday night."

"Wow! That is impressive. Good luck. Not to take away from your good news but I think Wizard needed to go out," I pointed as he was relieving himself on the floor. To his credit he was cowering in shame, Wizard not Kirk. "It's not your fault your owner didn't take care of you," I said to Wizard as I opened the back door for him.

"Oh Crap!" Kirk said. "I'll clean it up. I guess I forgot to let him out last night when I got home. Poor guy couldn't hold it any longer." Kirk grabbed some paper towels and cleaned up the mess. As he put the soiled paper towels in the garbage he looked longingly at my scrambled eggs and said, "I don't suppose you'd make me some?"

"Not on your life. Unlike you, I need to get to work."

He sighed, which moved me in no way.

"Where is Dad?" he asked as went to the cupboard to get some cereal.

"He must have spent the night at Karla's."

"Do you think they'll get married?" he asked me.

"I don't know. Would it bother you if they did?" I replied.

"No, he is happy again, especially when he's around her." He opened the door for Wizard as he walked by the kitchen door to get a clean bowl out of the dishwasher. Wizard blew in the door as fast as his legs would carry him. When Wizard moves that fast, you know he is up to something. As he flew by me heading for the living room I noticed a streak of something black dragging along him.

"I think Wizard brought something in with him," I pointed at the trail of black sludge he had left behind him.

Kirk muttered a cuss word, and went running out of the room after him.

I emptied the clean dishes out of the dishwasher and put the dirty ones in it, a never-ending cycle, then hollered at Kirk that he better clean up any mess Wizard had made and I headed to the farm. On the way to the shop I stopped by the prairie blazing star field and was pleased to find no new moths or caterpillars survived the spraying. I was thankful to observe bees humming happily around in the field. It was a good sign to me that my spraying hadn't affected them. I met up with Nick at the shop.

"How are you this morning?" he asked.

I considered his question for a few seconds and answered, "To my surprise I'm doing great. I slept the entire night, the moth is gone in the prairie blazing star, and Wizard is causing problems for Kirk. It would be a perfect day if the prairie blazing star wasn't behind from last year. It's bad enough the dry conditions already reduced the yield, but now we have to worry that it won't make seed before we get a frost." This was always a danger with the type of crops we raised. There had been no plant selection to breed robust varieties. This kept the plants genetics from being modified and therefore they ripened at their own pace, however Mother Nature and the growing degree days allowed. The fact that the prairie blazing star was still flowering made it unlikely that it would mature in time before a frost.

"How is your morning going?" I asked him in return.

"All the equipment is ready to go. No qualifiers today."

That was great news. Nick had been telling me the equipment is ready to go except for; and then he'd tell me some minor item, for the last few weeks. It was nice we were finally ready. Our harvest took about two months with each crop variety ready at different times. If we were lucky we would finish combining one crop before the next one was ready; if not, it became a mad panic, as again, not being genetically modified, the seed would fall off in the wind if you weren't there to get it in time. I wasn't expecting a bumper yield in any of our crops this year, as it had been too dry. We had irrigation which was a blessing or we wouldn't have any crop at all, but the crops respond better to rain.

"This is the roguers last day too," Nick said.

"Yes", and we both smiled at each other. While we appreciated and greatly needed the help they brought us, it was a relief to have four less people around. Hired help, while necessary, tended to bring extra stress also. Harvest would be taken care of by me, Nick and when an extra hand was needed Dad or Kirk would be willing to help out. After my conversation with Gary I was going to make sure and call him before either of them as Gary needed the work and Dad deserved time to do what he wanted, plus Gary is much better help than Kirk. We also had two employees, Sam and Phil, who cleaned seed in our seed cleaning facility for us in the winter that would help us out sometimes depending on when their construction jobs ended for the season.

"So what is on your plate for the day?" I asked Nick.

"I'm going to get the last two bins cleaned and get a conveyor out so it's ready for the blue grama. Are you thinking that will be next week?"

"It should. I'm hoping for Monday, but I'll check it again today. Right now I'm going to head out to the cabin site and see how construction is progressing there."

"As you see the cabins becoming reality are you having any regrets?" Nick asked.

"No regrets, a little hesitation, but I'd say excitement is the primary emotion. I'm not sure how the workload will affect us, but Jessica and Edna are planning on handling all the food. We aren't offering daily housecleaning and they have to rent by the week. So cleaning once a week should be sufficient and I'm sure I can find a high school kid to do it. The extra work for me will be keeping track of reservations and being available to help people check in or out. Dad said he would help with that if I was busy in harvest or burning." As our crops were perennial crops the most important thing for native seed production along with insect control and weeding was burning the fields every spring. It was my least favorite part of the farm operation. A huge fire to start and take care of never failed to scare me senseless every year. We'd been fortunate and in over thirty-five years of doing this we'd never lost control of a fire, but the threat was there every year. It helped that we maintained fire breaks around fields that were located near adjacent land that might pose a hazard, such as wooded areas or homes.

"I'm sure you'll figure it out."

"Let's hope or I'm sure wasting a pile of money on cabins and advertising."

"Do you want me to swing by and pick you up Saturday night? I assume Jessica will be riding with James."

"We haven't figured out anything for sure yet, but I think we can all ride together with James. If it's okay with him we will pick you up around seven." I paused as I realized I had no idea where Nick was living. "I feel kind of bad, but I have no idea where you live."

"Why should you feel bad?" he asked puzzled.

"You came here not knowing anyone and housing can be difficult to find. I should have wondered and helped if you needed it."

Nick laughed, "If I would have needed help I would have asked. I'm living in a house by that old country school. The house isn't the greatest but I like that it comes with a thirty-acre yard, most of it wooded, which is nice, otherwise my view would be open farm land."

"Oh, it must be the old Erickson place. It's been sitting vacant for a couple of years. Did you buy it?"

"No, I'm renting it now. It is for sale, but it needs a lot of work so I'm taking my time thinking about it. It might be easier to build my own place from scratch."

"I hope that means you are planning on being here permanently."

"I like it around here, so far so good," Nick answered.

"Great. Well I'm off to the cabin site," I said trying to keep my happiness that Nick liked it here from showing.

I stood outside my pickup for a second and breathed in the fresh air. As I did I saw a sheriff's deputy car go by on the highway, taking away some of my enjoyment in the day as I was reminded of Matthew's death. I promised myself I would track Gary down at some point today and make sure he went to talk to the sheriff. I thought about calling the sheriff myself and asking him if Gary had talked to him while at the same time asking if Pamela had talked to him also. I came to the conclusion I'd better keep out of it for now. If Sheriff Poole was going to consider anyone else but Jessica he wouldn't appreciate me helping him. If I irritated him he might get even more bull headed. I'd give him until Monday before I bothered him. I got into my pickup and drove to the construction site. A large flock of geese were flying far above me heading south; further proof along with the color changes happening to the trees and grasses, that fall was on its way. When I arrived at the prairie the framing was already up on two of the cabins. These guys were moving fast. Mark looked up as I got out of the pickup.

"Good morning Carmen," he hollered.

"Good morning Mark. I can't believe how fast you guys are moving," I said surprised that Mark was even talking to me. I don't think he had ever initiated a conversation with me before.

"We tend to work faster in the fall than the spring that's for sure. No one wants to be working on an outside project in the winter."

"Well whatever the reason, it's working great for me."

"I have to warn you it that it will slow way down when we start on the inside of the cabins. Knotty pine takes a lot of time."

"As long as it's done before spring I'll be happy."

"We'll be long gone by then," Mark said.

"I sure hope so. Is Mitch around?" I asked him as Mark moved to the saw to cut some more plywood.

"I think he's over there working on the third cabin," he answered as he lined up the saw blade.

"Oh, I see him. Is it okay to bother him, or is now a bad time?"

"It should be fine. It's about ten-thirty", he said looking at his watch, "we typically take a break around now anyway."

"Okay, thanks," I said as I wandered toward the cabin. Mitch was busy pounding nails. It was amazing to watch him work. He was one fluid motion; nail, pound once, next nail, pound once. I'd have no fingers left if it was me. I was scared to say anything in case I startled him. I cleared my throat to get his attention.

"Oh. Hello Carmen," he said as he looked up.

"Do you have a minute?"

"Sure, time to stretch anyway. What's up?"

I proceeded to tell him about Pamela and how she felt there was another car that night, that Matthew had contacted her and told her he was coming back here to talk to someone. "Did you have any calls on your phone that you didn't recognize? Maybe Matthew tried to contact you?"

"That's tough to say, I get so many unrecognized calls. I try to dial most of them back, in case they are business related, but a lot go unanswered—telemarketer calls I assume. If Matthew did try to contact me I would have no way of knowing." He looked me straight in the eyes.

"What's going on Carmen? Do you think somebody at the party that night killed him?"

I shrugged my shoulders.

He put down his hammer. "Carmen you've got to be kidding. You think something from way back at a high school party caused Matthew to be killed now?"

"What other explanation can there be?" I answered defensively.

"How about Matthew's been up to no good all these years, came home to get some money or something from his sister and someone from wherever he's been living followed him."

"It's possible", I acknowledged, "but I don't believe it. He had just contacted Pamela and told her that he remembered another car being involved in the accident that night. She told him that her memory of the night also included another vehicle. She hadn't told anyone, as by the time she woke up in the hospital Matthew was gone and she assumed he was guilty like everyone else. He told her he was coming home to talk to someone and instead he ended up getting killed. It has to be tied to that party."

"I've thought about that party a million times. Matthew got upset, he walked out of the party. Jacob followed him and tried to talk him out of driving. Matthew drove away."

"Are you sure no one followed him?"

"Jacob and Matthew were the only ones that left the party early."

"Jacob left at the same time as Matthew?"

"He went outside to try and talk Matthew out of driving. But he did come back in after Matthew left. He told us how he tried to stop Matthew. When that didn't work he stayed for a while longer until he left to check if Matthew made it safely home. He was the one that came across the accident."

"That meant he was driving on that road too."

"Yes, but it was after the accident had already happened as he's the one that found the accident and reported it."

"Oh," I said deflated.

"Maybe someone else not associated with the party was on the road that night?" Mitch offered.

"That could be. Pamela thought by what Matthew said that he was coming back to talk to someone. I think he might have recognized the car, and if I'm correct it was someone he knew."

"It could have been anyone from town."

"Who else would have been coming from that direction except someone from the party? There isn't any farmland, just swamp and trees. I looked in a county plat book and there were two homes on that road, Gary and Pamela's. The Wicks wouldn't have run over their own daughter and left her laying there."

"True, but no one left," Mitch insisted.

"Do you suppose it could have been Jacob? It was a long time ago and everyone was drinking. Maybe you got your times confused."

"I don't see how. Matthew and Jacob left and spent some time outside arguing; Jacob came back in and said Matthew left. I remember seeing Jacob after Matthew had left and he was agitated. I know he was upset that Matthew drove away in that condition. It would be highly doubtful Jacob was involved. Plus, he was devastated after Matthew ran away. He kept saying he should have forced Matthew to ride with him. Nah, it wasn't him. At times he acted jealous of Matthew, but they were best buddies. They even wore matching sweatshirts at times. I remember them even buying the same kind of tennis shoes. Even if our perception of the time was off that evening I can't imagine him being involved."

"Then who could it be? How about before Matthew left? Did anybody come to the party and leave before Matthew?"

"Not that I remember. Let it be Carmen, it's the sheriff's job to figure this out. Besides if you are right, someone killed Matthew to keep whatever happened that night a secret. What makes you think they won't get rid of you if you get too close?"

That made me stop; for a second. "I can't. The sheriff is trying to pin this on Jessica and I'm not going to let that happen."

"Be careful, sometimes stirring up the past causes a lot of problems," Mitch stated, picking up his hammer again.

"Thanks for your time Mitch. I'd better let you get back to work." I walked away wondering if I'd just been threatened.

I got in my pickup and noticed my cellphone was lying on the seat. It must have slipped out of my pocket. There was a text from Nick asking me if I could pick up a new leaf blower as ours had quit working. We used them to clean out the bins. I called him back and told him I would. I checked the time on my phone. I had just enough time to get to town, pick up a leaf blower at the hardware store and get back to drop it off with Nick before he left for lunch. Unfortunately for my tight schedule, Melanie was standing outside of the hardware store when I came out carrying the leaf blower. Today she was wearing a bright lime green shirt with ladybugs and an orange ankle length skirt. I tried not to wince.

She saw me and said, "I don't know why people insist on using those things. What is wrong with leaves? Think of all the poor bugs that get blown away and killed from using those things, also leaf residue when left alone provides valuable mulch for the soil under them."

I cut her off knowing I would be there for hours if I questioned her thinking, "I know that, Melanie. Our purpose in using them is to clean out old seed from our bins. I would never disturb leaves in my yard." This wasn't an actual lie as raking leaves was something no one in my family had time for. Wind or mowing took care of them just fine in our opinion, but of course we didn't even attempt to maintain a beautiful, manicured lawn in any sense of the word.

"That is wonderful Carmen. It's fortunate I ran into you. I have the brochures ready for your cabins. They are in my car which is right around the block. I'll be right back with them."

She ran off before I could stop her. She was faster than I thought she'd be and came puffing back, brochures in hand.

"I think you should hang on to these brochures yourself as the cabins are a long way from getting finished and I may misplace them before that," I told her.

"I can always print more. You can share them with your workers or customers," she airily replied.

She must have been under the mistaken impression that I was now part of her advertising campaign. Rather than waste any more time I accepted the brochures and excused myself. I got in my pickup as fast as I could before anything else delayed me. I got back to the farm, managing to deliver the leaf blower to Nick before dinner. The roguing crew had finished for the year sometime mid-morning and the van they used was sitting there. I didn't have much of an appetite, so I decided to skip my own dinner, clean the van and get their equipment put away. This took longer than I thought, and it was close to 3:00 p.m. before I was finished. It always amazed me the amount of dirt and grime four guys could get in a vehicle and it would never bother them for four months. Nick pulled up as I was parking the van in the back of the building. I had to move a couple of combines and silage wagons to get it in, but we needed the van out of the way. If we ever built another building I was going to make sure there were doors on both ends of the building. We wasted a lot of time moving things in and out to make room for equipment.

"Did you need help?" he asked.

"Nope, I just finished. I think we can both knock off for the day though; it's 5:30 p.m. I want to get home, grab a bite to eat and take a shower." Somehow I'd managed to get most of the dirt from the van on me. "I also need to get a hold of Jessica to see how she is doing and verify the plans for Saturday night. I think picking you up at seven will work. Plan on that anyway—if it's different I will let you know."

"That sounds good. I'll see you tomorrow and tell Jessica hi from me," Nick said while getting in his pickup to leave for the day.

CHAPTER SEVENTEEN

*Native prairies provide necessary habitat to sustain resident
and migratory wildlife populations along
with butterfliesand other pollinators.*

I GOT HOME TO FIND AN EMPTY HOUSE. I was starving and made
myself a peanut butter and jelly sandwich and grabbed a handful
of chips. After I wolfed that down I called Jessica.

"How are you doing?" I asked when she answered the phone.

"Okay I guess," she replied sounding listless. Obviously her
improved spirits from last night had been temporary.

"Have you eaten anything?" I asked feeling guilty for not thinking of her before I stuffed my face.

"No, but I'm not very hungry," she said.

I made a quick decision, "It sounds like you need a chicken
strip basket. I'm bringing you one as soon as I take a shower."

"Thank you Carmen. You don't have to", she hesitated, "but it
does sound good."

"I'll be there as quick as I can." I hung up the phone and headed
for the shower.

Twenty minutes later I was in the drive-through lane at Dairy

Queen, the sole fast-food place in Arvilla. I was wishing I could have brought her a more nutritious meal from her own restaurant but it was only open for breakfast and dinner. She met me at the door when I got to her place.

"Oh that smells wonderful," she said when I handed her the food. "Didn't you get anything for yourself?"

"No, I ate at home." Although I was wishing I had picked up some for myself, as who doesn't love the smell of French fries?

We sat down at her kitchen table. "Is everything set up for the funeral tomorrow? Nothing came up today that we didn't already talk about?"

"Everything should be ready. Edna is already working on the lunch," she replied as she ate her French fries. She noticed me looking. "Did you want some?" she asked.

I replied with regret, "No", remembering the chips I had eaten. "Is it okay that I invited Nick to go with us on Saturday?"

"I think it's great that you invited him and I'm sure James will think so too." She stopped eating and gave me a look. "Is there something going on between the two of you at last?"

"No. Dad suggested it as he figured Nick hadn't gotten a chance to meet many people in the area yet. I felt bad that I hadn't thought of it myself."

"Hmm", she said, "do you want there to be something?"

"He is attractive," I sighed, shook my head and said, "but it would make work too complicated."

"True," she said, resuming her French fry eating. It didn't look like there would be any left over for me to sneak.

"I told him we could all ride with James and that we would pick him up at seven. He's living at the old Erickson place."

"That will be fun. I'll let James know." Then she asked, "How is construction going on the cabins?"

"Mitch and Mark are moving so fast. It's exciting, but a little scary. I hope it takes off, otherwise I'm going to feel awful for losing the money I talked Dad in to letting the farm invest in to building them."

"Have you done any preliminary advertising?"

"Not yet. I have the advertisements ready to go, but I'm planning on waiting until after harvest. I want to make sure I have the time to answer the phone and be able give my full attention to answering questions without feeling rushed. I also wanted to wait with the ads to make sure the cabins were going to get built this fall, and it looks like that is happening."

"I think it is great, and I'm sure you'll make a success of it."

"If it is a success, I'm sure yours and Edna's food will be a big part of it." We spent the next couple of hours visiting, until I realized the time. "I'd better get going. Are you okay to be by yourself tonight?"

"Yes. I am doing fine. I'm sad, but I am okay. Thanks for supper, and thanks for all your help," Jessica answered with a few tears in her eyes.

"I'll see you tomorrow at the funeral. I'll be there around six o'clock." We hugged and I headed home. I could see some lights on in the house when I drove up, but I didn't see anyone around when I walked in, which was fine as I was tired. Tabitha came inside with me since it was a chilly night and we both went straight to bed.

Friday morning I woke up to a mist of rain and a cat tail on my forehead. A fitting day for a funeral was my first thought as I shut the alarm off. I realized I hadn't been paying attention to the weather forecast, but I remembered Mitch had talked about the possibility of rain. I guess he knew what he was talking about. I double-checked the forecast on my phone and saw it was for rain all day. It was nice to see that it could still rain, which I was beginning to doubt. I decided to text Nick and tell him he could stay home for the day if he wanted. He replied instantly that was okay by him.

Dad and Kirk were eating pancakes when I walked in to the kitchen. Wizard was waiting by their feet, his eyes never leaving them, hoping something edible would fall to the floor.

"There is some in the oven if you want any," Dad said as he looked up.

"Where have you been the last day and a half?" I asked Dad, trying to get a rise out of him knowing perfectly well he'd been with Karla.

Dad didn't even blink, "Karla needed some help yesterday. James is gone at the bull sale and a couple cows got out of their pasture. We rounded them up and spent the day fixing the fence. By the time we finished and had some supper I fell asleep on her couch. I sure am glad we produce seed and not cattle. What are you guys doing today?" he asked as he looked at us.

"I'll be practicing with the band all day," Kirk said his mouth full, not even looking up from stuffing his face with pancakes.

"I'm not sure yet. I gave Nick the day off. Everything is ready for harvest and he might as well get some rest on a rainy day." I stopped talking, thought for a little bit and decided. "I think I'll run to town and get some errands done. I can't remember the last time anyone went grocery shopping around here. I think I'll pop in to the book store too and see if any of my favorite authors have anything new out. What are you going to do today Dad?"

"I think it's a good day to take a nap," he said.

"Are you feeling okay?" I asked. It wasn't normal for Dad to want to take a nap.

"I'm feeling fine, but I thought that was what retirement was about?" he said with a smile. "Yesterday was a long day and I think these bones could use a rest. Plus I'll be here when you get home to help unload the groceries."

"That would be welcome." I finished my pancakes and took a few minute to clean up the kitchen. Kirk grabbed Wizard and took off for his practice. "I'm heading out now Dad, don't forget the funeral tonight," I reminded him.

"Yes. Karla and I will be there."

"Thanks for breakfast, have a good nap." I grabbed my keys and walked out the door.

My first stop was the bookstore. It was a real treat to have a bookstore in a town our size. They didn't keep a huge inventory, but she was more than willing to search online for any book a customer would want and order it for them with free shipping. I usually took advantage of that but today I decided to peruse her shelves. I had some books on order with her but with my usual stack of books by my nightstand down to one I didn't have much patience to wait. There were a few customers milling around. I lucked out and spotted one of my favorite author's books on her new arrivals table. I grabbed it and headed straight to the checkout. As I got in line I noticed the person ahead of me was Jacob's ex secretary, Gwen. Not being able to help myself, I leaned forward and said, "Sorry you lost your job."

She was startled, until she turned around and registered who I was. "Yeah, well. I'll miss the pay, but he was a jerk. I know everyone around here thinks he is so wonderful, but he's not."

I was shocked into silence, and then it was her turn to checkout. She paid and left. When I stepped up to the counter, Judy, the owner of the store said, "I couldn't help but overhear. Don't pay any attention to her. She has a reputation around town for not being a very reliable employee. She was lucky Jacob even hired her. She'll be even luckier to find another job around here."

"I was kind of surprised by what she said", I said and followed up on that statement by asking, "I didn't think Jacob was such a bad guy?"

"I think Jacob has done a lot of good things for this community. Have a good day," Judy said and handed me my receipt and turned to the next customer.

As I walked out of the bookstore, I heard my name being called. Melanie came out of the bookstore. I hadn't even noticed her in there, which was amazing since today's outfit was a neon yellow jumper.

"You are looking in to Matthew's murder aren't you?"

"How did you know?" I asked her.

"It's a small community Carmen. We all know the sheriff suspects Jessica; and we know how close you are to her. It stands to reason you would want to find out who is responsible."

I was surprised to hear the town was talking about it, but after a couple seconds I realized I shouldn't have been. "I think it's tied to the accident that Matthew was in twenty years ago. Do you know about that?"

"Of course, my ex-husband was in the same grade as Matthew and Jacob. He always said his high school class was a bunch of insincere, fake people. I couldn't help but overhear that girl in the bookstore. My ex never liked Jacob. He couldn't stand Maggie either. That always surprised me as I think she does a marvelous job at the library. Then again I don't know how much value you should put on his opinion either, as he divorced me." She smiled and stood as though waiting for me to say something.

"I thought you were from here," I finally said.

"No my husband was. We met at college and we moved here when he got a job with the electric cooperative. When we divorced, he said he had enough of this town and got out of here as fast as he could. I always liked it here, so I stayed."

At a loss for anything else to say, and starting to get wet from the rain, I thanked her and excused myself. It was definitely the day to run into people; James was walking down the street coming toward me.

"Hey Carmen, what are you doing in town?" he asked smiling at me.

"I'm taking advantage of the rain and getting some errands done. When did you get back from the bull sale?"

"I just got back. I haven't even been home yet. I thought I'd swing in to the restaurant and say hello to Jessica."

"I have to stop by Edna's bakery first, but do you have time to eat dinner with me at Jessica's restaurant when I'm done?"

"Sure. I'll make sure to save us a table."

"Okay, I'll see you in a bit." I kept walking to the end of the street where Edna's bakery was located. She ran the bakery out of the main floor of her house. Edna was about eight years older than Jessica and I. We got to know her when we played in a sand volleyball league with her. She was about six feet tall and crazy fit and athletic which was surprising, considering she ran a bakery. We didn't stay on the same team with her for too long. Jessica and I weren't a good fit for her extreme competitive side. It was a good thing we quit as quick as we did, she was still able to call us friends. I opened the door. The bakery was empty so I was able to catch her attention when I walked in the door.

She looked up from decorating a cake, "Good morning Carmen, what can I do for you?"

"I was hoping I could help you for a change. Do you need any assistance with the food for the funeral tonight?"

"If you wouldn't mind I could use some help loading the van here at the bakery and unloading it at the funeral home later this afternoon."

"I'm eating an early dinner with James and getting groceries afterward. I can be here around three o'clock if that works?"

"Perfect. Thanks a lot."

"I'll see you at three." I waved goodbye to her as I headed back out into the rain.

It was a relief to reach the restaurant and take off my now-soaking coat. James was sitting at a table, waiting for me. I could see Jessica in the back, cooking furiously trying to keep up with the crowd. I was relieved to see she looked like she was in her element. I'd had some concerns about her working today, but she had wanted to stay busy.

James stood up and gave me a hug when I got to the table. "How is your investigation going?"

"Quite a few people have been asking me that. Isn't it the sheriff's investigation, not mine?"

"Not to anyone who knows you. You are loyal to your friends, you like a good mystery, and basically you are nosy. The minute I heard that a body was found on your property I knew you wouldn't be able to stay out of it," James said with a smile.

"I feel like I'm spinning my wheels. I am convinced Matthew was killed because he was coming home to talk to someone else about the accident. You know what Pamela told Jessica when she called her, right?" I asked James.

"That's the girl that got paralyzed when Matthew ran into her," James replied.

I nodded.

"Yes, she told me. That has to be good news. I understood she would be talking to the sheriff today, which should get Jessica off the primary suspect list. Will you be able to quit looking into this if that happens?" James asked.

"Honest? I don't think I can. My curiosity is aroused and I like to finish what I start."

"Have you come up with anyone you suspect?"

"No, the problem is that no one else left the party that night, at least not that anyone remembers," was my frustrated answer.

"That doesn't mean it didn't happen. Twenty years is a long time ago to remember anything in detail," James reminded me.

"I know. I have to admit I've been amazed that people are remembering that night at all. I imagine the accident left it implanted in their minds, yet be able to accurately remember everyone's comings and goings is a long shot."

"Why does it have to be someone from the party? Couldn't it have been anyone that was driving on that road?" he asked.

"That is what everyone has said, but in my opinion it had to be someone at that party. No one else lived out that way other than Pamela and Gary's families. Plus Matthew was coming home to talk to someone, and whoever it was didn't want that happening. I believe if it wasn't someone Matthew knew well he would have just contacted the sheriff's office and told them, especially as Pamela confirmed to him that there was another vehicle. I think if he remembered another car he had to have known who it was, and if Matthew was anything like Jessica he would have wanted to give that person a chance to explain. There are a limited number of classmates that live locally: Mitch, Gary, Maggie, and Jacob, and I can't believe any of them did this. Although I've had some people tell me Jacob and Maggie aren't who they seem to be."

"What does that mean?" James asked puzzled. "I don't know Maggie, but Jacob is a great guy."

"I don't know, but I'm not sure they are reliable sources. A couple different people have told me that Jacob in particular isn't the stand-up person he portrays himself as. I don't think I trust their viewpoint. I've had a lot of dealings with Jacob over the years and I like him."

"Why couldn't it have been a classmate that doesn't live here anymore?"

"That would be nice, but how could they have known Matthew was coming, or even better, why would Matthew have come back here to talk to them if they didn't live here?"

"Everyone has Facebook these days, easy enough to look someone up and maybe they decided to meet here."

"I suppose, but if they had to travel back home to kill Matthew wouldn't someone have known that they were here? Plus, I think Matthew would have gone to wherever they were living rather than meet them back here. He wouldn't have wanted to be recognized here if he could avoid it."

"True. Have you talked to the sheriff?" James asked.

"No. I'm trying to wait a few days, let Pamela talk to him and give him time to digest what she has to say. I figure he'll be more apt to pursue other leads if I'm not hounding him. He hasn't arrested Jessica yet, so that's good."

"Maybe he got the blood results back and found out he doesn't have any evidence," James suggested.

"I hope so. Actually, now that you say that, you may be correct. It can't take that long for blood results, although that could also be the reason he is so stuck on Jessica killing Matthew." Our meals came, a chicken pot pie for James and a chef salad with a cup of wild rice soup for me. As always Jessica's cooking was so good that it made conversation stop. Twenty minutes later, we came up for air and pushed our plates away. "I'd better get going. I have to get groceries and then help Edna with the food for the funeral. I'll see you and Jessica there at six."

I stopped and paid for our food. As I did I saw on my phone that it was already one-thirty? I'd need to hustle with my groceries to get to the bakery on time. I drove to the grocery store and parked as close as I could to the door. It had been awhile since anyone from our household had shopped so it took some time and ended up being quite the bill. I crammed everything in the back of my pickup, except anything that needed to be kept cold or that would be ruined by rain. Those items I stuck on my passenger seat and cranked up the air conditioning. I drove over to the bakery. Edna had already started by the time I got there.

I left my pickup and the air-conditioner running, and ran over to her van. "How can I help?" I asked feeling bad that I was late.

"All the trays inside that have a red sticker on them need to be loaded."

I walked into the bakery and came to a halt. Edna walked in behind me. "What is with all this food?" I asked. "Jessica isn't expecting many people."

"That is what she thinks. I happen to feel this town is going to show up in droves to support her. Especially when everyone knows that idiot sheriff thinks she killed her own brother."

"I hope you are right, otherwise a lot of food is going to go to waste."

"It won't, because I know I'm right," she said with her usual confidence.

It took us about fifteen minutes to load the food and when we were done I followed her over to the funeral home where we unloaded it and set it all up. It was close to four-thirty by the time I got home. Dad helped me unload the groceries. I popped a frozen pizza in the oven and went to change clothes. When I came back downstairs both Dad and Kirk were setting the table. The oven timer went off and we all grabbed some pieces.

"I need to leave. Are you guys coming with me?" I asked.

"No, we'll drive separate," Dad and Kirk answered as they cleared the table.

"I'll see you there," I said as I left.

Jessica and James were standing by the picture boards talking to the minister when I got there. I walked over to them, "hello Pastor Schiff."

"Hello Carmen." He turned back to Jessica. "I see by the amount of food that you are expecting quite a few people."

She gave a nervous laugh, "I think Edna went a little overboard, I can't imagine that many people showing up. Matthew has been gone for a long time."

We stood around making small talk for a few more minutes until people started filing in. Dad, Karla, and Kirk joined us so we walked in to the room and found a place to sit down. Nick showed up and sat down in the pew with us. More and more people kept coming in and it wasn't long before the place was packed. Jessica was sitting next to me trying hard not to cry, I nudged her and motioned for her to look back at all the people. Jessica looked at me in amazement and started to cry harder. James put his arm around her. Thankfully the service was quick and everyone went out into the large foyer to partake of the refreshments. Jessica and James moved through the crowd trying to thank everyone for coming. I saw them make their way to Edna, no doubt to thank her for all the food. After about two hours everyone left. Jessica was exhausted and James shuffled her out while I helped Edna and the funeral home people clean up. Nick also stayed and helped. The funeral home director and Nick and I were the last ones to leave. He let us out the back door, and with our vehicles parked at the other end of the parking lot, it was nice that the rain had turned to a light mist.

"It was a nice turnout," Nick said when we got to our pickups.

"Yes, I could tell Jessica appreciated it."

"I haven't been here long but even I know how she's loved in this town. It's too bad the sheriff wasn't here to see this."

"I thought law enforcement was always supposed to come to the funeral of the murder victim."

"Maybe that is only in books and movies. I'm not sure it would have helped the Sheriff to pin-point any new suspects besides Jessica anyway as it looked like the whole town was here," Nick replied smiling. "Is everyone still planning on going to hear Kirk's band tomorrow night?"

"Jessica assured me she wanted to. I think she is looking forward to a distraction."

"Are you picking me up?" he asked.

"Yes. We'll pick you up at seven," I answered him as he got in his pickup.

"I'll see you tomorrow night," Nick said through the window as he started his vehicle.

"Thanks for your help with the cleanup." He nodded and waved as he drove away. I got into my pickup and drove home.

CHAPTER EIGHTEEN

Native prairies contribute to water quality and storing carbon.
Prairie plants and their large root systems basically
provide an inverted rainforest.

I WOKE UP SATURDAY MORNING to a loud crash and the sound
of Wizard barking and Kirk yelling. I pulled on my robe and
rushed down the stairs.

"What is going on?" I asked grumpy at the noise.

Kirk was wiping up the floor. "I was making waffles and I
tripped over Wizard and dropped the bowl."

"He wouldn't be by your feet if you wouldn't drop him treats
while you cook."

"Whatever," he mumbled as he cleaned up.

"It was nice of you to try, thanks anyway," deciding I could give
him a break and be nice. "I assume cereal is a go?" I asked as I
grabbed a bowl and a box of cereal, which was half empty. We'd
been eating a lot of cereal; it was good I stocked up on our supply
at the grocery store yesterday.

Dad came in the kitchen from outside, looked at Kirk cleaning up the floor, wisely said nothing, grabbed a bowl and joined

me for some cereal.

"What are you doing today?" I asked Dad.

"I thought I'd drive over to the shop this morning to change oil on my pickup but instead I have a flat tire. I was going to put a plug in it but the hole is too big. Can I get a ride to town from either of you so I can pick up some tires?" Dad asked.

"I can't Dad," Kirk said. "I'm picking up the band and we are going to Parkville to get set up and practice again for a few hours before our performance. We found out last night that the record producer is for sure going to be there tonight."

"That's great Kirk. I hope it goes well for you," Dad said as we both got up to hug Kirk.

It was nice to see Kirk rewarded for all his dedication to his music. Dad and I gave him a hard time for his ineffectiveness in all farm-related activities and if I'm being honest, in most other things too. However, to give him credit, he had never wavered when it came to his music. Dad had been frustrated a few times over the years with Kirk and had even considered making him move out with the hope that it would force him to focus on some way to make a living. He could never bring himself to follow through. Kirk had been seventeen when Mom died. Music was his connection to her and Dad came to the conclusion that as long as Kirk helped out on the farm when needed and continued to actively pursue a music career he would let him be. I don't think he planned on Wizard being added to the equation, though.

As we sat back down I said, "I can take you. I've got nothing else going on today. You might as well get four new tires. Yours are pretty old. We can spend the afternoon putting them on and getting them balanced. You'll have to make an appointment for an alignment on Monday, but we can at least get them on today."

It took Dad and me the rest of the day to get the tires picked out, purchased, get his old ones off, and the news ones on his pickup. We stopped once to grab a couple of peanut butter and jelly sandwiches for a quick dinner. He decided to test drive his tires by driving to Karla's for supper and some card games with another neighbor couple.

As I walked to the house I could hear Wizard frantically barking. Kirk must have left him out as he was in the fenced-in backyard barking at Tabitha who was taunting Wizard by sitting on the other side of the fence serenely cleaning her face with the remains of a mouse in front of her. I opened the door and called him in the house, poured some food in his dish, and decided a quick piece of toast would tide me over until we got food at the bar. I was surprised to find that I was excited to go tonight. Most of the time I was going to hear Kirk's band play I dreaded it, although I did it anyway as a show of support. I realized, if I was being honest, it was due to the fact that I was excited to spend a night away from work with Nick—I might find out more about him on a personal level. I'd better be careful though. I did not want to be too intrusive and mess up our working relationship. With that thought in mind I went upstairs to take a shower.

James and Jessica picked me up twenty minutes before seven, giving us plenty of time to swing by the old Erickson place to pick up Nick. While the house itself was standing straight with the exception of the front porch, the place looked in need of paint, new windows, and a lot of yard work. Nick had been mowing around various pieces of junk left behind by previous renters and judging by the stack of wood next to a rickety shed, he'd been working on getting rid of the dead trees also. He hadn't been exaggerating when he said the place needed work. He was waiting for us on his front steps petting an enormous black cat that looked like it had seen better days.

"Where did the cat come from?" I asked Nick when he got in the back seat of the vehicle next to me.

"He showed up a couple days after I moved in. I felt bad for him as he looked pretty tough so I put out some food, water, and a box with an old rug for him to sleep in. So far he appears content, but

I guess I'll have to get something a little better rigged-up for him before the weather gets too cold."

"That's awful nice of you," I said realizing this made me like him even more, as who could dislike a man that likes cats. "We have a couple enclosed boxes built that we added heat lamps to for the cats at our place if you want to take a look at them for some ideas. We have three outdoor cats that are quite pampered. You met Tabitha when you stopped by the other day. I can't imagine not having cats around, not just for mice control but they even keep Wizard under control."

"That dog is a maniac—is it a puppy?" Nick asked.

"By his behavior one would think so, but no, he's six years old. I believe his behavior stems from his owner. Kirk has never grown up either," I said while Jessica and James laughed in the front.

"Speaking of, is this a legitimate band playing tonight?" he asked with some doubt. "The way everyone talks around town his music is kind of unbearable."

"Surprisingly he has quite a following among the younger generation. A record producer is going to be there tonight so there must be something to his music even if I fail to appreciate it," I answered shrugging my shoulders.

"That's great news for the band," Jessica injected.

"To be fair, their shows are usually packed," James chimed into the conversation.

"Why do you guys go?" Nick asked. "I assumed the reason was to help fill the crowd."

"I guess it's because there isn't much else going on socially around here unless you want to hang around a bar, which isn't really our scene. Don't get me wrong, I don't have a problem with people drinking, but standing around in a bar all night gets old," I answered.

"We are in a bowling league that gets going in the winter," James said. "That's at least one night out a week."

"Hey, we are a person short with Kirk quitting as he's had more bookings for his band. Do you bowl and enjoy it enough that you'd like to join our team?" Jessica asked.

"I bowl, but you might want to rethink your offer if you want a good bowler," Nick said with a laugh.

"If that was the case, Carmen wouldn't be on our team," James offered.

"Ha, ha, thanks guys. I also want to input here that we try to watch when Kirk's band plays as a show of support. His music, while not the kind I like, is the only thing he takes seriously, so I do try to support him. After all if he makes it big someday, I want him to remember me," I said with a smile.

We pulled up to the bar where the band was playing. Although we tried to get there early enough that we could get a table way in back, rather than stand all night, by the number of vehicles in the parking lot it looked like the place was already starting to fill up. Kirk's fan base was definitely growing. We walked in and noticed with relief his fans were more interested in being close to the stage than sitting, leaving a high table with bar stools open for us in the back which is what we liked. The waitress came over as we sat down in the chairs.

"What can I get for you guys?"

Nick and James both ordered Cokes while Jessica and I decided to have water for the time being.

"Aren't you guy's hungry?" Nick asked.

"I'm planning on getting some food a little later, but go ahead if you are hungry," I answered.

"If I get a pepperoni pizza, is anyone interested in having any?" Nick tempted us.

"Go ahead, I'm sure we can help eat it," James said with a grin.

"That does sound good, why don't you make it two pizzas," Jessica said to the waitress.

"Ok guys, I'll be right out with your drinks."

We settled onto our barstools and looked around. I spotted Gary next to the wall towards the front. I couldn't imagine him enjoying Kirk's music, he was probably here as a show of support, as he worked with Kirk. He looked up and caught my eye, we nodded at each other. I'd have to work my way over to him at some point and find out how his conversation with the sheriff went.

Nick noticed me looking at Gary. "Is there a problem?"

"No, I was surprised to see him here, but I guess I shouldn't be; he and Kirk get along pretty well."

"Did you get a chance to talk to him about his behavior at work?" Nick asked me.

"Yes, his wife is an alcoholic and she relapsed. He doesn't know where she went and he's taking it pretty hard."

"Oh no," Jessica said. "She has done so well for so long. I wonder what set her off?"

"He didn't say. But he's hoping he can help with harvest as he wants to get out of the empty house as much as he can."

"That will be handy," Nick said. "We won't need your dad as much; I was worried about that. How did your bull sale go James?" he turned to James.

"We got the bull we were hoping to get," James answered. "I had to pay a little more than I expected to, but he is ours and will bring some good genes into our herd. That reminds me, Carmen, thank your dad for me for helping Mom with the cattle that got out when I was gone."

"He didn't mind in the least. You know he likes spending time with your mom," I said with a smile.

James and Nick got into a conversation about ranching. Nick talked about it with knowledge, surprising me again and making me wonder once more about his background.

I nudged Jessica, "Let's go talk to Gary before it gets too busy and loud in here."

We stood up as the waitress returned with our drinks and some bowls of peanuts. The guys looked up.

"We're going to talk to Gary a minute. We'll be right back." They went back to their conversation.

Gary saw us coming and moved to a bar table, motioning for us to have a seat.

"When I saw you I figured you'd be heading over here pretty soon. You want to follow up on my visit to the sheriff I assume?"

"How did it go?" I asked.

"About as expected with Sheriff Poole. It didn't make any difference. All he could say was that Matthew must have been coming home to talk to his sister about the inheritance."

"That's ridiculous, if that was the case Matthew would have named her when he talked to you."

"I tried to tell him that, but he's stuck on this being an open and shut case. He has an election coming up you know."

"Do you know if Pamela Wicks talked to him yet?" I asked Gary.

"Who is Pamela Wicks?" Gary asked with a puzzled look on his face.

"She's the girl that was paralyzed in the accident. She called to tell me Matthew had contacted her and that they both remembered a second vehicle at the accident," Jessica told him.

"Wow! That's amazing. She must not have talked to him before I was there or I think the sheriff would have put more stock in what I had to say," Gary said, scratching his head.

"Well thanks for trying, Gary." I started to get up.

"Hold on, I've been thinking back to that night, been thinking about it a lot actually, and I can't be positive, but I think Maggie was there after all. I remember seeing a girl outside, running around the back side of the house when I was looking out a window."

"Why do you think it was Maggie? She told us she wasn't there that night," I asked, surprised and sat down again.

"I can't tell you with any real certainty, but it feels right. I remember being surprised when I saw her because I didn't think she had been there and I knew I hadn't seen her inside."

"How sure are you about this?" Jessica asked.

"Well it's nothing I could swear to in court, but it gives you a reason to talk to her again. If she was there, it's kind of funny that she would deny it."

"Unless it was a normal teenager thing and she was embarrassed about something that happened that night," I offered as an explanation.

"Well I think she's worth taking a look at. Haven't you ever been curious how she can afford all the fancy cars and clothes she has on our small-town librarian salary."

"I can't say I've ever thought about it. To me, she's just Maggie the librarian," Jessica said. "She's in my book club but she's never said much about her personal life."

"Well I do know her family never had any extra money in high school, but that's not to say something significant hasn't changed in the last eighteen years. She also was a little off during high school," Gary said as he picked at the label on his bottle of beer.

"What do you mean?" I asked him leaning in to hear him better.

"I don't know how to explain it." He studied the wall while he thought and said, "she never actively joined in with anything we were doing, but she was there lurking. Sometimes it was kind of creepy. You'd turn around and she'd be there—it would startle you and then she'd scurry off."

"I've been going to the library for years. Maggie has been nothing but helpful," Jessica said.

"I have to admit I don't use the library much, I tend to buy my books, but she acted nice that day we talked to her," I said.

"People certainly change. It was just my impression, I didn't know her that well, or take the time to know her I guess. But I'm almost positive she was at that party," Gary said as he shrugged and took another drink of his beer.

"Well, thanks Gary. We appreciate your help," I said as we started to stand up.

"I liked Matthew, and if he didn't cause that accident he sure got a raw deal," Gary said, looking down at his drink again.

"I agree, but he did bring some of it on himself by running," Jessica surprised me by saying.

She noticed me looking at her funny.

"Maybe it's a stage of grief, but I am mad at him right now. He caused Mom and Dad a lot of heartache by running. I used to kind of understand it because he was young and scared, but now when we know he was perhaps innocent, if he would have just stuck around . . ." her voice trailed off.

I hugged her, "We'll figure this out."

"We better, or Sheriff Poole is going to have me in jail," Jessica said squaring her shoulders in determination.

"Let's head back to our table—did you want to join us Gary?" I asked him.

"No, I'm here to have a drink, listen for a bit, and get out of here before I lose my hearing. I don't mind supporting Kirk for a little bit, but my ears can't take a night of it."

"That is the exact same plan we have." We laughed and headed back to our table.

The guys were still absorbed in their conversation. It was good to see Nick and James getting along. There weren't a lot of people our age left in town so it was great when the ones that were got along. They looked up when we sat down. Nick opened his mouth to say something, but before he got it out, a loud cacophony of noise startled us all. We turned to look at the stage. There was Kirk's band warming up. A moment later, they started in on their most well-known song. The noise was deafening but the crowd was ecstatic. Our pizzas came about five minutes into the music. We wolfed them down, stuck it out for another forty minutes until we couldn't take it anymore, paid for our food, and we stumbled shell-shocked out of the bar.

"Was that actual music?" Nick asked.

"It's not what I think of as music," James and Jessica answered shaking their heads.

"Nor I, but we did our part, now let's get out of here." We climbed back in to James' pickup.

"Let's head over to my place," Jessica offered. "It's early yet and we can visit or play some cards. Anyone want to?"

"Sounds great," I answered and when no one disagreed, James started the pickup and we headed to Jessica's house. We had a fun night and I managed to keep any amorous thoughts of Nick at bay. Two hours later James, Nick, and I left. James dropped Nick off leaving just the two of us in the car.

"How is Jessica really doing?" I asked him.

"I think she's doing okay. Did Gary have anything for you?" he asked me.

"A few little snippets. I'm going to keep on asking questions though. Gary did tell us that he thinks he remembers Maggie being at the party after all and he confirmed tonight that Sheriff Poole isn't planning on looking at anyone besides Jessica; at least that was the indication Gary got from him. That may change once the sheriff talks to Pamela, although we don't know for sure if she has gotten a hold of him or not yet."

"Be careful, there is a murderer out there," James said.

"I keep getting reminded of that. Kind of gives you mixed emotions, if we do find something, we may put ourselves in danger, and if we don't find anything, Jessica may end up in jail."

"I can't imagine Sheriff Poole can lock her up without any real proof, and we know there isn't any of that," James said with a sigh.

That's true, but this is too small of a town to have her living here with people thinking she may be a murderer. I have to figure this out." We pulled up in front of my house. The lights were on so Dad must be home.

"Are you okay with our parents dating?" I asked him

"Yeah, I think it's great they have someone. It's tough to be lonely at any age."

"Too true," I agreed.

"How about you and Nick, is there anything there?" James asked looking at me, intent on reading my face when I answered him.

"I don't know, maybe. But we work together and to be honest I need him as my foreman more than as a boyfriend, so I hate to mess that up."

"I don't think you need to worry about it. He acts interested in you, besides life's too short to not pursue it. You both are mature enough adults that if it doesn't pan out you could work through it. I don't think he's going anywhere; the way he talks, he likes it here."

I got out of the pickup. "Thanks for the ride and the advice," I said as I smiled at him. I watched as he drove down the driveway. Tabitha appeared out of the dark and followed me to the house. I scratched her back and held the door open for her but she must have had other plans, as she took off, tail twitching, back towards the trees. I walked in to the house. Dad wasn't around. He must have gone to bed and left the lights on for me. I followed his example and went to bed leaving the lights on for Kirk.

CHAPTER NINETEEN

Blue grama has green to grayish leaves less than 0.1 inches wide and 1–10 inches long, with an overall height of six to twelve inches.

M Y EYES OPENED SUNDAY MORNING and I realized I had a smile on my face. It took me a few minutes to remember why. It had been a fun night. In fact it had been a long time since I'd enjoyed an evening so much. My mood sobered when I remembered what Gary had told me about Maggie. I decided she was definitely worth talking to again. It was Sunday and I wasn't sure if the library would be open. I grabbed my phone and looked up the library hours. They were open from one to four. I would head over there after church and with any luck Maggie would be working. I could go to her house, but I think that would be too strange, after all we didn't have the sort of relationship where I could show up unannounced at her house. But what could I use for a reason to talk to her, specifically at the library? I thought for a few minutes and decided that I could ask her for some help with researching how to reach out to birders to find out what amenities would be useful in the cabins I'm building and maybe even what kind of magazines, newspapers or websites to advertise in. But first I needed to get up and check if the blue grama was ready for harvest. After I did that I'd come back home, change clothes, go to church and then I'd head to the library. I swung my legs out of bed, slid my feet into my slippers, grabbed my robe, and went downstairs. No one was awake yet, so I decided to make some French toast and bacon. I also started the coffee brewing. I knew the smells would wake up Dad and Kirk shortly. Well maybe not Kirk, I never did hear him get home and most likely had only been in bed for a couple hours. Sure enough, about the time the bacon was ready Dad came downstairs.

"That smells good, are you sharing?" he asked with an expression on his face that was similar to Wizard's begging face.

"I sure am. I made plenty even if Kirk wakes up."

"How was your evening?" he asked me.

"Pretty good once we left the bar," I laughed.

"It was that noisy huh?"

"It isn't my type of music, but I have to say Kirk's band is packing in a crowd. Maybe we are going to have to stop giving him so much grief."

"He is sticking to it, which is something for him. Speak of the devil," Dad said as Kirk stumbled in the kitchen rubbing his eyes, Wizard right on his heels. He went straight for the coffee, while Wizard stood by the door wanting out.

"What are you doing up so already?" I asked him.

"I have some awesome news that I couldn't wait to share, plus I smelled the food," he said starting to look a little more awake as the coffee worked its magic.

"What is the good news?" Dad prodded him.

"Hold on; let me put Wizard outside."

Wizard bounded out the door happy to experience the beautiful day. Even better, the squirrel that liked to taunt him was waiting by the far side of the fence. He took off in a blur.

"So what kind of news gets you out of bed before noon the day after a show?" I asked, trying to urge him to spill the beans faster.

"The record producer was in the crowd last night and he wants to talk to the band this afternoon," he said with a huge grin.

Dad and I sat in stunned silence.

"Aren't you guys going to say anything?" he asked giving up waiting for us to respond.

"Is this for real?" I blurted out.

"What do you mean? Just because you guys don't appreciate my music doesn't mean others don't," he said indignantly.

"I'm sorry Kirk, of course you are right. Honestly I didn't believe a record producer would come all the way up to Northwestern Minnesota."

"I told you he was coming. He is from Minneapolis. I know it is a six-hour drive but it isn't like he traveled from California. I've been sending him YouTube videos links of the band for almost six months. I think he got sick of me and came to shut me up," Kirk said with a smile. "Anyway, long story short, he is interested. The only bad thing is I might not be around for harvest if we have to head to the cities to record."

"I think our equipment will appreciate you not helping," I said as I nudged his shoulder.

"Thanks a lot big sister," he said knowing what I said was true.

"I'm just kidding, I'm super thrilled for you and we'll manage. Gary wanted more hours so it will work out fine."

"One small problem though . . ., I can't take Wizard."

"That's not a small problem, but I'm sure we'll manage," Dad answered. "Wizard will be fine; we might not be, but he will be."

"Sit down and have some breakfast and tell us all about it," I said as I put some French toast on a plate for him. "But try to make it quick, I need to check the blue grama and get to church." I got going a lot later than I planned to. Kirk was excited and told us every little detail. But I had to admit it sounded like a great opportunity for him. After all these years my little brother was getting his big chance. He went back to bed to get some more sleep before picking up the rest of the band for their meeting later this afternoon. I asked Dad if he was going to ride with me to church and he said he was going with Karla. I cleaned up the kitchen, said I'd see him at church, and headed out the door.

Wizard was busy barking at his squirrel friend. Our old tom cat, Clyde, was sitting on the hood of my pickup, watching the show. I scratched his head, picked him up and put him down on a cushioned bench next to Tabitha, who was sleeping there in the sun. It was nice someone got to appreciate the comfortable benches; we rarely had time and when we did get a chance the cushions were so covered in cat hair that no one wanted to sit on them. I got in the pickup and drove to the blue grama field. I spent about twenty-five minutes crawling around in the field, trying to decide if it was ready for combining. It was a tough call as the whole seed head rarely ripened at once and a judgment call had to be made for when to harvest to get the maximum amount of seed. After going back and forth I came to the conclusion it needed a few more days as long as the weather cooperated. At this point there were no strong winds forecasted for the next few days. We would start on Tuesday. I went back home, changed clothes and left for church.

I have to admit my mind traveled during the sermon, but I told myself I would appease my conscience by going to the annual meeting tomorrow night. When church was over I talked to Jessica a few minutes to find out how she was. She told me she was doing fine as long as she kept busy. I was about to ask her if she wanted to come with me to talk to Maggie when she said James and her were going to Parkville for the afternoon to see a movie and have supper after. We hugged; I visited with a few more people for a couple of minutes and left. I swung through the Dairy Queen and got a hamburger that I wolfed down so fast I didn't even taste it. A couple salads should factor into my diet soon as I hadn't been eating very healthy lately. I stopped to fill my pickup with gas and throw away my garbage. Knowing I'd put it off long enough, it was time to see if Maggie was working and talk to her.

The library looked pretty empty, which was good. Now with any luck I'd find Maggie working. Luck was on my side. I could see her by the computers helping a teenager. I walked closer waiting until they were done.

Maggie looked up and saw me. "Can I help you Carmen?"

"Hi Maggie, I was wondering if you had time to do some research for me?"

"Sure, I'm done here, what do you need?"

"We are building some cabins in one of our prairies to branch out into tourism. Some of the clients we are hoping to attract are birders. I was wondering if you could help me find some possible birding magazines or online sites on which to advertise? I'd like to look over the magazines also to see if they have any ideas of some amenities to put in the cabins that might be attractive to birders."

"Why don't you have a seat at the table over there and I'll try to find something for you."

She disappeared for about fifteen minutes and came back with her arms full. She put them down on the table and sat down.

"Why else are you here?" she asked bluntly.

"What do you mean?" I asked trying to act innocent.

"You're not stupid Carmen. You wouldn't be building cabins if you didn't already have this kind of research done."

"Okay, you busted me. I do need some decorating ideas, but I also want to talk to you some more about the senior party when Matthew had his accident."

She looked puzzled, "I told you before I wasn't there."

"Well Jessica and I have been talking to a few more people and they claim you were," I bluffed.

"That's impossible, I don't know who they saw but it wasn't me."

"Come on Maggie, level with me. You were there. I just want to find out some more about that party."

She looked at me for a long moment; I could hear the second hand of the clock ticking. She came to a decision, shrugged and said, "Fine, I was there, I'd prefer to forget about it. It wasn't the greatest night of my life. I was such a mouse in high school. I never got invited anywhere, and honestly, never wanted to be, but I thought, what the heck it's our last party as seniors so I decided to go. Matthew and Jacob were so nice to me when I showed up, I wasn't expecting it, but it felt so good to feel welcomed. Then I heard Jacob talking to someone when he thought I wasn't around. He was laughing and telling them that he and Matthew were being nice to me because they were hoping I would give them the answers to the upcoming biology final test. I was a teacher's aide. I had never felt so humiliated and I ran out of there as fast as I could." She hung her head.

That jived with what Gary had told me he had seen. But something didn't feel right about her story. Everything I had ever heard about Jacob and Matthew made this story ring untrue, it was unlike them to treat anyone that way.

"Are you sure you heard them correctly? It doesn't sound like them." I looked at her trying to stare the truth out of her.

"I know what I heard," Maggie's voice got loud. It surprised the few people that were in the library. She quieted down. "I know everyone thinks they were so wonderful, but they weren't," she hissed vehemently, pushed back her chair and walked away. I looked at the other people that were staring at me, put out my hands in a what-can-you-do position, stood up and walked out of the library, thankful I bought most of my books and doubly thankful I hadn't brought Jessica with me. I had a feeling I wouldn't be very welcome in the library any time in the near future.

CHAPTER TWENTY

Blue Grama rapidly uses water when available,
yet becomes dormant during less-favorable conditions.

I DECIDED SINCE IT WAS SUNDAY, and harvest would be starting this week, I could take the rest of the afternoon off. The problem was, work is what I enjoyed doing. I tried to put it out of my mind and let the rest of the day stretch invitingly out to me. I looked down the street, wondering what I should do with an afternoon off when I saw Maggie run out the back door of the library. She went rushing down the street. I thought about following her, chided myself as isn't that what every amateur detective does in the mystery books I read? I decided what the heck, they always have good luck. The drawback to that idea is our small town doesn't have a lot of foot traffic to hide me as I trailed her. I took off walking anyway and lucky for me Maggie didn't even look back once. I sped up walking as she was approaching the one lone stoplight in town and I wanted to make sure I knew what direction she was going. The light turned red, forcing her to stop at the crosswalk. I stopped quick and looked in the nearest store window thankful it was the local hardware store. They had some shovels and hoes on display in their windows so it was easy for me to realistically pretend to be looking. Out of the corner of my eye I saw Maggie look back, but she didn't seem to register me. The light turned green and the crosswalk signal gave the okay; she crossed the street. I stood and watched to see which store she'd go in. I didn't need to follow her any farther since there were only a couple businesses along that street and not many of them were open on Sunday. One of them was Edna's bakery. I was going to feel foolish if all she was doing was getting some rolls to treat the library staff to a morning snack, but no, she turned into Jacob's office. Now that was curious. Of course it could be anything; Jacob handles all the legal work in town, but it was strange she went to him so soon after I had talked to her, and Sunday isn't a day Jacob is open for normal appointments. I decided to wait and see how long of a meeting it would be. Thank goodness I always carry a book in my purse, and there was a nice gazebo in the park kitty-corner from Jacob's office. I settled on the bench, opened my book and had read about five pages when out of the corner of my eye I saw Jacob escort Maggie out. They didn't look happy. Maggie shook Jacob's hand off her arm and stormed away. Jacob walked back in to the office. I decided Jacob warranted another visit. I decided to wait a few minutes and then saunter by. With any luck Jacob would be visible in the front window. I was hoping I could feign surprise that he was in and stop to talk to him. But as I started toward his office, he came out, locked the door, got in his Escalade, and drove away. Well I guess a visit with him wasn't meant to happen today, but I was certainly going to figure out a way to talk to Jacob soon. I remembered the annual meeting at church tomorrow night was also a potluck. There was no way Jacob wouldn't be using it as a PR appearance for his campaign. I decided I'd be making a hotdish tonight, as I was going to the meeting and potluck for sure now, especially as the blue grama wasn't ready to combine and it would be the perfect opportunity to talk to him. He wouldn't be able to avoid me at church. But in the meantime, I had a whole afternoon to myself. It was a perfect day for a walk. I'd go home, grab Wizard and head to one of our prairies. I turned around and started back to my car.

As I turned around, I heard my name being called. It was Nick coming my way.

"What are you doing?" he asked when he got close.

"You caught me doing some sleuthing," I admitted.

"How is that going?" he asked, looking like he was worried by my answer.

"Not sure. How about you, what are you doing in town?" I asked, deciding I wasn't in the mood to get into the details about what I had been thinking and doing, or hearing another person warn me to be careful.

"The hardware store had a sale on paint and I decided I couldn't take the puke green entryway in my rental house anymore," he said as he held up two gallons of paint.

"Are you supposed to be making changes when you are renting?" I asked.

"I'm confident they won't care, nobody in their right mind would want that color to stay," he answered with no hesitation.

"Well if you need help I'm free." What did I just hear myself say? Where was that coming from? I hate painting.

"That would be great, but you don't need to," he said looking at me trying to figure out if I was serious.

"Got any food at your place to feed me when we are done?" I asked trying to convince him I was serious.

"I have some frozen burritos."

"That'll work. You just hired a painter's assistant. I need to swing by home and change clothes first. Do I dare bring Wizard? He's been locked up all morning and Kirk won't be home this afternoon."

"Sure, I'm far enough from the main road that he should be safe running around. My yard might not be safe from him though," Nick replied with a laugh.

"That is true," I said not laughing back as I thought about the damage Wizard could do given enough time. "I'll see you in about a half hour."

I walked back to my pickup wondering what I had gotten myself into. It wasn't often I had a day off and I had volunteered myself to paint. I must be insane or listening to another part of my body than my brain.

I drove home. Dad and Kirk were gone. I changed clothes, left a note and grabbed Wizard. Twenty minutes later I pulled into Nick's driveway, noticing a huge pile of stuff on the front porch. Nick walked out of the house with another armful of things that he added to the pile.

I walked up to the porch carrying Wizard. "That's a lot of junk."

"Yeah, I rented this place as-is. They did tell me I could clean it out if I wanted too. I'm going to end up putting so much work into cleaning this place that I might as well buy it." He grinned not looking like the thought of it bothered him too much.

I put Wizard down, he looked up once, then his nose went down and off he went tail wagging with excitement. As I walked into the house I noted the color of the entryway. "Whoa, you weren't joking, this is horrible."

"Now you understand why I want to paint." He stared at the walls with amazement, "who would pick this color on purpose?"

"Maybe it was on sale?" I suggested. "What color did you pick to replace it?" Not that it mattered; any color would be an improvement.

"I picked out a light tan color for now."

"I hope you bought enough paint; it looks like that color will take a few coats to cover."

"I have a white quick-drying primer and enough for two coats of the main color, but I'm hoping for only one. I'm not a huge fan of painting."

"Me neither," I said as I grabbed a roller.

"In that case I'm honored you are helping," Nick said bowing to me.

"Where do you want me to start?" I asked ignoring him.

"I need to finish taping around the windows. You can grab yourself a paint tray, fill it up, and get started on the primer." Nick grabbed the tape and continued taping.

"What about the ceiling?" I asked, dreading his answer. I really hated painting ceilings.

We both looked up. "Thank goodness it's already white. I'm going to leave it for now. I'll have to wash it though," he said.

"Do you want me to trim?" I asked hoping that my holding a roller was a hint that I didn't want to trim.

"No I'll do that. I know it's the worst part of painting so since it's my place I'll do it, try to get as close as you can."

We worked together in silence for about ten minutes until Nick asked, "You avoided my question before; how is the investigation going? Have you learned anymore?"

"As I told James the other day, I'm not sure it's a good thing that people keep referring to it as my investigation."

Nick laughed and said, "I know you love farming, but I have noticed a certain sparkle in your eyes when you talk about the murder."

That took me off guard and I put my roller down. I said, "I have to admit it but you're right. I know I love a good mystery, but am I a sick person to be even slightly enjoying this? After all, my friend's brother was murdered and she's being accused of doing it."

"I think it's natural that with your love of mysteries you'd be somewhat enjoying it. Besides you are trying to help a friend."

"Yes, but I wonder if I'm using that as an excuse for a reason to be involved. It's not like Jessica has actually been arrested."

"Maybe that's due to you," Nick offered.

"I doubt it, but there is some promising news," and I told him about Pamela and what Gary had said.

"That sounds promising for Jessica."

"It would if Sheriff Poole would be open to a few ideas other than Jessica. Right now he's not seeing anything but her, and he's not willing to listen to any other options either. To be fair, I don't know if Pamela has called him yet. Maybe once she talks to him he'll place more importance on what Gary told him. Gary also told me last night at the bar that he remembered seeing Maggie at the party the night Matthew supposedly ran into Pamela."

"Who's Maggie again?" he asked.

"She's the librarian in town. That is why I was in town this morning. I wanted to talk to her."

"How did that go?"

I told him what she said about Jacob and Matthew, and how she got so aggravated, and how I followed her to Jacob's office.

"She could be seeing a lawyer for any number of reasons," he reminded me.

"I know. But I think it was strange. Jacob doesn't keep office hours on Sunday. I'm going to talk to him tomorrow night at our church potluck."

We heard Wizard's frantic barking, never a good sound, and peeked out the window. His whole body was quivering as he barked at Nick's cat that wasn't bothered in the least bit and was cleaning his tail while sitting on top of a barrel out in the yard.

"He doesn't look too threatened," I said relieved.

"No. I've seen him chase the neighbor's German shepherd out of the yard. No need to worry."

We left them to it and kept painting. With the two of us working it only took an hour to get the primer coat on.

"How long does it need to dry?"

"The can says about an hour. Do you want something to drink? We can sit on the steps while we wait."

"Do you have any Coke?" I asked looking forward to a jolt of caffeine.

"I do. I'll be out in a minute."

I sat down on the porch. Wizard abandoned the cat and ran over for some scratches. I gently pushed him away as of course he had found something ripe to roll in. He happily headed off in another direction. Nick came out with two cans of Coke and two glasses with ice. He handed one can and glass to me, sat down, and sighed.

"Do you like it here?" I asked

"Do you mean here at this place or here in this town?"

"Both I guess. I'm just curious if you are content with working for us and living in this area? I know you've said you are, but is it the truth or something you say to your employer?" I asked hoping he was telling the truth.

"Yeah, I am. I enjoy the work and I like that we don't have a lot of workers to supervise. That is what drained me at my last job. I like some time to myself," he said sounding content.

"That is one of the best things about our farm. Of course we have our seasons like the summer with the roguing crew and harvest when we sometimes have extra people around, but for the most part it's pretty solitary. We have Sam and Phil around during the winter for seed cleaning, but other than my setting the mill for each crop they are self-sufficient. It can be tough to meet people our age though, as a lot leave after high school and not many new people move here. There aren't enough jobs to attract people to come here."

"I enjoyed myself last night, and I did get on a team for a trap league when I first got here. I've gotten to know a few people. I like it here."

"I'm glad as I've told you before we sure appreciate your work," I said knowing that once again he wouldn't be able to accept a compliment. "What made you decide to become a mechanic?" I paused and decided to go for it and be intrusive. "I remember on your job application you didn't decide to go to diesel mechanic school until you'd been out of high school for a few years."

Nick took a long drink, almost like he needed time to think before answering, swallowed and said, "My home life was, let's just say unstable. I squeaked through high school, left right after graduation, bounced around awhile at numerous jobs and saw a lot of the country. At one place I stayed with an older gentleman who was a mechanic. He took me in and I helped him in his shop. I took a liking to it. I owe him a lot as the time with him finally gave me a direction. From then on I worked at various places until I had enough money saved up for school."

I sensed there was a lot more unsaid, but since he was talking I tried one more question. "Why did you decide to work on farms instead of a big shop somewhere?"

Nick was staring off in the distance now, but he answered, "I found I enjoyed the variety that farming offered. I never have to do the same thing over and over and I get to work outside at times."

"That is the best part of farming. I couldn't work in an occupation where I had to be inside all day," I agreed.

"Speaking of work, we better get at it. Let me put the burritos in the oven so they will be done when we are finished." He walked back in the house again, effectively ending the discussion.

We painted for another hour and a half, finished, and stepped back to check it out.

"I can't believe it, but along with the primer, one coat did it," I said so very thankful.

"I think it did," Nick agreed eyeing the wall critically. "The burritos should be ready. I don't have much to go with them, but they will fill your stomach."

"All food is good, well except for liver, that is," I answered.

We made the burritos disappear quickly and as he said, it wasn't much but it filled the stomach. I helped him with the dishes and said, "I better get home and get my hotdish made for the potluck tomorrow."

"You mean your bait for your next round of questioning," he said and smiled to let me know he was kidding.

I laughed, glad he wasn't upset with me for my interrogation of him and said, "I guess that's true". I whistled for Wizard, he came running and I scooped him up, and put him back down. I had forgotten about his aroma. "Can I borrow a hose?" I asked Nick.

Nick took a whiff, stepped back, pointed and said, "The hose is right over there. I wonder what he found to roll in."

"I noticed your garbage can isn't tipped over so it wasn't that." I commented as I bent over, grabbed his collar and lead, or rather dragged, Wizard while following Nick to the hose. We cleaned him off the best we could without any dog shampoo. Nick loaned me a towel to dry Wizard off. "He smells much better," I said as I carried him back to my pickup. I turned on the pickup; made sure the air conditioner was running and stuck Wizard inside. I turned to Nick and said, "I'll take some time and find out what Wizard rolled in and clean it up before I leave."

"I'll help", was Nick's welcome reply.

We walked around his yard, with his big black cat following us and Wizard mournfully crying in the pickup until we found the remains of an old compost pile a previous renter must have attempted. It was an obvious failure, as with some determined digging through its surface, Wizard managed to find kitchen waste that had not composted.

"That's nasty," Nick commented unhelpfully and said, "I'll get a couple shovels." He left and returned with two shovels and handed me one. We spent about ten minutes digging a hole, shoveling the waste into the hole, and covering it back up again.

When we finished, I stepped back and said, "I don't think Wizard will be visiting here again anytime soon."

"No, I would assume he'd dig it up again." Nick laughed, followed me to my pickup and said, "Thanks so much for your help painting today, Carmen."

"It was fun, well that may be stretching it, painting is never fun, but I was glad to help."

"And I was glad of the company," Nick said with a smile.

I smiled back not sure how to take that, but decided on a casual, "I'll see you tomorrow. It will be a short day as the blue grama isn't ready. I'll also be leaving for the potluck before the end of the work day. If you want, you can leave early too; you might as well get some rest when you can. We'll start the blue grama on Tuesday." I waved goodbye and drove out of his yard.

I got home around seven. Dad wasn't home, but he'd left a note that he was at Karla's and would be home later. Not knowing if he would have eaten at Karla's I decided to double my hotdish recipe. I was sure Karla would feed him, but it would be helpful to have some leftovers for the workweek, especially with harvest starting. I made a mental note to thaw a roast tonight so I could put it in the crock pot tomorrow. We would have roast beef for sandwiches as I'd have to start packing lunches. I decided to make a Tater Tot hotdish to share at the potluck. My secret twist was to leave out the usual green beans or corn that most people used and add some grated cheddar cheese instead. It was almost always a hit with anyone who tried it and most important I could make it quick. I got two pounds of ground beef out, sliced up some onions and got it frying. I had a momentary panic attack when I dug through the freezer but I finally found two packages of Tater Tots. I realized Wizard was probably hungry. I put some food in his dish and made sure his water was full. He was so tired from his day running around Nick's place he didn't even lift his head when the food hit his dish, just opened one eye. He must have decided it was the usual dog food and not worth his time to get up, as he closed his eye again. I heard a door slam and Dad walked in as I put the hotdish for the potluck in the refrigerator and ours in the oven.

"Have you eaten?" I asked him.

"Karla had a salad for supper, so I can always eat more."

I knew Karla and I knew that whatever salad she had made was more than just lettuce. But you were never going to convince Dad that salad was an adequate meal. In his opinion salad was nothing more than a side dish.

"It's not ready yet. I'm making Tater Tot hotdish for the church potluck tomorrow and I decided to make an extra one for us. It should be ready around eight-thirty."

"That sounds good, but you don't ever stay for the potlucks after the annual meeting. Is something going on?"

"I want to talk to Jacob, and I don't want to act too obvious by stopping by his office. I figured he'd be campaigning and he would be more approachable at a church potluck."

"What are you planning on talking to him about?"

I told him about Gary seeing Maggie at the party that night, about her strange reaction and what she said about Jacob and Matthew. I also told him about following her to Jacob's office. "I guess I want to hear if his story matches hers and if he'll tell me why she went to his office."

"Jacob is a lawyer you know, he's not going to give anything away."

"I know, but I'm hoping if I handle it right I'll at least be able to tell if he's being truthful or if Maggie is just cuckoo. Maybe it'll turn out that he's handling some sort of legal matter for her and that's all there is to it."

"Do you really think Jacob had something to do with the accident?" Dad asked.

"I don't know. I find it hard to believe he could have, but I'm sure someone else was involved. The little bit of nosing around that I've done so far has already stirred up some memories that people had forgotten about. I'm hoping that someone will suddenly remember and say, 'oh yeah, so and so drove away right after or before Matthew.'"

Dad frowned, "Keep in mind someone killed Matthew to keep that 'ah ha' moment from coming to light."

"I know. I'm going to go take a shower while the hotdish cooks."

"I was going to ask you what you've been doing. I didn't think we had anything that needed paint around here?" Dad asked.

"I ran into Nick in town this afternoon, he was buying paint and I offered to help."

"Is he buying the Erickson place?" Dad asked with interest.

"He's not sure yet, but he couldn't take the horrid puke green in his entryway any longer. I don't blame him, it was awful."

I ran upstairs and decided I had time to soak in the tub so I could scrub off the paint easier. I don't know how I managed to get paint on parts of my body that were covered by clothes, but I always did. I may have dozed a little bit in the tub and by the time I got out of the tub, dressed, and back downstairs, Dad had the hotdish sitting on the counter and was talking to Kirk who had arrived home while I was in the tub. He was excitedly talking to Dad about his meeting with the record producer. I heard him say two weeks.

"What's two weeks?" I asked as I walked into the kitchen.

"He wants me to come to Minneapolis and do some studio recording. If they turn out he'll take those recordings and shop them around to both radio and some apps like Spotify. If he can get our music out there the band may be on its way."

"I'm happy for you bro, that's great news." I went over and hugged him. "Have you eaten? There is plenty of hotdish if you want any."

"I'd love some," he said grabbing another plate while Wizard pranced around his feet hoping for a treat.

We all sat down and listened to him prattle on excitedly. It was a welcome change of topic from murder. By the time Kirk wore down and the kitchen was cleaned up I was ready for bed.

I woke up feeling well rested on Monday morning, which was surprising as I was expecting a few sore muscles from painting. I could hear Wizard barking and by the time I got dressed and downstairs, Wizard had been let out and was running around outside. Kirk must have been still sleeping as only Dad was up.

"What is your plan for the day?" he asked as I got myself some cereal.

"I should get a hold of the sheriff and find out if he ever talked to Pamela. Other than that I have nothing planned, it will be a short day as I want to be done in time for the annual meeting. Speaking of which, will you be around at four-thirty today to stick the potluck hotdish in the oven if I'm not home in time?"

"That shouldn't be a problem, but I'll put a reminder in my phone." He pulled out his phone and pressed a few buttons. One of these days I was going to have to get caught up with technology. Nothing like your dad knowing how to use a cellphone better than you did.

"I'm going to run by the cabins first thing this morning. I haven't been there for a few days. Did you want to come with?" I asked him.

"Yeah, I would like to see them, but I think I'll drive myself. I need to run to town afterwards and pick up a prescription at the drug store."

"Okay, I'll be leaving here in about ten minutes. I'll see you when you get there."

I walked out to my pickup and scratched Clyde who was once again sitting on the hood. He jumped off when I got in and started it. I drove out to the cabins taking my time, enjoying the day; for once not speeding. I was amazed as I parked and looked around. All three of the cabins were fully framed and enclosed with plywood. Two of them were shingled and they were working on the third one. They must have worked at least some of the weekend.

Mitch looked up from the trailer where he was unloading some shingles. "Good morning Carmen."

"Good morning Mitch. As usual I'm amazed at how much you guys have done."

"Everything is moving smoothly that's for sure. The weather has been fabulous, even the rain didn't slow us up. Say, I'm glad you stopped by. I remembered the other day that Edna was dating a guy that was in our class. She was a couple years younger than us, but she might have been at the party that night."

"Thanks Mitch. I'll stop by and talk to her this morning. It'll give me a reason to stop by and get some fresh long johns, not that I ever need much of an excuse," I smiled.

Dad drove up, got out of his pickup and came over to where we were standing. "Wow Mitch. It looks like you guys are doing excellent work as usual."

"Feel free to look around both of you," Mitch said.

Dad and I spent an hour walking around. It helped me get rid of any lingering anxiety about the project and move to excited and fully committed. After we finished we both went our separate ways. I pulled up in front of Edna's bakery and was glad to see there wasn't more than one car parked in front of the bakery, and the occupants of that car were already sitting at a table eating when I walked in.

"Hi Edna, do you have a minute to talk?"

"Sure, what do you need?"

"As you know I've been looking into Matthew's death for Jessica."

"Yes, Carmen I'm aware." She looked at me like I was losing my mind if I thought she didn't know this.

"What you may not be aware of is that I think it has something to do with the party the seniors had the night Matthew supposedly hit that girl with his car."

"Why would you think that," she asked puzzled.

"Too many reasons to get into right now, but Mitch told me that he thought you had been dating someone from their class and that you might have been there that night."

"Hmm, I was there, but it was a long time ago. I don't think I remember too much," she said looking thoughtful.

"I guess my main question is, do you remember when Matthew left and if anyone else left around that time?"

"The only thing I remember is being surprised that Maggie was there as I had never seen her at a party before. I also remember being surprised that Matthew was drunk as I didn't think that was normal for him."

"What about when he left, did anybody else leave?"

"I can't say for sure, but I don't think I saw either Maggie or Jacob after Matthew was gone. But that doesn't mean they left; I just might not have seen them. It was a big party. Come to think of it Gary was acting strange that night too."

"What do you mean?"

"He acted like he was upset with Matthew. At the time I thought it was because Matthew was drinking so much and Gary was getting mad at him because of that", she paused and squinted her eyes as she tried to remember, "but the more I think about it I'm almost positive Jacob left at about the same time as Matthew. I remember thinking it was silly of him to have left as he had already tried to stop Matthew from driving and it didn't work—so why was he trying to catch him. Then again I'm pretty sure I saw him again later at the party too. Who knows if these old of memories are correct? Things are always different when you look back at them after some time has passed."

"Thanks Edna," I said as I paid for my long johns.

"Do you think any of it helped?" she asked as she gave me my change.

"I don't know. The more information I gather the more everything gets muddled."

"Memories tend to be that way," she said. "Good luck, one thing I know for sure is that Jessica didn't kill her own brother."

I absolutely did not want to, but it was time to head to the sheriff's department for a visit. The dispatcher looked up when I walked in.

"Is the sheriff available?" I asked.

"He's on the phone right now. Did you want to wait?" the dispatcher asked me.

"Do you happen to know if Pamela Wicks has called him?"

She looked at me in surprise, "That is who he's on the phone with right now. Did you need me to interrupt?"

"No, not at all. I just wanted to know if she had contacted him. I don't need to wait," I said as I turned to leave.

"Should I let the sheriff know you were here?" she asked.

"That isn't necessary. In fact it might be best if you didn't mention that I was here. Thanks," I said and walked out the door. I headed to the shop next where I was surprised to find Nick busy cleaning and reorganizing the bolt drawers. "Are you bored?" I asked him.

He looked up and smiled. "I couldn't think of anything else to do, and this shop is always in need of organization."

"That's true. I'll give you a hand." We spent the rest of the day in the shop. I took a quick break and drove to town to grab a couple sub sandwiches from the restaurant for our dinner. The restaurant was busy and Jessica only had time for a wave when I picked up the food. Nick and I ate the sandwiches while we cleaned and by the time we were done I hardly recognized the place.

"This looks amazing," I said wiping some grime from my face.

"I'm sure the organization won't last long," Nick said.

"I would bet not," I agreed. "But I think that is enough for today. The forecast is good so I'll see you in the morning, your first harvest with us will be starting tomorrow."

"Are you going to check the field again?"

"No. There is supposed to be strong winds in the forecast by Thursday so we need to go get what we can or Mother Nature will take care of it for us."

"I'll see you tomorrow morning," Nick said. "I'm looking forward to starting harvest."

I got home with plenty of time to make myself presentable for the annual meeting. Dad had put the hotdish in the oven so it would be ready by the time we left. It wasn't often I bothered with makeup but I thought it would give me a little more confidence to question Jacob if I was feeling good about myself. When Dad and I got to the church, he went to sit next to Jessica while I stuck my hotdish in one of the ovens on warm, along with the others that had been brought. I got a few surprised looks as most knew I sometimes attended the meeting but I never stayed for the potlucks after. I joined Jessica and Dad in the pew, but not before looking around to make sure Jacob was there. He was sitting in his usual spot, a few pews from the front of the church. I was glad the meeting was short as the longer I sat there the more nervous I got about how to approach Jacob. The meeting ended after a minor disagreement over whether or not the youth pastor's salary should be increased.

People started either rushing to the kitchen to put out the food or standing in line to get first dibs on the specialties that the good cooks in town were known for. I purposely stood back letting others go first as I wanted to make sure Jacob was already sitting down so I could join him with my plate of food. This didn't go according to my plan as by the time Jacob sat down after visiting with several people, he chose a table that had a group already there. I sat down dejected next to Dad and Jessica.

"Jacob looks a little busy," Dad observed.

"I kind of forgot to factor in his politicking when I assumed I'd catch him at supper. Of course he'd be talking to as many people as possible."

We lingered over the food and when I got up to refill my glass and grab a dessert, luck was finally on my side as when I walked back to my table the people that had been visiting with Jacob got up to leave. I slowed my stride so they would be gone when I came by his table and I quickly sat down next to him before he could get up.

He looked at me in surprise, "Hello Carmen."

"Hi Jacob, do you have a few minutes?" I asked.

"Is something wrong with the construction site easements?"

"No everything is good, I wondered if I could bother you some more about the accident the night of the senior party."

His eyes narrowed, "what do you mean? I already told you everything I remember about that night."

"I've learned a few more facts since I last talked to you," I said deliberately calling them facts to get his attention.

"Like what?" he asked irritated.

"For instance, Maggie was there that night. Gary and Edna remember seeing her. Did you?"

"I'm not sure", he paused, "it was a long time ago."

"I talked to Maggie and she confirmed it, but she claimed that she left soon after getting there because she heard you and Matthew making fun of her. But that didn't sound right to me. Also Gary thought he saw Maggie not that long before Matthew drove away, which doesn't jive with her story. So what do you remember?" I stopped, realizing I was rambling, and needed to take a breath.

"Maggie said we were making fun of her?" he asked slowly.

"Yes. Were you?"

He took his time with his response, which either meant he was trying to remember or he was attempting to come up with a story.

"What do you know about Maggie?" was his surprising response.

"Just that she's the librarian in town."

"Maggie was always one of those people who wanted to be popular, but could never bring herself to actually join anything."

I thought that was kind of a strange response although it agreed with what Gary said about her hanging around. Also, just because you joined in, it wasn't a guarantee you were going to be popular, if that was the case high school would have been a lot more enjoyable for me. Jessica and I were in all kinds of activities yet we never "fit" in with the "cool" kids.

"Her family was very poor, and no one held that against her, but she acted like she had a chip on her shoulder. She always hung around us, lurking, it was creepy. If she was there that night I don't remember. Did we make fun of her? I doubt it, but I can't say that her name wasn't mentioned and if she had snuck in she might have misinterpreted something." He stopped and acted like he was mulling something over and finally said. "She did have a crush on Matthew. Maybe he turned her down or something that night if she was there. That would explain why he was drinking more than usual—he would have felt bad."

"I thought you said it was because of a drinking game?" I asked.

"It was, but it didn't make sense that Matthew was even participating in one." Jacob answered.

I continued, "That's not all; Pamela, the girl that was hit that night, she contacted Jessica. Pamela told Jessica that she remembers seeing another pair of headlights. She's positive there were two cars involved. She also told Jessica that Matthew had contacted her wondering if she had seen another vehicle that night. Gary also told me that Matthew had contacted him."

Jacob interrupted me and questioned, "Matthew contacted Gary?"

"Yes." I said surprised at his reaction.

"What did Matthew tell Gary?" he asked me.

"Matthew told Gary that he was coming back home to talk to someone."

"Did he tell Gary who?" Jacob asked.

"Not that he indicated to either Gary or Pamela," I said.

"Really; well Maggie would be a good candidate. If she was there and Matthew turned her down, maybe she was waiting for him down the road a ways."

Jacob looked pleased with himself after saying that, and he continued. "It would make sense I suppose. Too bad Matthew didn't stick around. Maybe if there had been an investigation, something would have cleared his name."

"Edna was there also," I prodded him some more.

"Why would she have been there?"

"I guess she was dating someone in your class."

"That's right. I'd forgotten about that."

"She doesn't remember you or Maggie being around after Matthew left."

"It was a long time ago. She was mistaken. I can't vouch for Maggie but I was there after Matthew left. Have you learned anything else?" he asked.

"No that's about it. Nothing is helping. Sheriff Poole hasn't changed his mind about considering anyone except Jessica."

"Maybe I can help with that. I'll swing by and talk to the sheriff about Maggie myself tomorrow. Maybe he can be convinced to question her—do you think that would that help?" he asked.

"That would sure be appreciated, Jacob. It will also help verify Gary's story about Maggie being at the party and maybe it will be enough to get the sheriff to consider another motive besides Jessica's inheritance."

"Any time. I'd better get some more campaigning done, it looks like the crowd is starting to thin."

"Sorry for taking up so much of your time."

"Good luck with your inquiries. If you are correct, remember there is a murderer out there."

"So everyone keeps telling me." I got up, threw away my uneaten dessert and went to find Jessica and Dad.

"How did it go?" Dad asked when I joined them.

"I'm not sure. I don't really think he knows anything, but I was surprised by how quick he threw Maggie under the bus. But both Gary and he have said she was a little strange in school. Maybe she is the one. He is going to talk to the sheriff for us and mention Maggie to him. With any luck it will at least get the focus off you Jessica."

"Let's hope," she said.

"Although it feels like I've said that a few times before. Let's hope Jacob has more influence with the sheriff than I do." I grabbed my hotdish pan, now empty, and we went our separate ways. Jessica headed to her restaurant to catch up on some book work. Dad left to visit Kayla and I decided that it was early enough in the evening to go on the walk I had missed out on yesterday. I called Kirk to ask him if I could take Wizard. I could hear the band practicing in the background, so they weren't finished. He said sure, so I drove home to change clothes and grab Wizard.

By the time I got out to the prairie it was nine. It was a beautiful evening but it was starting to get dark. Looking at the cabins I was amazed again at how far MM Construction had gotten. I knew though that their pace would slow when they finished outside and moved to the interiors. I parked next to one of them, got out and looked around. Wizard had already run off, so I went to catch up with him. I was glad I'd made the time to get out here when no one was around. It was exactly what I needed to ease some stress before harvest started. There wasn't as much evidence of deer as normal, but I assume the carpenter's activity had changed the movement of the deer. They'd be back when the cabins were finished. Wizard and I walked about three miles. It never failed to surprise me how those tiny little legs could cover so much ground. He was starting to tire when we neared the pickup, so I bent down to pick him up and carried him the rest of the way. He was going to sleep well tonight, guaranteeing there was at least one night he wouldn't get into any mischief. We got home a little after ten. There were no lights on so I wasn't sure if Dad and Kirk weren't home or if they were in bed. I shoved Wizard into Kirk's bedroom and when I opened the door I could hear snoring so I knew Kirk was home. I climbed the steps and barely had enough energy to get my pajamas on before I fell into bed. As I started to fall asleep I remembered the dirty hotdish pan I had forgotten in my pickup. Oh well, it wasn't going anywhere and would be there in the morning was my last thought.

CHAPTER TWENTY-ONE

Sideoats grama has small oat-like seeds
hanging down uniformly on one side of the seed stem
and takes on a reddish cast late in the summer.

I WAS UP AND OUT OF THE HOUSE Tuesday morning before any-one else was stirring. My pickup smelled like Tater Tot hotdish from the pan that had sat in it all night. I shrugged and decided there were worse things it could smell like—Wizard came to mind. I met up with Nick at the shop where he had the combine already running. We couldn't start for a couple hours as the grass was damp from the dew, but there was a nice breeze that would dry it in no time. It would take around an hour to get the equipment moved as the field was about six miles away from the shop. Nick took off with the combine while I followed pulling a silage wagon. Our crops didn't flow out of the combine augers smoothly like most grain crops. We had to do a lot of manual shoveling-out of the combine hoppers. Modified silage wagons worked the best for transporting the seed. The quantities we got off our small fields didn't justify big trucks. I'm sure we amused the locals with our archaic equipment but it worked for us. By the time we got the combine and wagon to the field and I took Nick back so he could tow another wagon, the grass was dry. We made one round in the field before we got all the settings correct on the combine. After that the day went by in a blur. This field of blue grama that we started in was a small one, about twenty acres. We finished up around 6:00 p.m. and decided to hold off until tomorrow to open up a new field. I drove home feeling tired but satisfied with how the day went. The beginning of harvest was always exhilarating. I enjoyed the feeling knowing it would soon turn to exhaustion.

As I pulled out into our driveway at home I was surprised to see the sheriff's vehicle in the yard. He was waiting for me on the porch.

"Good evening Sheriff Poole, can I help you with something?" I asked as I walked up to him.

"I don't appreciate you sticking your nose into my investigation," he said clearly agitated as he paced and fidgeted.

"I don't appreciate you accusing my best friend of murder," I responded back. "But just what is it you think I've done?"

"Jacob called me this morning and was full of information about Maggie. He thought I should be suspecting her instead of Jessica. He had all kinds of fancy notions that this was all tied in to that accident from years ago. I even have Pamela Wicks coming to see me in person tomorrow; apparently she didn't think I understood the seriousness of what she told me when she called me. I'm telling you to back off," he said as he glared at me.

"I'll back off if you agree to at least consider what you are being told and listen with an open mind to Pamela tomorrow. I'm positive this all ties back to that accident."

"I will listen; I know how to do my job. That paralyzed girl making the trip all the way here deserves to be listened to; but like I told her on the phone, she is wasting her time. Nothing she told me made me change my mind and showing up in person isn't going to change that. This isn't anything other than a sister not wanting to share her inheritance, and even if there was a slim chance

Matthew wasn't guilty of causing the accident there is no evidence that his death has anything to do with what happened at a high school party twenty years ago."

"I guess we will have to agree to disagree. I know Jessica and there is no way she would have killed her brother. Are you going to at least talk to Maggie?"

"I don't have much choice after Mr. high and mighty asked me to look into it. I can't have a possible future state representative thinking I didn't do my job," he said as he walked back to his patrol car.

I watched him drive out of the yard before I walked into the house. Dad wasn't home but I could hear music coming from Kirk's room. I knocked on the door, and when I didn't get an answer I cracked the door open wide enough to ask if he'd had dinner. Kirk was busy doing some composing with headphones on. He looked up when Wizard nudged him with his nose, smiled and waved at me—Kirk, not Wizard. He took off his headphones and confirmed that he had eaten. I closed the door and went to find myself something to eat. I'd had the roast beef on sandwiches for dinner today and I knew I'd have them again tomorrow. Instead of a third meal of roast beef I decided my favorite meal of fried eggs, over medium, and toast sounded like it would do the trick. While I ate I thought about what Jacob had said. I wasn't sure who to believe, but I tended to believe Jacob and Gary, especially as I had gotten a little glimpse of the crazy Maggie had in her when I was at the library Sunday. I needed to talk to her again, but decided it would be better to catch her somewhere other than her work place. I was not going to her house, that was for sure. I wondered how I could find out where else she might frequent. Maybe Jessica would know. I checked the time to make sure it wasn't too late to call her and was surprised to find it was only seven. It had been a long day and it felt like it should have been a lot later. I picked up my cellphone and dialed Jessica's number.

It rang a couple times and Jessica picked up, "Hey Carmen."

"Hi Jessica, how have you been doing?"

"I'm doing okay," she said sounding like she was in good spirits. "The restaurant has been busy, which helps, and James has been really sweet spending as much time as he can keeping me company. What are you up to? Has your harvest started?"

"We finished our first field today, but I'm calling because I was wondering if you could tell me anything about Maggie."

"What do you mean?" Jessica asked, not surprisingly sounding puzzled.

"After what Jacob said I'd like to talk to her again, but I don't think doing it at the library is a good idea and I want wherever I run in to her to be a casual occasion. Do you know anyplace she happens to frequent that I might arrange a chance meeting with her?"

"Sure, I know just the place. My house tonight at seven-thirty; you have twenty-four minutes to get here. I told you before she is part of my book club and we are getting together tonight."

I hesitated, "Are you sure I should come? Won't it look strange when all of the sudden I show up?"

"Possibly, but I have mentioned to the group that I've been trying for years to get you to come to a meeting, and you always have some excuse."

The truth was I'm very particular about what I read, others would say narrow minded. I get so little time to do it and going to a book club and having to discuss a book that would more than likely not be a mystery held little interest for me. But I was willing to give it a try if it gave me access to Maggie. "I guess if you'll have me, I'll rush over. I might be a couple minutes late but you'll be glad I am, as I need to take a shower."

"Great, I'll see you when you get here. I'm sure Maggie will be here; she hasn't missed a meeting yet. By the way we all bring a snack to share. You don't have to, but I know you would feel guilty if I didn't tell you and you showed up empty handed."

Knowing I was running out of time I still had to ask, "Could you quick tell me what you think of Maggie? I know you like her as a librarian, but what about her on a personal level? Both Gary and Jacob indicated they think she's a little wacky."

"I don't know, she seems fine to me. Wired a little tight and sometimes gets fixations on guys that she meets online. They never pan out into anything serious, but that's online dating. I don't know her too well, we don't have any other contact outside of the library or this book club."

"Okay. I need to get moving, I'll see you in a little bit. What book are you discussing by the way?"

""The Boy in the Field" by Margot Livesey, you might actually enjoy it as it's a mystery," Jessica answered with a laugh.

I hung up the phone and raced for the shower.

I got to Jessica's as everyone else was grabbing some snacks and starting to sit down. They all looked up when I walked in. Besides Jessica and Maggie there were four other women. They all owned businesses in town. Edna was there along with Judith who was the dentist in town, Helena who owned the drugstore, and Karen who owned the theater with her husband Paul.

"Hi everyone," I said as I put down my plate of cut vegetables that I had hastily thrown together. I filled my own plate with the snacks that everyone else had brought, glad I had eggs and toast and not a bigger meal for supper, and sat down.

"Carmen is going to join us. I've been trying forever to get her to come and tonight it worked for her," Jessica announced to my embarrassment. It made me uncomfortable whenever my name was mentioned in any sort of announcement no matter how small.

Maggie gave me a hostile glare, but turned her head when I caught her looking at me. I was pleasantly surprised by how quick the time went. There was a lot of animated discussion and I found myself enjoying the evening very much. I might have to make more of an effort to attend in the future. It ended too soon and I was left with trying to figure out how to broach the subject

of Matthew with Maggie. As I was sitting on the couch, the problem was solved by Maggie standing in front of me, hands on her
hips.

"I don't quite buy that you all the sudden decided to come
tonight, so I'm assuming you wanted to talk to me again."

She was being blunt so I guess I could be also. "Gary and Jacob
both said you were a little strange in high school and Gary believes
you were obsessed with either Jacob or Matthew."

She sat down with a thump.

"I was. I assume this is what the sheriff is planning on talking to
me about tomorrow also."

"I would assume so," I said, surprised Sheriff Poole had acted
that fast.

"I did like Jacob, but he never had any time for me. I wish I had
liked Matthew; he at least was always nice to me. Like I told you
before, Matthew knew about my home life and would go out of
his way to talk to me. I did consider him to be a true friend, which
makes what I did all the worse. That night Jacob asked me to come
to the party. I was so excited, but scared too. I had enough brains to
wonder why Jacob would want me to come, especially as he hadn't
even acknowledged I was alive up to that point. But I decided to
go, hoping that Jacob had a change of heart towards me. I got there
late and snuck around until I found Jacob and Matthew. They were
playing darts with a bunch of people. I remember standing there
wondering why I had ever come as I so didn't fit in." She paused
then continued, "Jacob eventually noticed me, came over, took me
by the arm and led me over to a corner away from everyone. I was
so excited to be getting that attention—that's the best explanation
I have for why I did what I did. Jacob spent around thirty minutes
talking to just me. He made me feel so special and once he had
me buttered up he asked if I wanted to help him play a joke on
Matthew. He wanted me to spike Matthew's drinks. When I asked
why, he said Matthew was hilarious when he was drunk and he
wanted to liven up the party. I went along with it. I don't know

how Gary managed to get a hold of all the booze he had on hand that night but everyone was enjoying both beer and mixed drinks. Matthew had one drink in his hand that he hadn't drank from. I grabbed it from him and told him I'd replace it with some pop for him. Instead, I grabbed a bottle of Everclear and added a bunch of that along with some Coke. I couldn't believe he didn't notice, but he drank it all—after that it was easy to keep serving him spiked drinks. I soon figured out Jacob must have lied to me as far from getting boisterous, Matthew got more mellow. I have felt so guilty all these years. If I hadn't done what Jacob talked me into, Matthew would have never crashed into that girl."

"Why did you tell me earlier that you left after hearing them make fun of you?" I asked her not sure I believed this latest version of her story.

"Would you want to admit what I just told you."

"No. So why now?" I asked her still not convinced that her story was true as it was so horrible.

"Before, it was you being nosy and I didn't care, but now the sheriff is asking. It feels a little more serious," she said her tone dripping sarcasm.

"But why didn't you say anything when the accident happened?"

"I wanted to, but Jacob told me no one would believe me over him."

Jessica had wandered over while she was talking and had been listening. When Maggie finished, Jessica plopped down on the couch next to me. We both sat there stunned. "I can't believe Jacob would have done that to Matthew," Jessica said, sounding shocked and disbelieving.

"Well he did!" Maggie hollered, "I told you those guys weren't what they acted like." And she stormed out of the house.

We looked at each other, "Could this actually be true?" I asked Jessica.

"It does explain why Matthew drove. He didn't realize how much alcohol he'd actually drank, he just thought he was tired.

Jacob should have told him what he and Maggie had done and
never let Matthew drive." Jessica now sounded furious.

"We need to talk to Jacob again," I said.

"It's only nine-thirty. Let's call him now," Jessica insisted.

I pulled my phone out of my pocket and dialed Jacob's number.
He picked up on the fourth ring.

"What can I do for you now Carmen?" He sounded annoyed.

"Jessica and I just talked to Maggie and we'd like to visit with
you tonight if we could?"

"What has that ding-a-ling been telling you?"

"We'd prefer to talk to you in person."

"I have an early morning press conference tomorrow. Can't this
wait?"

"She told us you had her spike Matthew's drinks that night," I
spit the words out.

There was silence until he said, "I guess you better come over."

"We'll see you in ten minutes," I said and hung up.

We took a minute to pick up the dishes, stack them in the sink,
grabbed our coats and rushed out to my pickup.

CHAPTER TWENTY-TWO

Sideoats grama is usually associated with drier upland sites.

WE PULLED UP IN FRONT OF JACOB'S HOME with time to spare. As befitting his wealthy philanthropist position in the community, it was a fabulous bricked two-story colonial. It even had a circular driveway with a small fountain and a perfectly maintained lawn. I was sure he hired someone to take care of it all. While his home and yard was beautiful, it was a little too opulent and over-the-top compared to the rest of the homes in this rural agricultural area. Jacob was waiting for us on his front porch.

"I can't believe she told you about those drinks," were his first words to us as we walked up the steps. He opened the door and motioned for us to follow him into his house.

"She has been blackmailing me for years," he continued to say as he led us into an elegant yet comfortable-looking living room, and told us to have a seat on the couch. He sat down on the love seat across from us.

"I guess this will end my political career, but in a way I'm relieved the truth came out. I have felt so much guilt over the years. You don't know what a relief it was to hear you guys say there was another vehicle involved and Matthew being drunk may not have been what caused that accident."

"It doesn't change what you did." Jessica said sounding mad. "Why did you feel the need to spike his drinks—some sort of stupid prank?" Jessica wasn't mad she was furious.

He hung his head ashamed, "Matthew was my best friend but sometimes it was hard. He was so perfect, all the time. He was the better athlete, had the better personality, teachers loved him, he had more friends. Everyone flocked to him. Grades were the only thing I did better, but no one cared about that in high school." He stopped.

"That doesn't explain why," I prodded him.

"I don't have a good answer. I guess I hoped that if he'd get drunk he would make a fool of himself, and just for one night he wouldn't be the best. Maggie was the perfect person to do it as she never got invited to parties and would be thrilled to be there, plus I knew she had a crush on me and would do it if I asked her to. Never in my wildest dreams would I have thought what happened would happen. I truly did try to get the keys from him."

"Why didn't you tell someone what happened? At least Matthew would have known it wasn't his fault. Maybe he wouldn't have run away?" Jessica asked her voice choking, whether from rage or sadness I wasn't sure.

"By the time I worked up the nerve to tell someone; Matthew was gone. I know it was horrible, but by then it was easier to keep quiet. I have spent every year of my life since trying to do things for the community, trying to be a better person. It doesn't make it okay but in some small measure it helps to know there was another vehicle involved, perhaps I wasn't solely responsible for the accident." He said as he hung his head.

"Did you kill Matthew?" I bluntly asked.

He looked up with a surprised look on his face. "What? No! Why would you even ask that?"

"You are running for state representative and he was coming home to open it all up again."

"If that were the case I would never have pointed you in the direction of Maggie."

"Why did you? You had to have known she would tell us what you had her do."

"I thought she would, but I did hold out a small hope that she wouldn't say anything, after all she collected enough money over the years from me to keep quiet, but I decided I didn't care. I owed it to Matthew and it is time for the truth of that night to come out. Especially after I found out that another car was involved and I am sure she must have been the other car."

"Why do you think that?" I asked.

"She was the only one that left the party that night the same time as Matthew."

"Do you have any proof?"

"Just my word, which should count for something," he said looking indignant. He stopped talking when he saw our skeptical looks.

"After hearing about the drink-spiking that you've never told anyone about for twenty years, your word doesn't mean much, at least to us," I stated disgusted with him.

He looked down at the floor and admitted, "I guess that is true."

"We've talked to several people and no one has been able to say with confidence that anyone left at the same time as Matthew."

"I know Maggie did," he asserted again.

"Have you told the sheriff any of this?" I asked him

"I didn't tell him about the spiking of Matthew's drinks, but yes I told him about Maggie being there, her leaving at the same time as Matthew and how I thought she might have been the other car."

"Well that explains why he is talking to Maggie tomorrow. Isn't it ironic how he listens to you, but hasn't been listening to us all this time," I said appalled.

"I don't think I convinced him that Maggie killed Matthew, just that she was involved in the accident. He believes Jessica killed him, and to be honest while I don't think Jessica killed Matthew, there isn't any evidence that Maggie did either."

Jessica and I looked at each other and both groaned.

"Do you think it is at least possible that Maggie killed Matthew?" I asked Jacob.

"I don't want to believe it, but I don't want to think anybody I know could have killed Matthew. I have definitely seen another side to her than the perfect librarian she depicts to the town. She had no problem blackmailing me all these years," he said.

"Blackmail isn't murder though," I said.

"No, I suppose not. But I don't know who else would want Matthew to not talk. He must have remembered her car," Jacob said.

"Whoever killed Matthew tried to frame Jessica, and when we questioned Maggie at the library she said she didn't know Jessica and Matthew were related. Her reaction rang true to me, I believed her," I said.

"I don't know what else to tell you other than I know it wasn't me," Jacob said with a note of finality in his voice.

"It's late and we've taken up enough of your time, thank you for being honest with us at last Jacob, and I'm sorry." And I was sorry. This was something from his teenage years and he had done nothing but volunteer and work for the town ever since. It was a shame it would derail his political career and yet he had done a horrific thing. Jessica and I walked out to my pickup.

"Do you believe him?" she asked when we got in the vehicle.

"Don't you?" I asked surprised by her question.

"I don't know. He was so quick to throw Maggie under the bus. She's been blackmailing him all these years and now he remembers her leaving after Matthew. It seems", she paused searching for the right world, "convenient".

"You're right, but I do believe Jacob is a good guy, I think he's just been protecting himself all these years."

"And maybe with Matthew coming back, and along with his political campaign Jacob figured it would be better if Matthew was never allowed to talk." Jessica said surprising me again.

"But Jacob knows better than to put Matthew's body in our field. He knows about our farm and business."

"Does he? I know it may surprise you, but a lot of people have no clue what you guys actually do on your farm. It's not exactly conventional farming. About all most people know is that you burn your fields and combine them. And sometimes you don't even combine all of them. Maybe Jacob assumed that field wouldn't be combined and the body would burn up in the spring."

"I suppose, but the same could apply to Maggie also."

"I can't see Maggie physically being able to haul a body all the way out to your farm, I do believe Jacob when he said that Maggie had something to do with that accident, in fact I'm sure she caused it, but I don't think she killed Matthew at least not by herself. Someone had to have helped her." Jessica stopped talking for a moment and continued, "I think I can prove she was involved in the accident."

"How?" I asked her.

"Do you remember that sweatshirt of Matthews we found in my basement with the blood on it?"

"Yeah," I answered wondering where she was going with this.

"Do you remember how I said we couldn't figure out why there was so much blood on it? It was unlikely that it was Matthew's, as other than a small cut on his head, he didn't have any external injuries that would have bled like that. Do you suppose Maggie and Matthew would have tried to help that girl, or maybe Maggie got hurt herself and Matthew got her blood on him?"

"But how would Matthew have ended up back in his own car?" I asked her.

"I don't know, maybe she hit him and put him in there. Maybe she tried to help him in his car when he was unconscious and transferred her blood on him then," Jessica argued. "Either way maybe some DNA could be obtained from the sweatshirt that would implicate her."

"Sheriff Poole will never agree to sending it in for testing", I stated, starting to get a glimmer of an idea, "but, he might be willing to use it as a bluff to get Maggie to confess about the accident."

"I doubt any of this is going to help with changing the sheriff's mind about me killing Matthew," Jessica stopped. She put her hand up to her temples and rubbed. "I know the sheriff keeps treating this as two separate incidents but we know it's not. They are tied together; I know it. I'm going to talk to the sheriff in the morning and tell him about the sweatshirt. I'll try to catch him before he talks to Maggie. If nothing else we can at least clear Matthew's name."

As she opened the door of the pickup I said to her, "I wish I could go with you but I need to combine. Thursday is supposed to be bad weather. Good luck and please let me know how it goes; I'll be watching my phone."

"Okay, thanks for all your help Carmen. I'm so thankful you decided to dig into all this this."

I reached over and gave her a hug before she got out of the vehicle. I backed my pickup out of her driveway and went home, still puzzling over who could have killed Matthew. It had to be either Maggie or Jacob. I didn't want it to be anyone I knew, and I didn't have any idea on how to figure it out.

CHAPTER TWENTY-THREE

Little bluestem grows 18 to 36 inches tall with mature plants acquiring a distinctive reddish color late in the growing season.

I WOKE UP WEDNESDAY TO A WET WORLD. Sometime between getting home from Jacob's and this morning it had rained. This reinforced to me how much my mind had been focused on this case. I had been worried about Thursday and neglected to check the most recent weather forecast. There went my plans for combining today. While I was thankful for the rain it was frustrating that after months of begging for moisture it had to show up during harvest. I got dressed and went down to get breakfast. Dad was eating some oatmeal. He looked up when I stepped into the kitchen.

"You got home late last night. There is extra oatmeal on the stove," he added when he saw I was stumbling around the kitchen in a daze.

I sat down next to him, "We were at Jacob's late."

"What were you doing at Jacob's house?" he asked in a puzzled voice.

I shared what Maggie had told us about Jacob making her spike Matthew's drinks and how we went over his house to talk to him.

"Did he have a good reason?"

"No, just jealousy, unfortunately a fairly typical high school emotion."

"An emotion not reserved for high school," Dad reminded me.

"True. But I'm frustrated. Other than knowing why Matthew was so uncharacteristically drunk it doesn't help with proving he wasn't responsible for the accident. Jacob is convinced that Maggie was involved in the accident, but we have no proof."

"You girls have been busy. You shouldn't be so bummed, you are making progress."

"We have no idea yet who killed Matthew. All we've done is figure out what may have happened in that accident. Jessica is going to talk to the sheriff today about trying to bluff Maggie into admitting she was at the accident."

"How is she going to do that?"

"Her mom had saved the sweatshirt Matthew was wearing the night of the accident. It has a lot of blood on it and Jessica's mom didn't think it could be his, as other than a scratch on his head he didn't have any other marks on his body. Jessica wants the sheriff to bluff that they know it is Maggie's blood. We figured the sheriff would never agree to test it for DNA, but we are hoping he'll agree to the bluff. But even if it does work it doesn't solve Matthew's murder. Jessica is going to continue being the sheriff's main suspect."

"That is true, but clearing Matthew's name is a big deal too. I know you don't know who was in the other vehicle involved, but Pamela's testimony along with the accident investigation that showed no bike paint on Matthew's car should be enough to at least exonerate Matthew. I'm sure that will bring a lot of healing to Jessica."

"I know, but I thought when we found out who caused the accident it would be the same person that killed Matthew."

"It might still be."

"I don't think Maggie would have been physically able to move Matthew's body." I said dejected.

"Why does the body have to have been moved?" Dad asked.

"Blood was found in Matthew's truck at Jessica's house," I answered Dad.

"I thought you believed that it was planted there to incriminate Jessica. If you're right about that the body wouldn't have been moved, just the blood, Matthew could have been killed anywhere."

I sat in stunned silence. "You're right Dad, some detective I am."

"You were focused on disproving the evidence the sheriff was using against Jessica," Dad said trying to make me feel better.

"Maggie could be the one who killed Matthew but I still can't think of a way to prove anything. Maybe I should go meet Jessica at the sheriff's department and support her."

"You have a knack of antagonizing the sheriff. It might be best if you stayed away," Dad said.

"True. I think since combining is off for the day, I'm going to head back to the big bluestem field where they found Matthew's body and see if I can find anything the crime scene technicians might have missed. It isn't likely, but I know those fields and irrigation paths better than anyone. I have to do something. I had kind of forgotten about it until I was about asleep last night, but didn't that old trail used to connect to a township road, that in turn leads to Jessica's?"

"Yes. It got abandoned the last ten years or so as it is very swampy back there and the crossing where it connected to the township road was always under water." He paused and said, "But it has been very dry this summer and fall, it could be passable, and the sporadic rains we've gotten the last few weeks haven't amounted to much."

"That would explain why the sheriff never got anything from our security camera other than a red blur which could have been one of our vehicles. It would also explain how the killer was able to plant the blood in the pickup parked at Jessica's."

"Don't forget the body shop owners are going to be back from their trip today, I'll check in with them and get a look at their security cameras."

"I had forgotten all about that." I was starting to feel a little excited again. My cellphone rang. It was Nick.

"I assume we aren't combining today and I'm at loose ends. Do you have any projects for me?"

I hesitated for a couple seconds while I decided, and finally said, "I'm in the investigating mode again. Do you want to come with while I check over the crime scene?"

"Sure, I'll help. I can be a Hardy boy to your Nancy Drew. What are you hoping to find?"

"No idea, but I don't have any other plans for what to do today."

"When do you want to meet?"

"I'm going to eat my breakfast first; I'll meet up with you at the break room in about thirty minutes. Have you eaten anything?" I asked looking at the pot of now unappetizing congealed oatmeal.

"A stale donut," Nick answered.

"I'll make you an English muffin with an egg and cheese if you'd like."

"That sounds good. Thank you."

"Don't forget your rain gear," I reminded him.

"It looks like the sun is starting to shine through the clouds, so it may not be so wet when you get here," he responded.

"That's good. You better give me a few extra minutes. I'll see you in forty-five." I shoved two English muffins in the toaster and got some eggs frying. Once the muffins were assembled and wrapped in tinfoil, I grabbed an extra cup of coffee for Nick and took off.

He was standing outside the break room when I drove up. I parked and walked up to him, handing him the food and coffee.

"Thanks, this is so much better than a donut."

"It's the least I can do to thank you for being willing to hunt around in a soppy field with me."

"Not a problem. Are we looking for anything in particular?"

"I don't really know." I told him what we had found out from Jacob yesterday and the plan Jessica and I came up with for the sher- iff to use the sweatshirt to entrap Maggie. "Everything is pointing to Maggie being involved in the accident but nothing we've come up with proves she had anything to do with Matthew's murder. The sheriff is resolute in his belief that Jessica is guilty. I guess I hoped if we could look over the crime scene maybe we'd find something that they missed."

Nick looked at me in skepticism.

"I know, I know, highly unlikely but when we couldn't combine today I felt like I had to do something."

"Good enough for me. Where do you want to look first?"

"I thought we'd start back at that old bumpy field road and try to find where they might have walked in, assuming my premise that they drove in on that old field road is accurate. I know the sheriff thought the killer was in one of the vehicles that drove by my camera, and that the red blur was Jessica in Matthew's old pickup. But since we know it wasn't Jessica, I think it was someone going fishing, after all we know there are plenty of red vehicles around. I'm sure the sheriff found that out also otherwise he would have arrested Jessica by now if it was Matthew's pickup. Most likely the pickup didn't start as it has been sitting there for years."

"That makes sense," Nick said, looking a little more interested. "Let's drive back there. Didn't you tell the sheriff about the field road though?"

"I did but they looked on the west edge of the road where it connects to our field. I'm sure they never drove past the gravel pits as he was positive the killer came in from the highway. I did also tell them that once you went past the pits the road didn't go any-where. When I talked to Dad I remembered that it used to hook up to the township road by Jessica's. I want to check if somebody could have made it through."

We both climbed into my pickup and headed across the aban-doned railway and drove along it until we reached the field road on the west side of the big bluestem field. I parked, we got out and started walking around. There were a few old tracks, but nothing looked new. We kept walking farther down the edge of the field.

"Any tracks we do find could be from any of your employees or even from some hunters. How are we going to recognize the path a killer might have taken?" Nick asked.

"I don't know. I guess I was hoping something would jump out at us," I said as I continued to walk while looking down. I came to a stop, causing Nick to stumble into me. I pointed, "Is that what I think it is?" Right in front of me was what looked like a trail leading into the field. Some of the crop was broken off.

"Could be a deer trail," Nick said.

"I don't think so, that would be more defined—they tend to go over the same trail repeatedly. And it can't be our roguing crew as they would never walk this pattern in the field. It goes against the rows. It's a place to start anyway, let's follow it." We walked into the field. A couple feet in we came across one of the wheel paths from the irrigation system. "Does that look like something was dragged there?"

"Yes; and that is a footprint." Nick pointed down.

"I don't often say this, but it's good there haven't been any hard driving rains or these prints would be gone. It could be from one of the rogueing crews, but I don't think so. They hadn't made it this far in the field before they found Matthew's body, and they haven't been in this field since that day. Let's keep following it."

We kept walking, and suddenly the sun broke out from behind the clouds. I kept scanning the ground in front of me as we walked following the broken crop stems.

Nick put out his arm. "Carmen, do you see something shining over there?" I looked where he was pointing. Just off the trail we were following was a pair of sunglasses laying on the ground. We would never have seen them if the sun hadn't come out and if they weren't lying exactly as they were. I started to bend over to pick them up, but Nick stopped me. I looked at him. "Fingerprints," he said.

I felt stupid, "You're right. Can we mark this spot somehow until we get the sheriff out here?"

"Let's stomp down some more of the crop around it, we'll be able to follow the same trail in," Nick suggested.

We went about stomping down crop. We continued to walk following the path until we got to another irrigation wheel row where the trail seemed to disappear.

"Where did the trail go? It's another two hundred feet or so until we reach where the sheriff had marked the crime scene."

"I don't know", Nick said, "but that would explain why the sheriff didn't find it. The trail we are following doesn't meet up with where the body was found."

We stopped and looked around. "I bet whoever it was followed the irrigation wheel row back to the road, and followed a different one back in, to where the body was found."

"Why would they do that?" Nick asked. "That would be a lot of extra work, plus walking around you'd be taking even more of a chance of being seen."

"To make it look like the vehicle came in on the main road, just like the sheriff did think. This person was smart and very brave. Matthew was probably being led by gunpoint," my voice trailed off.

"Are you going to call the sheriff?" Nick asked when I stopped talking. "Carmen, what are thinking?" he questioned me when I didn't answer.

Something was bugging me, but I couldn't figure out what. I held up my hand to stop him from talking. Something was on the edge of my brain, something to do with the sunglasses.

"Jacob," I said.

"What about him?" Nick asked.

"When I was in Jacob's office that day, he was coming out after me, and he was looking for his sunglasses. He couldn't find them. Do you suppose it's been Jacob all this time?"

Nick looked at me. "I don't know, Carmen. It could be, but you're taking a pretty big leap. The first step is for the sheriff to get fingerprints off the sunglasses. There would be no other reason for his sunglasses to be out here if they are his. Let's call the sheriff."

"No, I think I'll go to town and talk to him face to face. I want to find out how it went with Jessica and Maggie this morning anyway. I'm also hoping Pamela has made it there by now." Nick and I walked out of the field and found ourselves by the break room.

"I'll give you a lift back to your pickup," Nick said. As we climbed into his pickup, my cellphone rang.

"Hello," I answered. It was Dad.

"Carmen, the owners of the body shop let me review the security cameras. You'll never guess whose vehicle was shown to be heading out on the highway towards Jessica's place around the time they think the body was put in the field?"

"Jacob's vehicle."

"How did you know?" Dad sputtered.

"Because we just found an expensive pair of sunglasses near where Matthew's body was found and I suspect they are Jacob's. I'm on my way in to town to talk to the sheriff right now."

"I'll meet you there," Dad said.

"I take it that it's not such a remote possibility that the sunglasses are Jacob's anymore," Nick said to me after I hung up.

"No, I don't think so."

"You look a little shook—why don't I drive you in to town. We can get your pickup later. I'd kind of like to see the sheriff's face when you present this stuff to him anyway."

"I'd appreciate that." I buckled my seat belt and we turned around and drove towards town.

CHAPTER TWENTY-FOUR

*Prairie cordgrass has coarse, tough blades with short points
or teeth on its edges and is sometimes called "ripgut."*

As we drove up to the sheriff's office we saw Jessica coming out looking frustrated.

"It wasn't Maggie", she said when we got out of the pickup, "either that or she's a very accomplished liar."

"She didn't have anything to do with the accident?" I asked dumbfounded.

"She did admit that she spiked the drinks, and she acted surprised that Jacob had told the sheriff about her blackmailing him over it. She didn't deny it but she insists she was not responsible for the accident. She claims that she never left the party that night. She said she was so upset she spent the rest of the evening sitting outside in the gazebo. The sheriff asked her how her blood got on the sweatshirt. She didn't even blink. She said the tests must be wrong as she wasn't there. I even believed her. So after everything we've been through I guess I continue to be the main suspect in Matthew's death."

"I don't think you will be for long. Do you know if Pamela ever showed up?" I asked Jessica.

"That's her handicapped van over there," Jessica pointed to a brown modified van on the other side of a sheriff's department vehicle. "She's waiting to talk to him when he finishes with Maggie. I talked to her awhile after the sheriff kicked me out of his questioning of Maggie."

"How did that go, talking to Pamela?" I asked her.

"She was so apologetic about Matthew getting killed which was crazy. As much as it hurts to admit it, Matthew caused a lot of this himself. Things would have been so much different if he hadn't run away. She does think the same as we do that Matthew was killed by whoever else was present when she was struck by their car."

"Do you think she'd mind if I talked to her?" I asked Jessica.

"Not at all, she's very sweet and friendly."

Nick had been patiently waiting by the door while Jessica and I talked. He opened it for us when he heard Jessica's answer. All three of us walked in. Sitting along the wall in the waiting area near a bench was a beautiful woman with black cropped hair and green eyes in a wheelchair. We walked towards her.

Jessica said, "Pamela these are my friends Carmen and Nick. Carmen is the one I told you about. She has been working so hard trying to figure out what happened to Matthew. Like you and I, she believes that whoever killed Matthew was likely responsible for your accident too."

I held out my hand, "It's so nice to meet you."

"Same here. I understand you're the one who convince that other man to tell the sheriff that Matthew had also called him?" Pamela asked me.

"You mean Gary, yes, I did. Not that it did any good. The sheriff doesn't believe an accident from twenty years ago has any bearing on Matthew's murder now."

"Which is the reason why I'm here," Pamela said. "He was so dismissive over the phone that I had to come in person to give him a piece of my mind."

I smiled at that. She was feisty, leaving me wishing she still lived here as I was certain we'd be good friends. "Is the sheriff still in with Maggie?" I asked her.

"Yeah, I understand he's about finished, or at least that's what the dispatcher said." Pamela replied with a shrug.

Jessica said, "When I was in the room with the sheriff and Maggie it sounded like she's going to have some charges brought against her. I wish we had been right about her being involved in the accident though, as it would give her a motive for killing Matthew, and I wouldn't feel so bad for accusing her. Now I'll never be able to use the library again."

"I don't know that I'd worry about her being at the library, I can't imagine she'll have a job after this gets out, after all she did help spike Matthew's drinks that night, plus instead of telling anyone about it she spent years blackmailing Jacob."

"That's true," she answered brightening up a little that the library wouldn't be off-limits to her.

I looked at Pamela and told her, "I'm sure glad you came. I hope what you tell the sheriff in person will add to why we believe Jacob killed Matthew, which must mean he was in the other vehicle at your accident."

Jessica heard me and asked, "Jacob killed Matthew? Are you sure?"

"Almost positive," I answered her hoping we weren't wrong.

Right on time, Dad walked in waving a thumb drive at us.

"What is he doing?" Jessica asked.

"Let's wait and talk to the sheriff. I don't want to have to explain twice why I think Jacob killed Matthew."

"Are you positive it was Jacob?" Jessica repeated her question as she sat down agitated and started to bounce her leg.

"I believe Jacob killed Matthew. Maybe he was even responsible for the accident."

"Is she for real?" Jessica looked back at Nick.

"I think so. Let's see what the sheriff has to say."

Dad sat down next to me. Behind the counter I saw a deputy escorting a sobbing Maggie down the hallway toward the jail cells. The dispatcher finally looked at all of us gathered there and said, "Can I help you?"

"Can we visit with Sheriff Poole?"

"You'll have to wait a bit. He has to talk to Ms. Wicks before he can see the rest of you."

Pamela spoke up, "It's okay with me if the sheriff talks to all of us at once."

"I'll ask him," the dispatcher said. She pushed back her chair and walked towards his office. As she reached it, his door opened. He saw her, stopped, looked beyond her at us and we heard her telling him we all wanted to talk to him. He looked like he was disagreeing but she pointed at Pamela and he looked at all of us again. He must have realized from our expressions that we weren't going anywhere. The dispatcher motioned for us to come their way.

"I think I'll put you in the conference room, his office would be a little tight for all of you," She said. Dad, Nick, Jessica, Pamela and I followed her down around the corner where she opened a door to a larger room with a table and chairs in it. We all piled in and waited for the sheriff.

"What do you folks need now?" he said with a sigh as he walked in and sat down.

"We need you to look at this security tape from the local body shop and we need you to come back out to the seed plant and look at some evidence we found in the same field as where Matthew's body was found."

"Evidence you found. Something we missed I suppose?" he asked clearly irritated with me.

"Yes. Evidence that was missed, but to be fair, I don't know how you could have found it. We happened to stumble across it because of the sun and rain."

"Now you've got me confused. Why don't you just tell me what's going on," he said finally sitting down indicating he would listen to us.

"First let's look at this security tape. Can I use the computer over there?" I asked pointing at one on a cabinet in the corner.

"Go ahead."

I turned it on; waited for it to start up and stuck the thumb drive in. I looked to Dad and indicated he should take over.

"This is from the security camera at the body shop," he said. "On the night that Matthew was killed there were only two cars that drove out of town toward Jessica's house during the hours the coroner says Matthew was killed. The first vehicle came by at nine-thirty. It was a rusty brown Chevy citation that belonged to the minister of the Baptist church."

"You don't think Reverend Challing killed Matthew," the sheriff snorted.

"No", I answered exasperated with him, "I know he lives a few miles down the road from Jessica. Let Dad finish please."

Dad motioned for me to relax and he continued, "Just wait. The next car was a black Cadillac Escalade. Isn't this Jacob's vehicle?" he asked.

"It looks like it, but that doesn't mean it is," the sheriff said, but he started to look interested.

"Oh come on, how many black Cadillac Escalades are there in this town?" I interjected again. Dad fast-forwarded about one hour and the black vehicle came by again.

"What does this prove?" the sheriff asked.

I replied, "An old field road that goes from our big bluestem field, where you found Matthew's body joins up to a township road by Jessica's house. We didn't remember it because no one has used it in years as it's been too wet and the gravel pits were as far as you could get. But this year has been extremely dry and I bet if you sent somebody out to check the crossing you would find that it is in good enough shape to travel on. I'd say that hour was enough time for him to drop off Matthew's body and get back to Jessica's to plant blood in the pickup in her yard."

"It still doesn't mean anything, even if it was Jacob, he could have been simply out for a drive. Besides, his vehicle doesn't show up on your camera at your seed facility."

"It wouldn't have if he used that road," I said frustrated. "I haven't finished yet, sheriff. Nick and I decided to check out the old field road and we found evidence of a trail coming off it, even where a body was possibly dragged. We also found a pair of sunglasses that I am positive belong to Jacob." Jessica gasped and the sheriff looked even more interested. He actually sat up straight.

"Did you touch them?"

"Of course not," forgetting that I would have if Nick hadn't reminded me to not touch them. "We left everything there. We were hoping you could send someone out there today."

"Are you positive they couldn't be one of your worker's?"

"Of course I can't be positive, but they are seven-hundred-dollar sunglasses. I doubt anybody that works on our farm including us, would spend that much on a pair of sunglasses. Also, Jacob would know about that field road, as he used to hunt with Matthew around the gravel pit. I would bet he remembered how he could get from Jessica and Matthew's house to our field."

"What reason would Jacob have for killing Matthew?" Jessica broke in.

"I think when Matthew realized he hadn't been the only one at the site of the accident he remembered something from that night and he realized Jacob was responsible. My best guess is that he decided to take a chance and contacted Pamela to check if she remembered anything that would reinforce what he was thinking." I stopped and looked at Pamela. She eagerly nodded in agreement. I continued, "I would bet besides Gary and Pamela he also contacted Jacob and asked to meet with him to hear his side of the story because that is what Matthew would do. With his election coming up Jacob didn't want any hint of this to come out so he offered to meet with Matthew and killed him instead."

"Why would he have admitted to his part in spiking the drink if he was worried about the election?" Sheriff Poole asked.

"Again I'm just guessing, but I would say he was planning on framing Maggie. Maybe he thought the voters would forgive the prank as a youthful indiscretion on his part, but knew they wouldn't forgive him for injuring Pamela, leaving the scene of the accident and letting Matthew take the blame. I imagine he knew that once her part in making Matthew drunk came out no one would believe she didn't cause the accident and kill Matthew to cover up her part in it, and even if the leap wasn't made to accuse Maggie of the murder, he knew the blood he planted at Jessica's would give you another suspect. Either way he wouldn't be suspected of being the other vehicle twenty years ago or killing Matthew now."

"Let me get our deputy to come with me and look at this field road, trail, whatever it is, and we'll collect the sunglasses and run them for prints. Even if they are his prints, I'm not sure it will be enough for a conviction," the sheriff said.

"I realize I read too many crime stories, but don't you have ways to track somebody's cellphone to find out where they were? At the very least you should be able to get a search warrant to examine his car. If he transported Matthew either dead or alive there has to be some evidence in his vehicle. I don't care how you get the proof, Sheriff; I just want you to quit believing Jessica did this."

The sheriff stood up, "Let's go look at your evidence and we'll go from there."

As we walked out of the conference room, he called a deputy over, had a hurried conversation with him, and said to us as we waited, "We'll meet you at the field by your seed-cleaning facility."

"Why don't you follow us and we can lead you to the old field road." He didn't look too happy with me again telling him what to do.

He looked like he was holding himself back from saying something and stiffly said, "Okay, give us a couple minutes to gather up our gear."

Nick helped Pamela into his pickup and put her wheelchair in the back while I got in next to her; Jessica jumped in with Dad. About five minutes later the sheriff's car came up behind us and we pulled out with them following. We drove the few miles out to Jessica's house, and went another half mile past it on the township road. Sure enough the crossing was still there. It was overgrown with grass, but you could make out where a vehicle might have come through and bent down some grass. We turned off on the field road. It wasn't a smooth road, more of a trail, and you could see holes where the wet spots had been but it was passable. We bumped along the road until we came to the gravel pit, stopped and looked around. Dad pointed from his pickup to a path that followed along the edge of the gravel pile. The road got smoother as the gravel company used the part of the road we were now on. We stopped where my pickup had been left and Nick and I had walked in the field earlier today. I looked back to make sure the sheriff and his deputy were behind us. They had slowed down but were still following. We parked, and when the sheriff caught up to us and got out of their patrol car Nick and I pointed out the trail in the big bluestem we had found. The deputy started photographing, and the sheriff asked us to follow behind them for fewer disturbances. Dad stayed behind with Pamela while the rest of us followed the trail until we came to the tramped down part of the field where we had left the sunglasses. The sheriff put on plastic gloves, picked up the glasses and put them in an evidence bag. We followed the trail to where Nick and I thought Jacob had left the field by walking along the wheel path of the irrigation system to make it look like he had entered the field by the break room. Then we all tramped back out of the field to where our vehicles were parked.

"I'll let you know what we find out," the sheriff said. "In the meantime, I shouldn't need to say that you don't tell anyone else about this right?"

We agreed and they got in their patrol car and left.

"That was kind of anticlimactic," I turned and said to Nick and Jessica.

"No kidding," Jessica answered.

"I think you got his attention anyway. I got the impression he believes us. They'll find a way to get enough evidence against him." Nick tried to sound positive, "all we can do now is to wait for the sheriff."

We walked back to Nick's pickup where Dad and Pamela were waiting. Dad drove Jessica and Pamela back to town. I got into my own pickup, Nick got into his and we both drove back to the break room. We got out of our vehicles and went in to sit down. There were a few donut holes that had been left there by somebody. Nick and I didn't say much, both thinking our own thoughts while we munched.

Coming out of my stupor I said, "Do you think this is over?"

"I think everything fits, but I don't know if there is enough real evidence to convict anyone," Nick answered me.

"I wish I felt better that Sheriff Poole could do the job."

"Maybe he'll surprise us," Nick said not sounding too confident.

"I hope he will. All we can do for now is get back to farming. With the sun shining maybe we'll be able to do some combining today after all." I stood up. "I'll head over to check out the other field of blue grama and give you a call. If it's dry enough you can drive the combine there and I'll come back and get the wagon. I'll talk to you in about twenty minutes."

I drove away feeling somewhat deflated. I don't know what I was expecting. There was always a satisfying conclusion in the books I read. I had hoped the sheriff would be more definitive in his reactions. We'd just have to wait and see.

CHAPTER TWENTY-FIVE

The appeal of a tallgrass prairie is that it can be duplicated on any scale, from a small backyard flowerbed to many acres.

THURSDAY MORNING DAWNED CLEAR AND BRIGHT with a slight breeze that would dry the dew fast. Contrary to the weather forecast I had checked earlier in the week it would be a wonderful day for harvest. I double checked the forecast on my phone and there was now no mention of strong winds. Better yet, with blue grama the only crop ready so far, Nick and I could handle it without any extra help, which was fortunate as Kirk and his band were furiously practicing and they would be leaving next week some time. I had already let Gary know that if the weather continued to cooperate we would need his help soon. Due to our late start yesterday afternoon, by the time we got all the equipment moved to the new field and organized we only had enough time to fill one wagon before the evening dew had shut us down. But everything was now set up and we should have a productive day. I also decided to make up my mind that I would not think about the murder today. I planned to do my best to put it out of my mind and wait to hear from the sheriff.

It was a busy day and around four-thirty Jessica called. "Do you want the good news or the bad news first?" she asked.

"I'd prefer there would be no bad news, but I guess I'll take the good news first," I said, nervous for what she was going to say.

"All the information we gave the sheriff yesterday must have convinced him that Jacob was guilty. He went to arrest Jacob late this morning."

"That's great news but I thought there wasn't enough evidence yet?"

"That is what leads to the bad news. The sheriff didn't have all his ducks in order and didn't have enough to hold Jacob. He would have been wise to remember Jacob is a lawyer. He should have waited a few hours as later this afternoon the sheriff got the result from the lab and not only did the sunglasses have Jacob's fingerprints on them, they also found blood on them."

"Was it Matthew's?"

"No idea, the results on the blood could take a week or so to come back. Anyway, when he went back to pick up Jacob again he was gone. It looked like he emptied out his closets and took off."

"Why would he do anything that stupid?" I asked.

"I wondered the same, panicking I assume. Once he heard about the sunglasses I imagine he knew the blood on them would match Matthew's. The sheriff checked with the bank and Jacob had emptied out his accounts. He's wealthy enough to hide out for a long time. Anyway, even though he got away it is still good news because I'm not a suspect anymore. They'll catch up with him sooner or later and when they do he'll pay for what he did to Matthew. It's over." She sounded happy

"That's great news Jessica. Did you let Pamela know?"

"I talked to her this morning. She was already traveling back to her home. I'm on my way to the restaurant. If you get a break from harvesting in the next few days let's all get together."

"I wish we could, but the weather sounds promising, so I doubt it will be anytime soon. Thanks for calling and Jessica I'm so happy for you."

As I hung up with Jessica, the phone rang again. It was the sheriff. "Carmen, I'm sure Jessica filled you in already," he hesitated . . .

I jumped in and said, "Yes she did. I'm thankful she's not under suspicion anymore, but I do wish it had been someone we didn't know."

"You and me both, look, I'm sorry I wasn't more attentive to your suggestions. My only excuse is that I felt like I shouldn't be letting citizens tell me how to run my investigation", he paused and continued; "I have to admit I was wrong. This whole business has shown me that I have a lot to learn about this job. I wanted to call and apologize and to also say I'm sorry that we let Jacob escape. We will catch him though. Of that I am positive." He said as I thought to myself that the sheriff wasn't so bad after all.

"Thanks for calling sheriff. I appreciate it," I said genuinely meaning it before we hung up.

We combined for another three hours before the moisture in the air made the crop too wet. It took us another two hours to get all the wagons unloaded, the crop in the bins and all the fans on.

"Well that was a productive day," Nick said when we were finished.

"Yes it was." I replied wiping sweat off my brow. "I'm going to swing by the cabin site on my way home. I haven't been there for a few days. Tomorrow morning I plan to check the sideoats grama. If that is ready I'll get Dad and Gary to help. They can finish up the blue grama since everything is already set up, and we'll move over to the sideoats field."

"Did you hear from the sheriff today?" Nick asked.

"Both he and Jessica called," I said and shared with him what they had said.

Nick said, "That's too bad Jacob disappeared."

"I agree, but Jessica is off the hook and her brother's name has been cleared, which is the most important thing."

"And that the mystery is solved and the detective in you can relax," Nick said with a smile.

"That too," I answered grinning back at him.

"I'm going to head home, I'll see you tomorrow morning," Nick said as he started to walk to his pickup.

"Thanks for all your help Nick. Those sunglasses wouldn't have been found without you."

"I was happy to help. It was fun to see your Nancy Drew side," he laughed and continued, "How many sides of your personality are there?"

"You've only started getting to know me," I answered and blushed as that felt way too flirty. "I'd better get going before it's completely dark. See you tomorrow Nick."

It would be hard to see anything at the construction site now that it was dusk, but I could use the flashlight app on my phone and I wanted to see how much progress Mitch and Mark had made. I pulled up in front of the first cabin, opened the door of the pickup and sat there enjoying the peace and quiet for a few minutes. The absence of mosquitoes was one good result of months of dry weather. The cabins were shingled, doors and windows installed, and they had started on the siding. After a bit I noticed it looked like the front door of the closest cabin was open. I turned on the phone flashlight app and walked that way. I didn't want a skunk or raccoon to get in. As I was about to grab the door and close it a voice said, "Hello Carmen."

I startled and screamed. It was Jacob. He was sitting on the floor of the cabin. As he stood up and came towards me I noticed he had a gun. "Is that the gun you killed Matthew with?" I asked my voice shaking.

"Yes it is," he replied in an emotionless voice.

"What are you doing here?" I asked as I started to edge towards the side of the cabin trying to get out of the open doorway.

"I was stopping by here to figure out where I was going to go. I didn't think anyone would be around, but of course you had to mess that up too."

"Why don't you turn yourself in to the sheriff? You have to know you'll get caught eventually," I said trying to make myself sound brave.

"Maybe, maybe not," he said. "Matthew managed to disappear for twenty years and he had a lot less money than I do."

"Are you going to kill me too?" I asked mad at my voice for trembling.

"I should for all the trouble you've caused, but I don't enjoy killing. I haven't made up my mind. If it was Friday I might consider being nice and tying you up as they wouldn't find you until the construction crew showed up Monday morning. That would give me plenty of time to disappear, but since it is Thursday you'd be found right away tomorrow." He scratched his chin while he considered what to do with me.

I couldn't believe this was the same person I had dealt with over the years. How could I have not picked up on how crazy he was?

Almost like he could hear my thoughts he said, "I'm not the upstanding citizen you thought I was, am I? You may as well turn off your phone flashlight and drop it on the ground. I wouldn't want anyone who might drive by on the highway to wonder what a flashing light is doing out here."

I turned off the flashlight but discretely turned my phone to video before I dropped it. It couldn't hurt to try. "Why did you kill Matthew? The accident happened a long time ago, Pamela didn't die. You wouldn't have gotten much of a sentence. Now it's a murder charge."

"Only if they catch me," he snorted. "I've spent my whole life in this one-horse town. The state representative run was my ticket out of here. If my part in that accident had come out it all would have been over. Getting rid of Matthew gave me a chance, but of course you had to get in the way."

"What happened the night of the party anyway?"

"I had Maggie spike Matthew's drinks. I wanted the adoration of him to stop for at least one night. I had hoped he'd be one of those people who got belligerent when they were drunk and that he'd act totally stupid. Instead he just got sleepy and decided to head home early. No one followed us outside and I knew they wouldn't notice if I was gone from the party for a few minutes so I decided to follow him and see if I could startle him into running off the road. I would claim it was a joke but perfect Matthew would have to report the accident and he would get in trouble for driving under the influence." Jacob said with a sneer and continued, "If I had stayed at the party the plan would have worked perfect as Matthew ran off the road without any help from me. When I caught up with him a couple miles down the road I was so busy staring at his vehicle rammed into the tree I didn't see Pamela until it was too late. I tried to see if I could help her, but I could tell she was in bad shape. I got blood all over my sweatshirt and then I remembered Matthew and I were wearing the same sweatshirt that night like we sometimes did. I switched sweatshirts with him and I checked my vehicle over to make sure there wasn't any noticeable damage. There was a dent, but I had hit a deer a few weeks before so no one would notice. I turned around and went back to the party."

"Nobody noticed how long you were gone?"

"No. I told everyone I had been outside arguing with Matthew, trying to get his keys and then I waited at the party for about an hour to make sure people saw me before I left to conveniently come across the accident and report it. Everything was going to plan until I heard a rumor that the sheriff was questioning why Matthew's vehicle didn't have any significant damage and some strange skid marks. Fortunately it wasn't hard to convince Matthew that it would be more honorable if he disappeared instead of making his family go through a trial."

"You are a horrible person. Why didn't you kill Maggie instead of paying the blackmail?" I asked trying to stall.

He looked at me and said, "Don't think I didn't want to, but she told me she had it all written down and if anything happened to her she had a plan for the information to be exposed, plus she didn't know about my true part in the accident, just that I was the one who told her to spike Matthew's drinks. Once I was elected, an accident would have happened to her though and if her information did come out at that point it would have been her word against a state representative. I was pretty sure I could weather that storm by claiming that she was a delusional, jealous woman. Anyone who knew her in high school wouldn't question it. But, after all this time, Matthew contacted me. He had figured out that that there was another vehicle present that night. The way he talked to me I was positive he knew it was me, and with Maggie knowing about the spiked drinks; well, I knew that between the two of them my political career would be over. Matthew had to die before he and Maggie could put their stories together. I didn't know he had also talked to Pamela and Gary. I told Matthew I would pick him up at the bus station in Parkville. When I picked him up I took him out by his old house on the pretense of showing him the place for old times' sake. Once we were that far out of town and no one would see us, I pulled my gun on him and made him drive towards the field road crossing. I knew with the dry weather it would be passable and was counting on no one else remembering it. We followed the road to where I led him into the field and shot him. He tried to get away once, we scuffled and I punched him in the nose. I imagine that is how I lost the sunglasses out of my pocket and how they got his blood on them."

I hoped my phone was getting all of this in case I lived to turn the recording over to someone. In the meantime I was trying to discretely look around for anything I could use to help myself. My eyes had adjusted to the dark and I noticed a three-foot piece of rebar. I was trying to figure out if I had the guts to try and grab it and hit him with it before he could shoot me.

He continued with his story, "When he was dead I took a rag out of my pocket, got some blood on it and drove back to Jessica's and put it the back of Matthew's pickup." He stopped talking and focused on me again, "it would have worked too. With a little word from me about the inheritance, the sheriff was convinced Jessica killed her brother until you got involved."

I tried to distract him again. "Why didn't you shoot him at Jessica's instead of in our field?"

"I didn't know if she was home or not and I couldn't risk Matthew making noise or getting away. I'm sorry Carmen, but that is enough questions for you." He started raising his gun towards me.

Sensing my time was running out, I tried the oldest trick in the book. I suddenly screamed, "What is that?" and pointed to my left while grabbing for the rebar. Jacob was startled giving me enough time to grab the piece of metal and nail him on the head as hard as I could. He dropped to the ground. I couldn't see where the gun went, but I quickly grabbed my phone, sat on top of him and dialed the sheriff.

"I have Jacob," I said when he answered.

"What did you say?" he asked.

"Please come out to where we are building the cabins. Jacob was here. I knocked him out. Just please come." I started to cry.

To his credit he didn't ask any more questions, he just hung up. I hoped that meant he was coming. It didn't take long, only about ten minutes before I heard the sirens. I turned on the flashlight app again so they could see me. By the time they found me I had gotten myself under control.

"Is he alive?" the sheriff asked when he saw I was sitting on Jacob and he wasn't moving.

"I'm pretty sure he is, but I don't really care if he isn't." As I finished talking he started to stir. The sheriff put handcuffs on him and helped me up.

"You'll have to come in and give a statement."

"Not tonight," I said as I handed him my phone. "I have a recording of everything on this. If you have any more questions I will stop by in the morning."

He looked at my face, and must have decided I was serious. He helped Jacob to his feet and led him to the patrol car as I walked to my pickup.

I was thankful Dad and Kirk were in bed by the time I got home. I really wasn't up to answering any questions. I fell into bed.

When I walked down the stairs the next morning, Dad, Kirk, and Jessica were all standing in the kitchen. They rushed over to hug me. Wizard barked frantically at all the commotion.

"I assume the sheriff got a hold of you guys already?" I said trying to talk loud enough to be heard over Wizard's barking.

"Yes he did. Are you okay?" Dad asked while Kirk quieted Wizard.

"I was pretty shook-up last night. I think I'm okay now. I need to get over to the farm. I need to get a hold of Nick, check the sideoats grama and . . ."

Dad interrupted me, "Combining can wait for a bit, and Nick is on his way over. I thought we could all have breakfast together."

I sat down, suddenly feeling a little shaky again and said, "That sounds good", just as there was a knock at the door.

It was Nick. He rushed right over to me. "I can't believe what they told me. Is it true that Jacob almost killed you?" He sounded furious.

"Yes, it's true, but honest I'm fine, a little shaky but so relieved it is over."

Jessica said, "You got that right. I can't believe we all thought Jacob was such a wonderful person. I'm glad he's in jail and I hope he goes to prison for a long time, and, and breakfast is ready," she exclaimed and sat down with a resounding thump.

We all laughed and Kirk, Dad and Nick joined Jessica and me at the table. I told them the whole story while we ate.

"It's all so sad," Dad said when I finished.

"I agree." I said. "But now it is time to get back to work. I know I'll feel much better once I get going on a combine. I will let you guys clean up the kitchen though," I said with a smile.

Nick walked out with me. "I sure am glad you're okay. We need you around here," he said shyly.

"So am I," I said as I got into my pickup. "This farm needs you too. You have been such a great employee, especially covering the slack when I've been running around like a chicken with her head cut off trying to figure out Matthew's murder."

Nick leaned in on my pickup window. "If I'm not being too forward I would hope I'm a little more than an employee at this point?" he asked questioningly.

I hesitated for a brief moment, my mind reviewing the possible ramifications if this went poorly, and about the things in his past he wasn't ready to talk about, but the overwhelming thought was how life was too short to be scared. I smiled at Nick, "I think it would be wonderful if you were more than an employee."

TARA RATZLAFF lives in the northwest corner of Minnesota (just about in Canada) with her husband of twenty-eight years, daughter, five fat cats and one eccentric dog that belligerently greets everyone as if she's never met them, including family. She graduated from North Dakota State University with a degree in Civil Engineering and became the first female County Highway Engineer in the state of Minnesota. She retired early from her career as a Civil Engineer when she and her husband purchased a native grass and wildflower seed farm/business which they operated for over twenty years before recently retiring. With her daughter in college pursuing her master's degree and the seed farm no longer keeping her busy, she decided it was time to pursue her dream of writing cozy mysteries. Her hobbies are reading (mysteries only, of course), long walks, swimming when the pool isn't froze and watching the antics of their pets.

CPSIA information can be obtained
at www.ICGtesting.com
Printed in the USA
JSHW031300230323
39302JS00005B/35